MW00657426

THE ELECTRONIC MOTHER

ALSO BY KIRK ADAMS

Left on Paradise

The Trouble with Girls

The Electronic Mother

THE ELECTRONIC MOTHER

KIRK ADAMS

KIRK ADAMS BOOKS

This is a work of fiction. All events and characters appearing in this work are either fictitious or used fictitiously. Any resemblance to actual events or real persons, living or dead, is purely coincidental.

The Electronic Mother

This book was published in the United States of America.

ISBN 978-1-7356062-6-2 (ebook)

ISBN 978-1-7356062-3-1 (print)

Kirk Adams Books, PMB #219

45591 Dulles Eastern Plaza, Suite 132

Sterling, VA 20166

Cover designed by Joelle Clapier.

Created with Vellum

ACKNOWLEDGMENTS

Passages from Plato and Aristotle have been lightly edited from the following editions: Plato, *The Republic*, trans., Benjamin Jowett (Colonial Press: New York, 1901); H.W.C. Davis, *Aristotle's Politics*, trans. Benjamin Jowett (The Clarendon Press: Oxford, First Edition 1905); George Henry Lewes, *The Ethics of Aristotle* (Walter Scott Publishing Company, Ltd: London and Newcastle-on-Tyne, n.d).

Passages from Genesis 2:23-24 cited from: *La Sainte Bible qui Comprend l'Ancien et le Nouveau Testament Traduits sur les Textes Originaux Hébreu et Grec par Louis Segond (Nouvelle Édition Revue: Paris, 1910).*

For Pamela and every mother,
natural or adopted,
who loves her children more
than her own life.

CONTENTS

PART I

Plato, *Republic*, Book V

The wives and children of our Guardians are to be held in common. Let women strip for physical training and share in the toils of war and the defense of their country.

Childrearing duties will be handed to the nurse and attendants. Authorities will take the greatest possible care that no mother recognizes her own child.

The proper officers will take offspring to the pen or fold, and there they will deposit them with nurses who dwell in a separate quarter; but deformed offspring will be put way in some mysterious, unknown place.

. . .

Guardians will appoint certain festivals at which we will bring together the brides and bridegrooms. Anyone who forms a connection without the sanction of the rulers is raising up a bastard to the State, uncertified and unconsecrated.

1

HOME SWEET HOME

Marie-Thérèse looked older than her twenty-four years. Her narrow shoulders were draped with an oversized and ill-fitting dress that fell to her calves and her thick, raven-black hair brushed the small of her back, giving the impression of matronly maturity beyond her years and the fashion. The young woman's cocoa-brown face was pale and her bloodless cheeks bloated; her breasts were swollen and her buttocks hung heavy with ungainly weight. Mostly, though, it was the bulge in the woman's abdomen that drew Sawyer's eyes. The skinny-armed boy couldn't turn his face away, no matter how repulsive he found the melon-round protrusion from the young woman's abdomen: the nurse was pregnant.

Sawyer Adams observed the maid as she spruced the flat, bending awkwardly to the floor or otherwise balancing herself with a steadying arm. He watched with undisguised disdain as the pregnant woman reached atop a bookcase to find hidden dust or stretched her bulky form toward an arched window to polish smudged glass and shook his head in disgust when she dropped to hands and knees to vacuum beneath a sofa with a cleaning tube, her distended belly brushing the floor. The boy responded in sheer horror when the pregnant woman twisted an arm behind her back to stretch the undergarment clinging to her hips.

"Ugghhh," Sawyer groaned as he cupped his hand to his mouth and turned his head.

For her part, Marie-Thérèse paid Sawyer little heed, being far too engrossed in her chores to trifle with the concerns of a boy—even if he was a superior and an Equal. Indeed, the nurse completed her cleaning with quiet efficiency until she heard rustling from the hall and noticed her young charge staring straight at her. As soon as Marie-Thérèse glanced back, the boy averted his eyes and started for his room, leaving the nurse to continue her work without further distraction.

Sawyer quickly reached his room at the end of a wide hall adorned with a platinum chandelier and plush velvet carpets and closed the door behind him, removing his shirt and turning toward a full-length mirror to examine his own flat stomach and skinny arms: which showed none of the maternal excess of the housekeeper. He stared at the sight of skin-starved ribs and flat abdomen until a voice startled him.

"Have your hairs darkened, son?" a woman's voice asked. "Are there more of them?"

It was Mother's words that echoed from the hall. Her tone was straightforward, though her voice was muffled by the centimeter-thick oak door that provided a facade of privacy.

Sawyer looked into the corner of the room, where he saw a red light flickering from a metallic optics box. "I'm changing shirts," the boy said, "if you must spy on me."

"Very well," Mother said, "but don't make too much laundry for the nurse."

"Not too much," Sawyer replied as he threw a wrinkled shirt down a laundry chute and pulled a pressed one from a drawer. "I do need to change for dinner."

"We eat in an hour."

"I'm going to call Gunther."

"Is," Mother asked, "your homework finished?"

"Everything except Current Events."

"What's the assignment?"

"To learn about the most recent truce with the Heavenly Socialist Empire."

Mother's voice sounded from the far side of the door after the slightest of pauses. "The Heavenly Socialist Empire of the Two Chinas?"

"Yes, Mother."

"Walter Cronkite," Mother said, "is doing a story on this year's truce. It's televised on Program Alpha Beta Three. You may watch it later. And there's an *International Culture and Geography* file on the no-man's land in the South Pacific region."

"Do I have to?" Sawyer asked.

"Would you like paper or port?" Mother said.

"A color print, I suppose."

"I'll send it to you."

"Thanks," Sawyer said as he rolled his eyes.

"You're welcome."

A moment later, Mother spoke again, her voice still muffled by the oak veneer of the closed door. "Son," she said.

"Yes?"

"I'm taking my nap now."

"How long?"

"Just a few minutes to rest my eyes," Mother said as the red lights stopped flickering.

SEVERAL MINUTES LATER, Sawyer walked down the hall to an adjacent room where scanners and printers were stacked on a titanium rack situated between two shelves stocked with papers and inks. A printer was spooling down, its export tray holding a half-dozen thick sheets of glossy paper: each one color-printed and time-stamped *15 May 2084* front and back. All six sheets remained warm to the touch as Sawyer retrieved the articles Mother so expeditiously had obtained. The downlinked story was dated November 2047—only months before the Second War for the Spratly Islands engulfed the entire Pacific Rim. Sawyer brought the hard-copy to his bedroom as his mother napped.

Sawyer's bedroom was fair-sized: not opulent, but spacious and orderly. It measured both six meters long and wide and was inset with opaque rectangular windows shaded by linen drapes. The platinum smooth-faced equipment throughout the room showed traces of cross-circuited strip wiring visible through thin screens of metallic transparency. Touch-squares and copper circuit lines were set across the digitized panels and not a single button or knob associated with the outmoded technology of earlier generations was to be seen. The opposite wall was fitted for grooming: with a wardrobe, closet, and bathroom that included a marble-walled shower and an oak-seat toilet. Sawyer's bed, centered in the room, was a dark-colored titanium sleeptech that measured nearly two meters in length and one and a half meter in breadth. Several shimmering zinc panels, so slender that two together remained thinner than one of the antique Memorial Lincoln pennies found at antiquities shops, draped from the sides of the bed as reflector screens. Fluorescent lights were set directly into the outer ceiling panels and the whole room was ringed with a flat umbilical strip embedded near the ceiling. The ceiling panels themselves sloped from the curved edge of a concaved recess (actually a shallow dome) crowned with a convex mirror. Lush carpet stretched to each of the four corners of the room: a carpet whose tint changed from grey to red to brown according to the diffusion of light and shade of the day. At present, nothing beyond the room was heard beyond a low hum of white noise emanating from every wall to maximize the solitude of the place.

Sawyer seated himself on a sofa near the window and stuffed two nylon-filled pillows behind his shoulders before shifting his weight backward. Light streamed over his shoulders, illuminating the ink-scented manuscript like a sacred text as images of indigenous life shimmered and gleamed with the intensity of undiffused light. The hue of the seas darkened, the shade of the skies lightened, and the reflection of the sands sharpened on the glossy paper. Several times, the sheen of the page proved blinding and the boy was forced to turn his face away from image and text alike, unable to fix his eyes upon the burning light of life immortalized in the refraction of a photographer's lens.

A single blink cleared his vision.

The first image was innocent enough: two girls swimming in a shallow lagoon, their dark hair streaming behind burnished backs like the flowing locks of sea maids of ancient lore. Other photographs also were without harm: a skinny adolescent boy surfing a breaking wave on a homemade board, three gulls falling on a flock of seed-throwing children, and a plate of fresh fish displayed for a harvest feast. There also were a pair of photographs of locals at work: hairy-chested old men repairing rusted automobiles and smooth-chested girls selling trinkets to tourists, both photos making it evident war hadn't yet come.

The first truly shocking image jumped from the report's next sheet. A young woman stood before a whitewashed cottage, her all-too-noticeable belly bloated as if from starvation or cancer and her teeth as white as the cotton summer dress that fell to her swollen knees. She was pregnant.

Wincing, Sawyer remembered Marie-Thérèse and wondered what Mother would think of maternography in the house and why the Chaperones had let the article filter through unsupervised. Checking the time-stamped publication date, Sawyer realized the journal was among the last gleanings of the paperbooks published before the establishment of the Universal Scriptorium. It wasn't a book properly called at all, but a hardcopy image, and one made before the eyes and memory of the Chaperones had matured.

Sawyer tried to turn the page, but was drawn back to the picture of the pregnant native. He touched her belly, almost expecting it to jump, but her immortality had been immobilized and the girl didn't move. Neither did her belly kick against his touch. Sawyer studied the girl's face until he could guess an age, a task that took several minutes since his only experience with pregnant women was watching the nurse presently stationed to his own home and he seldom saw women so nakedly female. He concluded the girl was perhaps eighteen years old: several years younger than Marie-Thérèse and probably about the age of older bedfriends who attended Gymnasium. She certainly was older than his class sisters. Sawyer forced himself to imagine Heidi or Freydis with bulges at their waists, but his mind recoiled at his perversity and he proved both unable and unwilling to keep such unnatural thoughts in mind. The boy shook his head in shame and turned the page to free himself from the obscenity.

If the photograph of the pregnant teenager proved troublesome, the next page brought utter disgust. A nurse held a small baby to one of her breasts in what was a full-page display of maternal indulgence. The baby's face was nestled into the cocoa dark-skinned chest of the grown woman, who looked older than even a Guardian: her eyes blackened from lack of sleep and face wizened from worry. The nurse (for that's what Sawyer reckoned her to be) cradled the child with both arms as the baby grasped the breast with two tiny hands, fingers clawing at soft skin and nose turned upward seeking breath. Tiny buttocks burrowed toward milk-gorged breasts and nakedness fell on nakedness as the nurse looked on the child with an air of wistful pleasure. The woman's belly remained bloated from after-pregnancy and her arms looked thick from the task of carrying life. Sawyer darted his eyes from the image, desperate to see anything but the pornography before him. He found the caption and read: *A Korean refugee nurses her three-month child soon after arriving on the island to join one of its many Christian sects. This baby was home birthed.*

The blood rushed from Sawyer's face. This wasn't a nurse, but a stead-mother and he had cast his eyes on the vilest of obscenities. He turned his head and dropped the article from sight, careful lest his mother should catch him reading it.

Sawyer could read no more and now rose from the sofa, walking straight to his desk. There, he looked straight at a small electronic optic embedded into the mirror and stood still until the optic recognized his cornea and flashed a small green light that signaled permission for a voice command.

"Open."

A lock clicked as Sawyer reached for a side drawer, pulling it open and depositing the article inside before pushing the drawer shut. Then the boy spoke another short command.

"Lock."

The hard click of a bolt sounded and Sawyer stepped back, the article secured from the prying eyes of maid and mother alike. Now, the boy turned slowly and looked into one of the unblinking optics staring from the room's hard-shelled umbilical cord as he shouted into the hall.

"Are you awake yet, Mother?"

When there was no reply, Sawyer returned to his desk, opened the upper drawer, and shuffled through a loose pile of keepsakes until he came to a photograph (not much larger than the size of his hand) of a newborn baby and its young mother. As Sawyer looked upon the picture, he smiled. Though his own features were imperfectly reflected in those of the baby, Mother was clearly recognizable, albeit somewhat younger in appearance, though she kept her hair long and wore calico. It was the only time Sawyer ever had seen his mother in such clothing and he laughed a little at the sight of her in such old-fashioned apparel.

Indeed, Mother stood before a Victorian-era white chapel with a large dark wood cross fixed above its front entry and a single bell tower whose dark planks contrasted with the whitewash of the chapel itself. The building looked new and was flanked on either side by palm trees, with a large, square-shaped stone a few meters from the main entrance. It was a place in Old California that no longer existed, having been (as Sawyer was told) restored to its natural state shortly after his birth. Sawyer himself, a mere infant, was cradled in the arms of the enigmatic woman whom he had long known and even appeared to be nestled against her breasts.

Mother reflected a disquieted smile and melancholic serenity Sawyer never had seen with his own eyes and her very being seemed weightier and more substantial than he'd ever before noticed. Sawyer touched his mother's face with a forefinger, then returned the photograph to its holder. Afterward, he closed his eyes and wondered how and why the photo was made and decided to ask Mother about it later.

A moment later, Mother announced her presence with a hollow cough. She arrived with gentle, noiseless steps across the carpet and wore denim jeans with and a button-down shirt. Her loose-curled tresses lay unmoved against her shoulders as she flowed through the room and her cocoa skin tinted like his own, though flickering different shades of brown as mutable light changed like a kaleidoscope.

Mother glided straight for her son. "Did you finish your homework?" she asked.

"Mostly," Sawyer said with a shrug.

"What does that mean?"

"It was gross."

"What was wrong?"

"You saw it."

"No," Mother said. "Occasionally, I'm unable to review hard copy images before they print."

"There was a woman who ..." Sawyer's words died on his tongue.

"Continue," Mother said after a brief pause.

"She," Sawyer said as he blushed, "had a baby."

"There's nothing wrong with babies."

"It was in her belly."

Mother said nothing.

"Besides," Sawyer continued, "there was an even worse one with a baby who was ..."

"Please tell me."

"It's an unsocial word."

"Spell it."

"S-u-c-k-i-n-g."

"It's only obscene," Mother spoke without pause, "if there's a letter L between the letters K and G."

"It sounds the same."

"Language," Mother explained, "is more art than science. You must pay attention to context."

"She held him," Sawyer said with a nod, "close to her ... to her chest."

"That's the duty of a nurse," Mother said. "Babies must be fed."

"But," Sawyer objected, "it wasn't a nurse. She was a stead-mother, I think. With her own baby. Born out of her own body."

"Old Believers," Mother's said with a voice that remained unchanged, "are eccentric people. Perhaps you shouldn't be reading about their oddities. Not until you're a little older. I'll speak to your father."

"They are strange."

"Fathers?"

"I mean," Sawyer quickly explained, "Old Believers."

Mother's voice was toneless when she spoke. "Dinner will be served soon."

"Can I eat in my room?"

"You may," Mother replied, "eat with Marie-Thérèse."

"I hate to eat with her."

"No matter. If you wish to play with your friend after dinner, you'll follow class rules."

Sawyer submitted with a tip of the head.

"What do you say?" Mother asked.

"I said I would."

"You said nothing I could hear."

"I nodded my head. Couldn't you see?"

"That's bad manners. It's proper to annunciate words to your mother."

"Yes, Mother," Sawyer replied with an exaggerated clarity.

"I believe dinner is ready. Wash yourself."

"Will you join us?"

"Not this evening," Mother answered. "It's not my time to interact with you. Children need to socialize outside the family as well."

"Can I play," Sawyer asked, "with Gunther instead of eating?"

"Boys your age," Mother replied, "must eat before they play."

Sawyer said he would eat before stepping into the water closet to wash his face and hands. Though a dry towel hung near the door, he rubbed his palms against the legs of his pants until they no longer dripped. By the time he finished, Mother was gone, so Sawyer went to the dining room. There, he sat at the table with the pregnant maid, though he was careful to angle his chair so his eyes wouldn't fall directly on her. Only after the nurse served the first course and took her own place at the table did Mother speak.

"Mind your manners," Mother said to her son, "and respect our house guest."

"Bonsoir, Marie-Thérèse," Sawyer said with a flat voice as he glanced at the maid.

"Bonsoir, Sah-yer." The nurse's tone was little more enthused than Sawyer's had been.

Sawyer turned to his meal of sautéed flounder, steamed carrots, and honey pudding. The boy said nothing more, trying hard not to stare at his dinner companion. Only once did his eyes fix on the nurse: when she stood to retrieve dessert, stretching and arching her back so far her belly seemed to cast its shadow over the whole table.

Mother noticed the breach of etiquette even before Sawyer's jaw dropped. "Marie-Thérèse," she said, "faites attention à vos manières."

"Oui, madame," the nurse replied with a noticeable curtsey.

Mother chided the nurse no more and Sawyer quickly finished his meal, then excused himself without further word while the maid remained at the table as she worked through her second plate of food. Sawyer requested permission to visit Gunther and was granted it, though reminded to dress warm. He pulled a grass-stained sweatshirt over his shoulders and raced for the front door.

"Open," Sawyer shouted a few meters from the door and it did so as the inch-thick steel door slid into a steel frame built into the hollow of the wall. Sawyer shouted for the door to close as he ran into the outer world and the double-steel door closed on cue. As floodlights illuminated the front porch, the boy emerged from his home. Indeed, a moving path of light guided his every step as he sprinted across the compound, passing rows of steel poles that lined the walkway leading to Gunther's apartment. Though the towers didn't move, globe-like lamps perched atop each pole rotated, allowing both lens and beam to alight the course of the running boy before fading to darkness.

Sawyer paid no attention. His mind was focused on play,

maybe scrimmaging in the commons or using simulators in the recreation room. Perhaps they'd battle barbarians with sword and spear or totalitarians with rifle and grenade; maybe they'd just finish their climb of Mt. Everest or even snorkel through the Great Barrier Reef. It didn't matter as long as Gunther could come out.

As matters turned out, Gunther wasn't allowed to play. He spoke to Sawyer through a locked door and explained he was grounded, this time for turning his back to his mother while she talked. Sawyer was clearly disappointed, but could do nothing to save his friend as his pleas to Gunther's mother fell on deaf ears. After several minutes of fruitless begging, Sawyer returned home by the same path crossed a little earlier and found himself readmitted to his own house after commanding a single word. The door opened upon voice recognition and the boy stepped inside.

Marie-Thérèse was taking personal time, so Sawyer took a seat in the Salon de Cinéma on a leather sofa and ordered the visual monitor to power up. He instructed the machine to digitize and the machine's two-meter screen flickered to life within a couple seconds.

"News," the boy said.

The monitor divided into quadrangles, each one displaying a different program. The upper left monitor displayed a golden-haired woman with broad shoulders and smooth skin talking to the camera with a panorama of The Hague behind her. The screen below it revealed a classroom in session, several wide-eyed children being lectured by a shaggy-haired instructor dressed in furs and bedecked in jewels and looking rather like Genghis Khan. On the upper right screen was a video of a snowstorm in the Rocky Mountains and below it an image of a flight patrol bearing west into the Pacific Ocean. It was to this screen that Sawyer turned.

"Security news," the boy said, "in Anglo-European."

Instantly, the screen was filled with the image of four long-range patrol planes. The four unmanned aircraft had the length of rockets, with suitable wingspans and fuselages wider than the outstretched arms of a grown man. The deep-voiced newscaster noted that patrols had been ordered into the central Pacific in light of growing tensions with the Heavenly Socialists. She also reported that flights of manned aircraft could remain aloft for nearly two days without refueling and unmanned aircraft could patrol upwards of two weeks with tanker support and suitable weather. It was noted that maritime squadrons had been deployed to forward staging areas.

Sawyer leaned forward at the rumor of war until a voice startled him. He jumped.

"What are you watching, son?" Mother asked.

"News of the wars."

"Do you really need to watch war so young?"

Sawyer stood and turned toward the hall, where he saw that Mother now stood near the door, dressed in a long nightshirt and a thick housecoat. The contours of her robe fell limp to the ground and were as unmoving as the frozen robes of a sculpture while her hair was fixed in a bun atop her head. She wore reading glasses which slipped a few centimeters down her thin nose. Sawyer noticed the incandescent sheen from her teeth when she talked.

"Someday," the boy said as he stepped toward his mother, "I'll be a Guardian."

"It's better to wait."

"The Chaperones didn't veto."

"The Chaperones," Mother said, "provide rules for all children your age. With the guidance of your father, I set them for your particular good."

"Well," Sawyer protested, "you didn't preselect channels."

"Sometimes," Mother said, "it's best to go through the process of discussion."

"Maybe," Sawyer answered, "but it won't be too long till I pilot a plane or a ship or command a missile squadron."

"Perhaps, but not tonight."

Sawyer said nothing.

"Besides," Mother added, "you haven't finished your homework. You were told to watch Cronkite's program on the Heavenly Socialist Empire of the Two Chinas."

Sawyer winced. "I forgot," he said with a more subdued tone. "Should I do it now?"

"It's too late. Get a snack and I'll read you a story before you sleep."

"Now?"

Mother nodded slowly, the rhythm of her head in perfect cadence with her speech. "Marie-Thérèse," she said, "baked your favorite cookies: honey-chocolate and spiced orange rind. I'll wait in your room."

Ten minutes later, Sawyer shut the door to his room and sat on his titanium-framed bed, a glass of milk and a plate of cookies on his lap. He looked to his mother, who stood before him dressed in her nightclothes, waiting for the boy to settle in.

"Which story would you like?" Mother asked after Sawyer stopped moving about.

"I don't care. Maybe a story about mothers and sons?"

"You like adventures."

"Usually," Sawyer said, "but tonight I'm in the mood for a story of a mother and her son."

"Since when," Mother said, "have family stories interested you more than adventurers and heroes?"

"I guess," Sawyer said, "since the nurse came."

"There are many stories of stead-mothers in the fairy tales."

"I want to hear of a real mother. Like you."

"There are no stories of mothers like me, but Mrs. Darling looks real. And her story also has pirates and adventures."

"Yes," Sawyer said, "I'll hear Peter Pan."

The lights went dim before the name of Peter Pan rolled from his tongue and Mother now moved near her son, narrating the story with a soft voice as the living images of Peter Pan, Wendy, Mrs. Darling, and all the lost boys of the tale appeared before Sawyer's eyes. Mother told of the mysterious Mrs. Darling, the corner of whose mouth held a kiss that her children never could quite find, and of Neverland—the dreamland in the mind of every boy. She told of adventures with pirates and American Natives and flying ships and mermaids swimming bare-breasted in tropical lagoons. Even as she spoke, Peter Pan flew through the room, Lost Boys fought savage natives, and Wendy braved the cruelty of Captain Hook. Characters appeared on cue from Mother's words, their images following her every word as they flickered and flew about the darkened room.

Sawyer finished his snack and lay down in his own bed. He watched till his eyes grew heavy and rolled to the back of his head. Only then did Mother fade from sight.

Sawyer heard no click of the door.

2

THE SCHOOL OF EQUALS

The scent of olive blooms drifted from groves rooted in the rocky soil of Attica. It was noon and the hard rays of the sun god streamed from the heavens, blinding every eye and burnishing every face. Pruners huddled in small groups throughout the groves, where they shared flasks of wine and rations of dried figs and salted herring while seeking refuge from the worst of Apollo's fierce fire. To the west, the sea was peaceful and still; Poseidon remained calm and unwrathful, now permitting the frothful play of Aphrodite to caress the shores of the Greeks. Several caravels sailed across the horizon, their sails puffed with the gentle breath of Zephyr as they carried the produce of Athens across the sea to trade for the gold and goods of barbarians. A single trireme lay anchored off the coast, no more than half a league away, perhaps training sailors or planning patrol. Virgins too delicate for nuptials (dressed in indigo and verdant chitons that brushed against clay-soiled feet and were held fast to trim waists by cords of spun wool) walked from nearby villages, heavy jugs of water stretching their arms as they inched toward brothers and fathers and sisters and mothers in the fields. Younger children played in the shade of the groves, some content to talk and others determined to wrestle in the manner of the arena.

The grove was planted southwest of Athens on a hill whose slopes streamed toward the sea from a rocky spur of earth from which rose the glory of the Greeks. To the east lay the great city, its stone walls shimmering in the sun and tile roofs absorbing the hard heat of the day. Stone and plaster buildings were congregated around the hill in a cluster of human needs and communal activity. Temples, markets, and even towers jutted toward the high walls of the Acropolis, which rose above every hearth and home. Crowning that summit was the temple of Athena, silhouetted against the blazing gaze of Apollo at which no mortal could stare and still see. From afar, the streets at the base of the hill looked alive: an undulating mass of artisans, merchants, and householders. Potters, tailors, wheelwrights, and blacksmiths (along with veiled wives and daughters of every class) filled the mountain with movement and mutability, so that the very earth appeared to dip and swell with the glory of mortal being. Beyond the limestone and brick walls of the polis lay the countryside—a panoply of natural beauty and human striving, of glory and grace and grapes and groves. The scent of blooming olives filled the air, seasoned with a dash of sea-salted winds that flavored the land with the foam of Aphrodite.

Twelve students, dressed not in tunics and robes, but in blouses and trousers, sat on a pew-length, felt-cushioned bench that appeared to be situated atop a small mound on the side of the mountain. Before them appeared a stout Greek teacher with thick hair and broad shoulders, dressed in a plain linen robe and sporting a thick-curled beard. The eyes of the students flitted among themselves with quick recognition, but looked on the ethereal serenity around them with a more measured gaze, taking long looks to identify the lay of the land or consider a strangely clad foreigner.

"Feast not your eyes on the beauty of temporal things," the old Greek declared, "but raise your thoughts to the forms of heaven: to ideas unchanging and truths undying."

One of the students, a brown-eyed girl with skinny arms and thick braces, raised a single arm above her head and was given permission to speak by the Greek philosopher.

"Master Plato," the girl said, "is this your republic?"

"Can any republic be mine?" the Greek replied.

When the student said nothing, the philosopher raised his right hand. "Who completed the class assignment?"

All but one of the students raised a hand.

"Digital or hard?" the Greek asked.

"Both," the students replied as a chorus.

Plato asked again whether any republic could be his and the brown-eyed girl stood to her feet. She was a head taller than the Greek virgins, though her shoulders were no less narrow and her face no less cherubic. Her hair was close cropped and uncovered.

"In your republic, in the one Socrates spoke of," the girl said, "the State belongs to each citizen equally. All possess an equal share. The exact same."

"Very good," Plato said, "and if the republic belongs to all citizens, do all citizens belong to the republic?"

"Each one," the girl continued, "must perform social service to the State for which his nature is best suited, or hers."

"Those are nearly my words. Explain them."

"Every person belongs to the government?"

Plato motioned for the girl to sit and asked for another

student to continue. A doe-eyed and thin-lipped boy raised his hand and Plato told him to stand and speak loud.

"What it means," the boy said, "is everyone lives for everyone else."

"Very good. Can you give an example?"

"I suppose," the thin-lipped boy said, "babies are an example."

"What about babies?"

"In your book, when they were born, the republic decided which ones were to be raised since they didn't have genetic coordination in those days."

"Continue."

"Some children," the boy explained, "were born with diseases that couldn't be cured, or even defects. Since such children could never make useful citizens, they weren't awarded citizenship."

"And?"

"They were left exposed."

"Meaning?"

"Meaning that they were abandoned to animals and the elements. They were left to die."

"By their parents?"

"No," the boy said, "not by the will of a father, but by the laws of the State."

"Very good," Plato responded. "You may sit down, Adrian."

The sound of shouting now echoed from atop the hill. Several Athenians had made a chance encounter along a road and begun to quarrel. Two of them looked middle-aged; others looked younger. A girl stood behind a hastily formed battle line of olive-skinned and thick-armed adolescents. The students on the bench didn't stir, though one did adjust a small microphone attached to the back of her ear.

"Explain," Plato said, "the significance of this brawl."

"They're arguing over the girl," one student replied.

"What's the point of the argument?"

"She was promised," the student said, "to one man in marriage, but taken into the bed of another."

The argument grew louder and soon a blow was struck and answered in kind. Before another olive bloomed, a brawl broke out. The middle-aged men parried staffs while their brothers, sons, nephews, and servants fell into a melee of closed fists and clenched teeth. Only the quick arrival of several onlookers, among them an armed hoplite with drawn sword, put an end to the fight. Two of the youth were bound with leather straps and marched toward the walls of the city while their kinsmen were dismissed with angry words and dire threats.

Plato spoke only after his pupils fixed their eyes on his face. "What," the philosopher asked, "is the real cause of this disorder?"

"Regime historians would've claimed," Sawyer now spoke for the first time, "it was the girl's unfaithfulness or her betrothed's honor."

"Excellent recollection," Plato said with a clap of the hands. "What's the underlying truth?"

Sawyer paused to collect his thoughts. "Jealousy," he said. "Possessiveness. Selfishness."

"Exactly. It was believed she belonged to another man: that one person might possess another as property."

Sawyer looked puzzled. "She didn't look like a slave," he said.

"Not a slave," Plato explained, "but a daughter and a bride. She was owned by one man and traded to another."

"So," Sawyer asked, "fathers sold their children for silver and gold?"

"It wasn't quite so simple," Plato said with a shake of the head. "Fathers gained money from the brideprice, but they often weighed more than silver and gold and even paid from their pockets to arrange suitable marriages. And that was the problem. The Greek father we saw a moment ago might have been placated soon enough if it only was a matter of market value, as with an ass or a sheep. A silver drachma would've settled the dispute. But honor and happiness also took their part and the possessiveness and jealousy of parents for the good of their children and husbands for the love of wives overruled every rational consideration or public spirit. Civil wars erupted when aristocrats preferred their own lineage to the common good and merchants left inheritances to their own offspring rather than public coffers. Factions rose from warring clans and alliances broke apart when marriages failed."

Plato continued to lecture as his students fell silent. "What did my mentor propose to resolve this tension? To break this spirit of selfishness, possessiveness, and jealousy?"

Sawyer sat down to let someone else answer.

A petite girl sporting a crew cut and showing few signs of physical maturation took her turn.

"He wanted," the girl said, "to abolish the family. Children were to be raised in public nurseries and the gymnasia so every child would call all adults father and mother and every man treat all children as his own."

"Precisely," Plato said, "and what did he say of women?"

"He proposed equality," the girl continued, her face lighted with pleasure from having been correct, "for he knew women must be freed from domestic slavery if a genuine republic was to be established. The principle of equality was to rule over nature. Socrates was the first to understand that the equality of mind in man and woman required differences of body to be transcended."

"How so?"

"Nurses," the girl said, "were to be drawn from the alien classes so citizens could devote themselves to public affairs. If women did no more than bear and raise children, they'd never become Guardians of the state. Women were to be spared all distractions from public service and even forbidden to get up at night to tend babies."

"What else did he propose?"

"He wanted women to bear arms and share power."

"Why?"

The girl shrugged.

Plato looked at the row of pupils. "Who," he asked, "can answer the question?"

For a second time, Sawyer raised his hand and Plato again motioned for the boy to speak.

"Because," Sawyer said, "women share equally in reason, they should share equally in public duties."

"And jealousy?"

"It has no place," Sawyer answered, "since it's irrational and selfish and is neither good nor just. It's part of mutable reality rather than an unchanging ideal."

"If women were to be allowed public service," Plato said, "then what of the patriarchy of the day?"

"It was to be abolished. Along with monogamy."

"Which was?"

"The social isolation and sexual segregation," Sawyer said, "of a single man with a single woman."

"Very good," Plato said, "someone else take a turn. What was to replace traditional marriage?"

"Socrates," the tall girl with braces answered, "wanted his republic to be unified more by friendship than self-interest, so he made marriage common between all men and women. His plan wasn't to divide citizens from each other by the passions of love but to unite society by sexual pleasure and controlled births."

"Excellent," Plato replied, "I'll give one last question before noon meal."

Several students stirred.

"When," Plato asked, "did the Greeks constitute this republic?"

"The Greeks," the petite girl with the crew cut said as she raised her hand, "never accepted Socrates, but made him drink hemlock"—now the girl paused for a moment, unsure whether her answer sufficed—"I suppose they thought themselves equal in a city of slaves and happy in a land of families."

Plato opened his arms as if to embrace the ethereal world before him. "Didn't," he asked, "each one of you feel the same?"

When no one answered, Plato repeated his question, sweeping his arm across the hologram of the ancient city. "Didn't you," he said, "feel for a moment the serenity and pleasure that ruled the land? At least until the brawlers came?"

Heads nodded and voices affirmed what he said to be true.

"You will remember," Plato said, "that the perceptions of this world are illusory and must be weighed against logic eternal and measured by thoughts unchanging. Sentiment and experience must be subordinated to policy and reason; they are powerful illusions we must resist."

As Plato's final sentence died, the world of ancient Athens also dissolved, first into multicolored pixels and then into absolute nothing. The twelve students found themselves sitting on a felt-cushioned bench in a sixty-square-meter circular hall ringed with cameras, projectors, speakers, atmospherers, and hologrammers. The voice of their instructor sounded one last time from the walls.

"Next session," Plato announced, "we continue our discussion of the ideal republic. Be sure to review your sources. Class dismissed."

All twelve students gathered their belongings, their backpacks and books stashed in individual compartments built into the base of the bench and left the room. As a group, they made their way down a high-ceiling corridor lined with digitized images displayed from hall-length monitors. Now a panorama of the Pacific coast was followed by an image of Les Halles Contemporaire. Scenes of fashionable boulevards were interwoven with pictures of unvarnished nature. Pixel changed to pixel in a whirlwind puzzle of mutability and transformation. The blue-green grass of a country estate morphed into the turquoise waters of a mountain river and the grey stone of an ancient castle was transformed into the sheer rock of an unbowed cliff. Images followed one upon another in the flux of transition: visions remade to follow unseen patterns of geometry and lucent physics embedded deep into the mind of the mural's programmers. The effect of the whole provided a sense of gradual change in a single purposeful direction as the twelve progressed toward their destination.

The students remained silent as they crossed the corridor, most of them silently viewing the creation of images and forms unlikely to be repeated. A faint echo of chamber music accompanied the panorama, sound sufficient to damper the step of leather soles on synthetic flooring and mute the rustle of shifting totes, and no more than five minutes passed before the students arrived at a large café in the center of several main halls. There, the students found several unoccupied tables on a cobblestone terrace, which they claimed for themselves with stacked books and rucksacks. Given the early hour, they were the first to arrive, excepting only three slender-waisted Guardians with thin mustaches and pointed breasts who kept to themselves across the courtyard. Three of the new arrivals remained at the table while their compatriots excused themselves to the lavatory.

SEVERAL MINUTES LATER, the twelve reconstituted themselves as a society and sat around the table while a coffee-skinned and youthful brunette dressed as an old-fashioned Parisienne hostess in a smock that clung to her chest and loose flowing curls that brushed her shoulders approached the table with an exaggerated curtsy. Her slender limbs bowed with rehearsed grace and her eyes dropped with accustomed deference. She spoke with measured inflection to her words, thoughtfully chosen and carefully rehearsed.

"Bonjour, messieurs et mesdemoiselles, s'il vous plaît—"

"En anglais, s'il vous plaît," one of the students interrupted.

The waitress curtsied and spoke in the common tongue. though with the noticeable accent of a native of Guyana. "For dinner, you would like?"

Sawyer ordered a spread of bread and cheese, along with tropical fruits and a chocolate religieuse. The others also placed orders, chosen not from menus but preprogrammed into the virtual chef's memory. Only Gunther's selection of fresh salmon was unavailable, with pork roast offered in its stead. After taking orders, the hostess then hurried to the kitchen.

"Guess what I saw yesterday?" Sawyer said as he turned toward Gunther, who sat to his left at the center of the table and beside the girls who had spoken during civics class.

Gunther responded with a shrug.

"Pictures," Sawyer announced.

"Of what?"

"Women."

"We see females every day," Gunther said as he looked at the two girls across the table and rolled his eyes, "hardcopy. Here's two right here."

"Are they naked?"

Gunther turned toward Sawyer. "Sometimes we see sisters," he said, "undressed at therapy or at exercise."

"With babies," Sawyer said as he grinned, "hanging from their nipples?"

Gunther let out a loud guffaw and Freydis, the smaller girl with a crew cut, let out a shriek. Her taller friend, Heidi, curled a lip in disgust, letting flash a glimmer of alloy-silver braces.

"That's really nasty," Heidi said, "especially at the table."

"Don't talk like that of nurses," Freydis added, "it's bad manners."

"But they weren't nurses. They were ..."

Sawyer took hold of his right ear and squeezed tight, blocking a diamond-sized, titanium transmission chip embedded in the lobe. The others followed suit as he spoke words so soft his friends needed to lean forward.

"They were," Sawyer whispered, "stead-mothers."

Both girls groaned and Gunther choked on his milk until he finally coughed it all over his own face.

"Can't you just imagine," Gunther said, milk dripping down his chin and glee in his eyes, "a baby chewing on Heidi's tasties?"

"That's beyond the sphere," Heidi said as she turned pale. "Don't say it again. Ever."

Gunther kept laughing. "Can you imagine," he said, "Heidi in bed with an old-fashioned, hairy-chested trew-father?"

Heidi's face turned deeper red.

"They'd be a happy family," Gunther said, "Heidi, her udder-sucking baby, and her very own mother"—even Gunther hesitated and limited his vulgarity to the spelling of his obscenity—"l-o-v ..."

Gunther didn't get far. Only the first syllable was spelled when a loud voice echoed through the open café.

"Gunther Stadtson," the voice sounded through the wall speakers, "please report to your fathers at once."

Gunther stared at Sawyer. "Now you got me in trouble," he said without a trace of a smile, "and I'll be grounded forever."

Heidi and Freydis laughed out loud. So did Sawyer, though with evident disappointment written into his face.

"Can't you stop getting in trouble?" Sawyer asked. "We never get to play. Next week is Festival of Virgin Conceptions."

Gunther clutched his right ear lobe as he answered with a whisper, "I'll be over first thing tomorrow."

Sawyer looked confused.

"My mother's going to be sick for the day," Gunther whispered with a lift of the eyebrows as he dropped his voice even further.

Sawyer and the two girls leaned closer and strained to hear.

"I hear," Gunther mouthed with almost no sound at all, "there's a virus going round."

Sawyer blinked and Heidi turned her head while Freydis

remained red-faced from the earlier vulgarity and Gunther sauntered to the main hall. Gunther's meal remained on the table, his drink warming and pork cooling to room temperature as Sawyer finished his own meal without speaking and both girls did the same. After a bell sounded, the entire class retraversed the digitized hall and returned to the austere room in which they had taken philosophy from Master Plato. As his classmates filed into the classroom, Gunther already waited on a bench, his eyes bloodshot and puffed.

When the last of the students took her seat, an electronic bell sounded from the walls and the room fell dark. The students looked about as the darkness lighted, a faint hue emerging from the blackness and muted colors emanating from the dim glow. Then a light flashed and its creative energy was diffused into a colored panorama of virtual existence. A sandstone hall, castle-like with towers and portals, appeared from the void: several stories high with cross-paned windows, a wide stone-arched entry, and a steep roof supported by corner towers. The red sandstone building stood against the backdrop of an azure lake that shimmered like a living tapestry and the deep blue of a cloudless northern sky which graced the scenery like a lower heaven.

Behind the students stood a high-roofed gothic-style church with broad oak doors and a limestone steeple at its center. Bascom Hill rose a steep-breathed walk to the west and the unpretentious shops of State Street extended east to the base of the mammoth State Capitol, a gilded age imitation of the former Federal Capitol building now known as the Confederated Assembly of Guardians–East Coast. A huge dome sat atop the white-washed walls (stained with a light layer of city grime) of the State Capitol and a patchwork of scaffolding led to a gold statue atop the dome. Other buildings stood closer to the students within the perimeter of the campus itself, some constructed of limestone or sandstone and others of pine or tin. The array was undisciplined and unaesthetic, having been built more for expediency and utility than harmony and grace. Yet, when set against the backdrop of Lake Mendota, the final impression wasn't unpleasant and the students didn't despise what they saw.

After a short wait, a middle-aged man with slender shoulders and a sunken chest stepped through the arched portal, a cigarette pinched between the fingers of his left hand and a pink-eared rhesus macaque held in his right hand. The man's face was leathered from age and his eyes darkened from overwork. His hair was close-cut to the ears, thick streaks of grey accentuating the fact that he retained hair well into middle age. He was accompanied by a female technician who looked half his age. Both wore the white coat of the laboratory.

The man nodded when he faced the students lined on their bench. "Miss Carson," he said with little emotion, "will you please return the monkey to its cage?"

As the young woman complied, the professor turned to his pupils, spanning the breadth of the campus with a single sweep of his arm. "I'm Dr. James Dower," the man said. "Welcome to Madison. Welcome to the University of Wisconsin."

A student raised her hand. "Professor," she said, "what's the date?"

"September 17."

"What year?"

Dr. Dower pointed across the campus with a forefinger

and told he girl to venture a hypothesis. When the student said nothing, Dr. Dower called on the entire class.

"Anyone?"

No one spoke.

"Give me the decade."

Still no one answered.

"The automobiles," Dr. Dower said, "and the skirts say 1959. You need to observe details if you're to be trained as scholars or scientists."

The students fell silent. No one rustled a paper or fidgeted a knee.

"Today," Dr. Dower continued, "we plan to discuss what is now called biopolitics. In my day, we referred to the field as human psychology."

Several students reached beneath the bench for totes from which they drew digital recorders and tablets.

"Tell me," the professor said, "of the importance of the infant I sent away."

Gunther raised his hand and Dr. Dower called to him.

"With monkeys like that," Gunther said, "you proved that orphaned children die or grow sick if abandoned. They need mothers."

"Be more specific, young man. State your name."

"My name is Gunther and you showed that—"

"The work was done by me and my colleague."

"You and your colleague," Sawyer said, "showed that babies without mothers grow sick. They need someone to talk to and love. You explained why orphanages are—"

"And foundling hospitals," Dr. Dower interrupted.

"Why," Gunther continued, "orphanages and founding hospitals are filled with sick children. The need for a mother is a biopolitical necessity."

"Precisely. Who can add to this?"

It was Heidi who stood to speak. "You also showed," she said, "that virtual ... I mean, real mothers could replace biomaternity since rhesus macaque infants willingly clung to stuffed dolls that could neither hear nor speak."

A pair of coeds passed behind the students: blonde girls with slender waists and somewhat wider hips, long ponytails swinging across their backs in rhythm to their step and dressed in knee-length skirts and buttoned sweaters. Three brunettes, who differed only in the dark shade of their hair, followed a few moments later, giggling and laughing out loud. Two held hands like young girls of old. Only after they passed by and faded into nothingness did class continue.

"What else?" Dr. Dower asked.

A boy raised his arm and spoke. "The third lesson is human beings need to be touched."

"Explain yourself."

"You," the boy said, "designed two types of surrogates: wire and cloth. Baby macaques turned away from the wire ones and hated them while they clung to soft surrogates and loved them. It showed that biolife needs touch and feel as well as communication."

"Very good," Dr. Dower said. "There were three lessons learned from our early experiments in biopolitics. First, children need mothers. Second, mothers need not be biologically related. Third, children need touch as much as food and water. What our research established was the reason why children consigned to orphanages wither and die even when provided the best material conditions. That is, humanity does not live on bread alone, as a first-century biopolitical observationist declared. Now, who can tell me what happens when a child is made motherless?"

Again it was Gunther who answered. "Your monkeys," he said, "grew sick and depressed."

"Be more specific."

Gunther said nothing and no one helped him.

"Did you read the assignment?" Dr. Dower asked.

"I understand the basic point," Heidi said as she raised her hand, "but the science was difficult."

"Then let me explain it to you. In plain speech."

The students turned took notes as the professor lectured.

"It's very simple," Dr. Dower said, "the offspring of primates are complex biopolitical organisms who require socialization as well as physical sustenance. If isolated to themselves, particularly if they lack a mother, they become unmanageable. Some become depressed and withdrawn; others grow aggressive and biopathetic. Such problems are most noticeable at puberty and during mating, when motherless children prove themselves unable to relate to the opposite sex or successfully breed. With nurturing, a few may be healed, but many are lost for their entire lives once reared motherless. Is this clear enough?"

Several heads nodded as Dr. Dower asked another question. "What is Dower's Syndrome?"

No one raised a hand, so the professor turned to Sawyer. "Tell me," the white-coated instructor said, "about Dower's Syndrome."

"As far as I could tell," Sawyer answered, "it's an adolescent disease treated by hormone therapy."

"What are its symptoms?"

"What you just said. The person is depressed or aggressive and unable to socialize with bedfriends."

"What's the cause?"

Sawyer looked confused. "I didn't understand that section," he said. "Since we all have our own mothers and the disease still exists, how can it be caused by motherlessness?"

Dr. Dower paused before answering. "Contemporary manifestations of Dower's Disease are caused in many instances by hormonal deficiencies resembling the hormonal attributes of motherless children. Even sons or daughters of irreproachable mothers may be stricken. It looks similar to the old regime social disease I described, but scientists now assign it to the class of genetic disorders. As such, it's generally treatable."

Sawyer nodded.

"Class," Dr. Dower said a moment later, "this brings us to the most important aspect of our discussion: tell me how and when modern government has dealt with this once-common disease?"

"I think," Heidi answered, "it was the casualties suffered in the First Taiwanese War and the Balkans and Ethiopian conflicts that caused the shift. When the orphanages filled up with thousands of children who lost both parents fighting in gender-integrated combat units, psycho-holographic parents were developed as mother substitutes."

Dr. Dower waited while Heidi collected her thoughts.

"The new technology," the girl continued, "gave women even greater equality in public service than previously achieved, especially with military service. Within a generation, before the class of 2065, systems and technology were in place. And they've been perfected for our class. For us."

"Very good," Dr. Dower said with a nod.

The discussion ended twenty minutes later, with Dr. Dower and the University of Wisconsin fading from view after the entire room flashed for an instant with a psychedelic pixilation of color. Students rubbed their eyes, then picked up their books and left the room. It was holiday and school was dismissed early. Students exited the front gate with identification bracelets and thumbprint recognition before running home to their own mothers or breaking into playgroups, both large and small, to enjoy the sun-filled afternoon.

Sawyer was disappointed, however, by the subsequent turn of events. Gunther remained grounded and even a best friend's entreaties fell on deaf ears when Sawyer tried to explain away Gunther's use of foul language. Ms. Stadtson refused to allow Gunther outside and told Sawyer either to go away or to be reported to his fathers. More than a little irritated, Sawyer left Gunther's front door and hurried to the playforest for a walk. But the trails were boring without his friend, so he returned home, where he moped until dinner. Even when Mother suggested that Sawyer visit Heidi and Freydis, the boy elected to spend the evening alone.

3

A DAY FOR PLAY

True to his word, Gunther arrived early. His mother didn't send an itinerary and the teenager simply showed up with a loud knock. Though Mother found Ms. Stadtson unavailable when she called, she nevertheless opened the door since maternal blackouts weren't unknown.

As soon as Sawyer heard his friend's voice, he hurried to the door and planned for outdoor play.

"You're free," Sawyer asked, "all day?"

"Gunther," Mother interrupted before the young guest could speak, "are you hungry? Marie-Thérèse has prepared hotcakes."

"Yes, Mater."

Mother directed her voice toward the kitchen. "Marie-Thérèse," she said, "apportez un peu de nourriture pour le petit déjeuner à Sawyer et à Gunther, s'il vous plaît."

"Oui, madame," the nurse said.

The boys moved into the dining room as Marie-Thérèse set their places with silverware and linen. Only when the nurse returned to the kitchen did a voice sound from the hall.

"Gunther," Mother asked, "is your mother well? I can't contact her."

Gunther gave Sawyer a glance, careful not to sustain eye contact since Mother's hidden eyes covered every stolen look and her many ears heard every spoken word.

"She's fine," Gunther said, his words spoken with a hint of irritation, "but she was a little ill this morning. I think she caught a cold."

"I was surprised," Mother said, "she didn't tell me you planned to visit."

"She was sick all morning. I let myself out through an emergency exit."

"Did you call a physician?"

"I couldn't—since her lines were down. I thought you might help."

"It's done. She'll be well soon."

"Thank you very much."

"I called a father to explain your situation."

"Thanks."

Sawyer suppressed a smirk (unshared by Gunther) just as Marie-Thérèse came from the kitchen: pale-looking and uncertain of step. The nurse carried a silver serving tray on which were set glasses of fruit juice and porcelain plates stacked with steaming hotcakes. As soon as breakfast was served, the boys ate and the nurse returned to the kitchen.

It wasn't long before Gunther spoke with his mouth stuffed from food. "Not bad," he said. "My mother didn't order breakfast and our nurse is taking leave."

"What'd you expect?" Sawyer said. "She was sick."

"Good point."

"How'd she get sick?"

"Don't know," Gunther said. "Maybe she's morning sick."

Sawyer laughed out loud.

Mother didn't. "Gunther Stadtson," she said, "please mind your manners."

"Yes, Mater. Sorry."

"Speaking of morning sick," Gunther continued, now filling his mouth with an oversized bite of hotcakes as he spoke a few muffled words, "what about your nurse?"

"I don't want," Sawyer replied, "to talk about it."

"She looks enormous."

"She's gross weight," Sawyer said with a grimace, "all fat and droopy. Mother says she's only at seven months and will grow even bigger before it's over."

"She's deformed. Like a hunchback."

"More like a hunchbelly. The hunchbelly of Notre Dame. She even speaks old French."

Both boys laughed, then Gunther finished his hotcakes and stood to leave. Sawyer followed his lead until Mother stopped him.

"Son," Mother declared, "you aren't finished eating."

"I'm full," Sawyer protested. "Can I play now?"

"According to the Guardians," Mother explained, "a boy with your size and metabolism should eat at least two medium-sized hotcakes and drink eight ounces of milk or juice for breakfast."

"The Guardians don't feel my stomach right now."

"Perhaps not," Mother said, "but you still have one hotcake to finish before I'll unbolt the door."

"I'm not hungry," Sawyer said.

Now Gunther caught the eye of his friend and whispered a message as both boys pinched transmitters embedded into their right earlobes.

Mother rebuked both boys for their poor manners,

noted that she'd already told Gunther's mother of his misbehavior, and made her own son eat another hotcake. Ten minutes passed before the boys were in the commons, where the miscreants kept their voices low.

"Don't do that again," Sawyer said as they passed into the open are, both boys again pinching their right earlobes to block transmission.

"What," Gunther said in feigned shock, "are you talking about?"

"You know."

"I know nothing."

"Don't pull me," Sawyer said, "into your pranks. The fathers will punish you if they ever find out."

"The fathers," Gunther observed, "don't know anything except what mothers tell them. And my mother sometimes forgets."

Now the boys reached the center of the commons, forty meters of open field displayed before them.

"Far enough?" Sawyer asked.

"I'll test. Moth ..." Gunther hesitated to finish the obscenity, "Mother-lover."

"Mother-lover," the boy repeated, this time even louder than before.

Both boys listened for a minute, but heard nothing.

"Like I told you before," Gunther said, "they can't hear us. It's a dead spot."

"Why?"

"Something about triangulation of radio waves or radio interference. At least that's what an older sister told me."

Sawyer sat in the grass beside Gunther. "Isn't Marie-Thérèse gross?" the boy asked as he pulled grass from the lawn and tore it.

"Gross weight," Gunther said, "but she's got big udders."

Sawyer threw grass at his friend. "You're uncivilized," he said. "That's beyond barbarism."

"I say what I see."

"You see everything as touch."

"Touch is better than seeing."

"Sister touch may be good," Sawyer said, "but Marie-Thérèse is a stead-mother, or will be soon. Besides that, how much do you know about touch? You're a naïve like the rest of us."

"Do you think," Gunther asked, "we'll get bedfriends at Festival?"

"Why would we?"

"I reach fifteen years next month."

"So?"

"I'm almost old enough."

"You're old enough," Sawyer said as he tore more grass, "a month too late. Besides, you still have to be allotted dates."

"I'm fifth seat."

"Maybe," Sawyer said, "but you've been grounded more times than the rest of the class combined. The fathers aren't going to let you couple this year."

"I'd like," Gunther said, "to try Heidi."

"She's a class-sister."

"Maybe," Gunther said, "but she's growing softies and matriculates next year."

"She'd kill you for talking about them. She hates that word almost as much as she hates busting out."

"Who cares what I say?" Gunther said with a shrug. "As long as my mother doesn't find out."

Sawyer surveyed the open field. "You sure about this place?" he asked.

"If the fathers could hear," Gunther said, "our mothers

would be calling us home."

Even as Sawyer relaxed, Gunther continued to speak. "I meant what I said about Heidi."

"What?"

"She'd be a good bedfriend."

"You wouldn't touch her," Sawyer said as he grimaced, "without a father's permission, would you?"

"I guess not," Gunther said. "Well ... maybe."

"Some girls do, don't they?"

"My older sister did."

"Did what?"

"Let me kiss her."

"At a tactile?"

"Not that kind of kiss."

"On the lips?" Sawyer asked.

Gunther nodded.

"Alone?" Sawyer said.

Gunther nodded.

Sawyer dropped his eyes. "I didn't know," he said, "you had a house sister."

"Before I transferred to Napolis."

"She lived with you?"

"We shared a mother."

"What happened?" Sawyer asked.

"My mother," Gunther said, "spied us and the sister was declassed."

"What about you?"

"I was under age, so they transferred me from Metroyork to Napolis."

Sawyer fell silent.

"Would you?" Gunther asked.

"Would I what?"

"Kiss a class sister. I mean, without permission."

"No," Sawyer said as he turned red. "Never. I don't like any of our sisters. Not for bedfriends."

"You'll get," Gunther declared, "a bedfriend in two years, at most. And sometimes the Guardians pair together classmates, even brothers with brothers and sisters with sisters. Especially for high marks."

"I wouldn't do it."

"What about Freydis? She has perfect grades."

"Don't talk like that," Sawyer snapped. "You're going to get us in trouble."

"Trouble," Gunther said as he grinned, "is the spark of existence."

"No, it's just trouble."

"Well, Freydis doesn't look bad and you know she wants you. You'd be stupid to shun her."

The discussion wound down with teasing and eventually a wrestling match which Gunther handily won given his twenty pound advantage. The boys stayed in the commons another thirty minutes, until a group of younger brothers and sisters arrived to play rounder football and claimed the common area for themselves. Sawyer and Gunther decided to move into the dinner hall to take ice cream sodas and return home. Though they had hoped to play at Gunther's house, one of Gunther's fathers barred their entrance, saying the boy's mother remained ill. The father noted that he himself was diagnosing her disease and sent both boys to Sawyer's flat for lunch, where Mother set up a digital and Marie-Thérèse prepared a meal while the boys watched an adaptation of *The Marionette Who Became a Real Boy*. As soon as the digital ended, Marie-Thérèse called them to the table.

Gunther ate slow, more engrossed in the nurse's appetite than his own. Indeed, the nurse ate for two, maybe more, as both boys watched stone-faced while she cleaned three plates of food before treating herself to two slices of chocolate cake and a glass of milk. When she returned to the kitchen for a tray, Gunther rolled his eyes.

"That was obscene," Gunther complained.

Sawyer looked at his plate, on which two rolls and a heap of potatoes remained uneaten. "I feel sick."

"Is she always like that?" Gunther asked, "I'd eat in my room so I wouldn't have to see it."

"Mother," Sawyer replied, "won't let me. She says it's bad manners. This was the worst ever."

"Marie-Thérèse is at seven months," Mother sounded from a wall. "Her fetus is completing a growth spurt and requires extra nourishment."

"Yea," Gunther said out loud, "but it's not just the fetus that's growing. Have you seen the belly on that woman? I'm surprised it's not dragging across the floor. She's the shape of a sow. Oink! Oink! Oin ..."

Gunther froze mid-word as Marie-Thérèse returned (serving tray in hand) and stopped in her tracks as she glared at him. After taking a moment to compose herself, the nurse continued her work in brusque silence—collecting plates with haste and slamming dirtied tableware on the serving tray in barely suppressed anger, without any pretense at manners. After clearing the table, she disappeared into the kitchen.

Only then did Mother materialize.

"You boys shouldn't be pleased," Mother said. "It's unsocial to ridicule the nurse as you did. Where would we be without servants? You were incubated by a nurse, weren't you, Gunther?"

Gunther nodded.

"And you too, son."

Sawyer didn't respond.

"Your sisters," Gunther continued, "will never be subjected to the travails and humiliation of pregnancy just as you'll never be forced to experience the tedium of a factory. But we enjoy these rights only because we employ aliens to perform them for us. If they ever stopped, we'd be required to labor for ourselves."

"They won't stop," Gunther said.

"The fathers have never declared so," Mother noted.

"Nurses," Gunther said, "don't make babies from love, but for money. They need the money. Babysitting and wet-nursing pay well."

"Perhaps," Mother replied, "you're right. Still, our code of behavior is structured to deal with the reality of the situation. You know perfectly well that good manners forbids poking fun at the distensions of pregnancy."

Gunther dropped his head and Mother pointed to the door. "You may go home now," she said.

"My mother is sick," Gunther said.

"She called during dinner to say she recovered. Apparently, she took a virus from your electronic slate."

"Really?' Gunther said. "I wonder how that happened."

"Did you take the slate to school?"

"I always do."

"Did you contact the library?"

"This week? A couple times."

"Perhaps you ingested a virus. Did you inoculate your system before you came home?"

"Oh no," Gunther said with exaggerated surprise that drew a smile from Sawyer. "I forgot to safe scan."

"The fathers will inspect your system."

"Won't help," Gunther said as he faked a grimace. "I recycled my drives just this morning. Just before I came to visit."

Mother didn't smile. "If Sawyer," she said, "forgot to scan his system and caused me to get sick, he'd be grounded two days."

"Well," Gunther said as he looked to the ground, "my mother won't be happy either."

"She's waiting for you now," Mother said. "I've already told her what you said. Your discipline is at the will of a father, who requests that you hurry home."

Mother pointed toward the main hall and Gunther stood to leave, his chin bowed toward Sawyer. After he left, Mother insisted Sawyer apologize to the nurse for his bad behavior, though the boy's apology remained terse. So was the response of the nurse (who had changed clothes to a long-sleeved sweater and loose-fitting pants). Neither made eye contact.

After completing his homework, Sawyer took dinner in his bedroom and retired early.

4

THE FESTIVAL OF IMMACULATE CONCEPTIONS

The week passed quickly. Class was dismissed by noon on the fourth day and suspended altogether on the fifth as celebrants prepared for the Festival of Immaculate Conceptions. Gowns needed to be fitted, diplomas signed, and ceremonies rehearsed. It was also necessary to prepare Napolis Mall for commencement exercises: stands were raised, tents pitched, and barriers erected. Years of practice had streamlined procedures so that ceremonies and students alike were readied by the morning of the seventh day.

Sawyer and Gunther arrived at Lincoln Gateway after an early morning rendezvous at Gymnasium, where the two boys collected passes and took breakfast while waiting for the required third partner for travel. When, however, the girl's mother called in her daughter's illness, the boys were allowed to set off as a mere couple. By midmorning, the boys had arrived at the plaza with thousands of young Equals and congregated on the Mall's thatched grass where they observed monuments dedicated to long forgotten valor: Korea, Vietnam, Fallujah, Tehran, Damascus, Rangoon,

Hanoi, Lagos, Tapai, Kabul, Manila, Jakarta, Nairobi, Cairo, Peshawar, Kampala, Pretoria, Kinshasa, and Bangkok—each war or battlefield commemorated by bronze and marble monuments. The more recent memorials, for Guam and Gibraltar, were little more than massive gravestones mourning lost wars. Everywhere, disrepair was evident: bronze faces weathered by neglect, marble smoothed by the elements, and granite chipped by vandals. Only after nearing the Obelisk of National Fatherhood were grounds groomed and monuments preserved.

The Obelisk stood 170 meters high: a single phallic symbol dedicated to the idea of national fatherhood. Plated with white marble said to symbolize the immaculate conception of the paternal state, the monument rose before the Mall of National Maternity (which stretched a fifteen minute walk to the marbled dome of the Confederated Assembly of Guardians–East Coast). Sawyer and Gunther paid no heed to the Obelisk (or Washington's Eleventh Finger as the coarse called it) as they passed many hundreds of congregates moving toward the commons. Some were classmates to whom the two boys waved while others were matriculates or transfers to whom scant attention was paid. Most congregated by classes of a dozen students per section and a few formed cliques of four or five students. Only a handful of graduates strolled the Mall as couples and no one at all walked alone since private fêtes were forbidden at public celebrations, along with most coupling. Friendships required three persons, except with special permission or from unforeseen circumstance as with Sawyer and Gunther.

Sawyer and Gunther reached the assembly point an hour before ceremonies commenced, so they found a shaded place on the grass and ate an early lunch, being careful to solicit a third student to join them. Sawyer pulled a loaf of bread and slices of cheese from sealed pouches in his knapsack while Gunther took a flask of fruited juice from his pack, along with recycled cups. After finishing their picnic, the boys joined their cohort, which was gathered in the central commons where Heidi and Freydis waited with a dozen students divided into three groups. Gunther went straight for the two girls and Sawyer followed.

Freydis smiled when she saw the boys approaching.

Heidi just groaned. "How," she said with evident disgust, "do you always manage to get out of trouble? I thought you were grounded for sedating your mother."

"Ha," Gunther said as he raised his eyebrows and crinkled his cheeks while covering his right ear with the palm of his hand and signaling for the others to follow his lead before he explained that his mother was under the weather.

"You'll get flogged," Heidi whispered as she shook her head, "for parricide."

"I didn't kill her. I just gave her a sleeping pill."

"She'll find out what you've done and you'll be summoned."

"My mother," Gunther said, "fell asleep before I left and what she doesn't know won't hurt her or me."

"What," Sawyer joined the conversation, "about the afternoon waking?"

"Doesn't matter," Gunther said, "she'll know I'm gone but not why. She won't remember what happened. Her eyes and ears were turned off and her memory asleep. What can she know?"

"A father will come for you," Sawyer said.

Gunther fell silent and the smile vanished from his face as conversation turned to a different subject.

"Virgins are becoming sisters today," Freydis said after a pause. "It's so exciting."

"They say," Heidi said with a smirk, "that I may graduate a year early. Maybe next cycle, if there's an opening."

"How do you know?" Sawyer asked.

"Because," Heidi said, "I'm already on sisterhood delay and an Equal can only take hormones one year before she donates her sack. I'm almost an Equal now."

"Sack?" Sawyer said as he turned red. "You mean an egg sack? You already have eggs?"

"All females do," Heidi said, "millions of them even before birth. But they're no danger till menstruation. That's when they litter the uterus."

"Nasty," Sawyer said with a quiver. "I thought eggs were created after the miscycle began. I didn't know girls already have them. At our age? I mean, your age."

"We've hidden them away since birth," Heidi said as she shrugged, "for safekeeping until society needs them. They're removed for protection and used to create the next generation. We've been told this for years. Where've you been?"

"Being a boy."

"That's a phallocentric view of the matter," Heidi retorted. "You're no different than us. If it weren't for surgery and hormones and contributions, you'd make a baby too."

"Don't talk like that," Sawyer said. "It's not decent."

"It's true," Heidi pressed her point. "Men can have babies. Old Believers do it every day. So do aliens. I've heard of trew-fathers having three or four children from one woman."

"Superstitious peasants," Sawyer replied, "naturalists and naturists. Why would anyone want to do that?"

"Maybe," Gunther said as he pumped a fist, "fathering's even more fun than touch."

Sawyer groaned and Freydis laughed while Heidi reprimanded Gunther for using dirty words.

A LOUDSPEAKER SOUNDED from the courtyard and the students turned toward it. The ceremony was beginning and it was time to find a chair. Sawyer followed his classmates into one of the stands, where they took reassigned seating reserved to Napolis Gymnasium 24. Not every student chose to attend and more vacancies remained than filled seats, so the four classmates sat separated by empty chairs. They waited until a single blue-robed Guardian led a section of white-robed sisters across the stage, the young women walking single file. One hundred sisters entered in four lines as the Guardian, a soft-shouldered man with slender arms and close-cropped hair, addressed the assembly.

"Good day, Equals," the moderator announced.

Applause was scattered.

"Welcome," the moderator continued, "to this season's Festival of Immaculate Conceptions."

As a second round of applause more subdued than the first sounded, the Guardian turned his back to the crowd. He faced the cohort of grown sisters and addressed them directly, his voice carried by a microphone.

"Sisters," the Guardian said, "this is your day to be honored. Each of you has donated, willingly and by your own free choice, your inheritance—your very heirs—to our society and our state. You've given the gift of life and today we honor you with filial gratitude."

The applause of the crowd was no louder than before. Sawyer fidgeted in his seat and Gunther yawned.

"Today," the Guardian continued, "you consummate your marriage to the state. Never will you conceive haphazard and random, like mating beasts of field and forest. Never will you be enslaved to unharnessed nature or organic life. Reason and science will be born of your bodies and the state will fuse your conceptions with the self-giving of the male to make true citizens: to beget sons and daughters worthy of our ideals and equality."

Again, Sawyer fidgeted and Gunther yawned.

"Neither shall you," the speaker continued, "be limited in your offspring to one, two, or even ten offspring. Thousands of unfertilized ova you have donated and thousands of begotten offspring you shall acquire. Every child conceived after this day belongs to you as if bone of your bone and flesh of your flesh. And soon you will complete your education that someday you might be older to younger, begetter to begotten, Guardian to Ward."

Sawyer closed his eyes while Gunther's eyelids fell shut of their own accord and his head slumped forward. Heidi and Freydis whispered between themselves, paying little attention to the ceremonies.

"I declare," the Guardian said, "without qualification, clarification, or equivocation that our society depends on these donations so that we might make the Equals and Guardians on whom our style of life depends. We have chosen to ..."

And so the speaker continued until Gunther dozed and Sawyer immersed himself in his own imagination. Heidi and Freydis talked through the ceremony and it wasn't until their voices were hoarse from whispers that commencement drew to its anticlimactic conclusion—with the new graduates donning scarlet sashes draped from the left shoulder to the right hip and filing offstage to sporadic salutes and scattered applause. The Guardian shared final thoughts (though still far too many for most of his young listeners) and finally followed the graduates offstage. Only then did the four young Equals feel themselves free.

"That," Gunther declared as he rubbed his eyes and made little effort to keep his voice low, "was more painful than last year."

"It wasn't too bad," Heidi said, "he said a few interesting things."

"I was talking about you and Freydis. The two of you never shut up. I could hardly sleep."

"At least we didn't bring bedrolls."

"I bothered no one."

Sawyer changed the subject. "Where next?"

Heidi told him they had to attend prom, so Gunther nodded toward the girl's chest and asked for first selection.

"Don't be crass," Heidi said. "We get to watch The Promenade of Friendship across the Mall later."

"Seeing is no fun," Gunther said.

"Neither are you," Heidi snapped.

"Anyway," Freydis interjected, "prom isn't till evening. What till then?"

"Banquet," Sawyer said.

"That's after prom," Heidi said.

"Let's go," Sawyer said, "to the Center for Aerospace Development or the North Atlantic History Museum."

"Why," Gunther said, "don't we just go to school for the day too?"

Both girls laughed.

"What else can we do?" Heidi asked.

"I know something fun," Gunther said with a grin.

"What?" Sawyer looked skeptical.

"Don't be gross," Heidi groaned.

When Gunther said he'd heard tactiles were scheduled,

Heidi said she'd read the same and Freydis asked if they were open to students.

"They were on the agenda," Heidi said.

"Where?" Freydis stroked a cheek with a finger.

"At the Tidal Basin."

Freydis stroked the back of an ear with two fingers and looked toward Gunther, who nodded his consent.

When Heidi said she'd go, only Sawyer was left to object. "Isn't there something else to do?" the boy protested.

"I'd really like," Freydis said, her voice growing soft, "some physical conversation."

When the other two classmates agreed, Sawyer had no choice but to follow their lead since he wasn't allowed to wander alone. Twenty minutes later, the four Equals reached the Tidal Basin and joined hundreds of celebrants milling around the edge of the pool and enjoying the shade of cherry trees. Nearby, a podium had been erected where a flight of marble steps reached the portico leading into a colonnade that comprised the outer ring of the Monument to the Pursuit of Happiness. Beneath the monument's shallow dome was a well-preserved white and black marbled sculpture of a middle-aged Anglo-European embracing a much younger Afro-European girl who lay on her back: the young woman's legs bent at the knee and arms holding fast to the unclothed man atop her. Behind the podium stood an amber-fleshed woman with broad shoulders and a shaved head who dressed in silk robes that fluttered with the gentlest breeze as she motioned for the crowd to draw closer. Communicants formed uneven lines at the foot of the marble steps, every participant soon sitting in a modified lotus position.

As the moderator lifted her hands toward the heavens, the crowd settled and stilled and the woman leaned forward to whisper into the microphone. "Close your eyes and breathe deep," she said.

The crowd settled. Every eye closed and every tongue stilled from habit at the sound of those few words. Only the cherry trees rustled.

"Lay on your backs," the woman said, "knees skyward."

Everyone did as told.

"Take a single finger and twirl your hair around it, if you can. If your hair is close cut, massage your scalp gently."

Everyone did so.

"Don't hurry," the shaved-head mentor continued, "we have the entire afternoon, if we need it. Bring your hand to your hair, or your head, and feel your hair between fingertips. Close your eyes and rub as gentle as you can until you feel a single hair across the tips of your fingers or fingertips in the soft of the scalp."

The woman let her words take hold. Indeed, for a time both long hair and shaved head alike were stroked between fingertips, curled around fingers, and caressed with the palms of hands. Then the mentor focused attention on arms and ankles and feet: caressing, stroking, and soothing. Only after toes were self-massaged did she tell the people to open their eyes.

"Now," the mentor announced, "take the hand of one person beside you. Hold one of their hands."

It took several minutes before the crowd was ready to continue (after accommodating friendships and preferences). Only after every person was seated close to a partner did the mentor lift a palm to the skies.

"I want," the mentor said, "both of you to caress the palm of your partner with your thumb. Do so with both hands. Gentle and soft. Again."

Freydis had paired Sawyer and they sat cross-legged, face-to-face, as the young Equal massaged her own scalp.

"Now," the woman said, "one partner place palms out, hands open. The other should caress."

Freydis extended her hands toward Sawyer, waiting for his touch, for any response.

None came.

"Feel the love of person for person," the woman said.

When Freydis quietly asked Sawyer to touch her hand, he didn't reply, so the girl stretched her fingertips until they brushed those of her partner. But even as Freydis reached forward, Sawyer turned away and closed his hands until the girl leaned back and continued her session alone, soon stroking her upper lip with the back of a forefinger. Freydis had just settled into routine when the mentor announced the session's end.

"Open your eyes," the mentor said, "and take hands from your partner. Our tactile is finished. Remember to cherish each other with gratitude."

Across the park, couples disjoined and returned to sociability as they broke into groups of classmates. Gunther held Heidi's hand as they returned to the Mall, now conversing without bickering and banter as both students remained subdued in the aftermath of a tactile. Freydis twice brushed Sawyer and another time tried to take his hand, but Sawyer just shied away.

Later that afternoon, the students attended a banquet at the State Rotunda with several hundred congregants and afterward gathered for Promenade. Scores of matriculates (along with their selected bed partners) marched west of the Mall along Old Constitution Boulevard, while crowds watched from sidewalks and curbs. Guardians paraded in full dress, with shoulder epaulets and waist sashes matched to dress boots and ceremonial rifles, and were followed by cohorts of robed fathers and choruses of naked youth (gendered and androgynous alike). Only after the parade was completed did a large number of associated commemorations and celebrations sound from the falling dark. Guardians ate, drank, and boarded together while Equals indulged in authorized caressing. Being under curfew due to tenderness of age, Sawyer and his friends returned home at an early hour.

5

A DAY AT HOME

Sawyer lay fast asleep when light pierced the darkness, its blinding beams emanating from every direction. His first instinct was to pull a blanket to his face, but they'd fallen to the floor, except for a cotton sheet which didn't dim the bright. The boy bolted upright, his face sour and lips curled.

"Leave me alone, Mother."

Mother's voice was unperturbed. "I need to talk to you."

"I need to sleep."

"You've slept," Mother said, "nine hours and three minutes, which is sufficient for a boy your age. You completed six cycles of REM sleep."

Sawyer rubbed his eyes and looked around. The curtains were raised and a breeze coming through an open window rustled papers on his desk. He looked to Mother, who stood near the door dressed in denim curved around her hips and a sleeveless blouse tucked into a red sash. There was neither a single roll of fat on her body nor the slightest distortion of her figure. Her hair was streaked with grey and her lips moved in flawless cadence with her speech. Mother's eyes sparkled as she spoke; she had been upgraded and the effect was noticeable.

"What about?" Sawyer asked.

"Yesterday."

"Can we talk after breakfast? I'm hungry."

"I received," Mother's said as her volume increased, "a call from a father."

"What'd they want?"

"He told me Gunther gave his mother a virus."

"Wh-what does that mean?"

"I believe you know what it means."

"No, I don't."

"Your father said you did and I believe him. Don't lie to me and don't be an accessory after the fact."

Mother's words were accentuated for effect and Sawyer fell silent as she continued with an even louder voice than before.

"Gunther," Mother said, "gave his mother a virus and ran away from home. He's restricted for a week and will take school at home. No play."

Sawyer mumbled a few words.

"What's that?" Mother asked.

"Nothing."

"I've audio enhanced," Mother said, "the memory of your words and what you mumbled was you told him to be careful."

Sawyer didn't respond.

"You knew of his plan?"

"He's always making plans."

"I'm not able to understand," Mother said, "such ambiguous answers. 1 or 0? On or off? Yes or no?"

"Yea," Sawyer snapped, "I thought he might try something. Usually he gets caught before he can do it or changes his mind."

"His father took him to a state home last night. He goes to Juvenile Rehabilitation today."

"For sneaking out of the house?"

"No," Mother replied, "for parricide. For assaulting his mother."

"Is she gone?"

"No," Mother said. "The Guardians rebooted her and she lost only a day."

"If she's not hurt," Sawyer said, "why should Gunther be punished?"

Mother put her hands to her hips when she replied, just as she always did when the subject was broached. "The trust of mother and child," she declared, "is the fundamental bond of our society. If a mother can't trust her own memory, how can she lead her loved one to a truly good life? All who violate their mothers will fall into the hands of the fathers. That is the rule of our law."

Mother paused for a moment, then spoke words that sounded from the walls that were accompanied by an unintentionally synchronized whisper from her son.

"Let it be known," mother and son said in near unison.

"What did you say?"

Sawyer smirked.

Mother didn't. "You've mimicked your mother," she said. "The penalty is grounding for three hours. You will stay in your room."

Sawyer moved toward the door as the panel bolted shut. He tried to hurry through Mother, who neither moved nor flickered, but simply fastened her eyes on her son.

"It's locked," Mother said, "until lunch."

Sawyer turned around and threw himself on his bed.

"Stand up, son."

Sawyer didn't move.

"Stand up," Mother said, "or you'll be grounded for the day."

Sawyer rose to his feet, his face contorted and chin quivering. "It's not fair," the boy protested. "I didn't do anything wrong."

"You were caught prowling with a parricide."

"I was caught having a friend."

"You were caught prowling with a parricide."

"I told you I didn't do anything."

"You were caught prowling with a parricide."

Mother had repeated the same sentence three times without movement and even her lips remained fixed as her words sounded. She was frozen in place, arms at her hips and eyes unblinking. A moment later, the hue of her skin turned green and she disappeared, leaving empty walls and a locked door. A voice sounding of static came from the hallway.

"I don't feel well," Mother announced. "I must take a nap."

Darkness fell briefly on the house, blacking out everything for the blink of an eye and the rebooting emergency system unbolted the bedroom door as a precaution. A moment later, Mother returned, now wearing a somber grey dress and sporting an unsmiling face.

"We need to talk," Mother said.

Sawyer said nothing.

"We need to talk about Marie-Thérèse."

Sawyer's eyebrows lifted and his jaw fell slack. Mother had forgotten their conversation, her short-term memory apparently lost at her rebooting. The upgrade was flawed.

Sawyer laughed.

Mother didn't. "Why are you smiling?" she asked.

"No reason," Sawyer answered. "Can I go out to play when we're done?"

"I don't see why not."

"You're a good mother."

"You were rude to the nurse-maid last week and your fathers asked me to speak to you about it."

Sawyer turned red. "I wasn't rude."

"Yes," Mother said, "you were. At the morning meal."

"Last weekend?"

"When Gunther visited. You made rude comments."

"Maybe Gunther did, but I didn't say a word."

"And it was unmannerly not to. You looked at the nurse as if something was wrong with her."

Sawyer's voice grew weak. "I just ... I just don't like to see her belly. It's not right."

"That's not true," Mother replied. "She's a nurse and carries a fetus. That's perfectly acceptable."

"Our women don't carry them. It's not ... social."

"Marie-Thérèse is a professional."

"I mean sisters. Sisters aren't impregnated."

"Do you understand why not?"

Sawyer said he didn't.

"It's because," Mother said, "they're Equals. We're a society of Equals: in mind and body alike. When women were enslaved to pregnancy and childbirth, they weren't equal. It was called separate but equal, but it was a synonym for slavery and servitude. Women swept floors after men built houses; women cooked meals after men earned food; women nursed children after men begat babies. Our sisters will never be subjected to servile inequality, for they are born equal under the law and not as afterthoughts."

Sawyer nodded.

"Do you know what an alien is?" Mother asked.

"A foreigner," Sawyer said. "Someone from a strange land."

"Like Marie-Thérèse?"

"Yes," Sawyer said, "she's an alien."

"She's not bound to our society. She doesn't follow our customs or laws and she's not privy to our rights."

"Why's she allowed here?"

"There's work," Mother explained, "unsuited for the hands of an Equal that must be done by aliens. They find no shame in picking fruit, digging ditches, or bearing babies. Aliens are paid in hard currency for their labor and we're provided raw materials for our society."

"But why," Sawyer asked, "do they come here? Why can't we just buy babies at the borderlands?"

"Because," Mother said after a brief pause, "we must control the quality of our conceptions. Pregnancy is complicated and dangerous and we can't permit it to be unregulated any more than we'd eat unrefined sugar imported straight from the filthy fields of Brazil. Marie-Thérèse will eat and sleep by our direction. She'll be kept from unhealthy recreations and spirits. And thus we will ensure the production of her womb is our conception: the flesh and blood of equality. Of Equals. We grow our life in her womb."

"I still don't understand," Sawyer said. "Why does she live with us? In our own house, I mean."

"It's your brother or sister she carries. That child will be your Equal. You must learn to love it."

"I don't know the child," Sawyer said. "I won't even see the child. I don't care for it."

Mother shook her head. "It's time," she said, "for you to speak with a Guardian. I'll contact your school. As for today, you must know Marie-Thérèse performs work the

Guardians deem necessary and must be treated by every rule of civility. You must apologize for your poor manners."

"But I don't want—"

"Son," Mother ordered, "apologize to the nurse."

Sawyer dropped his head and stepped toward the door, where he heard a lullaby sound from the kitchen. He followed the singing to Marie-Thérèse, whose belly pressed the table as she polished silver.

Mother appeared and spoke to the nurse with a hushed volume. "Marie-Thérèse," she said, "Sawyer doit vous parler. Faites attention s'il vous plaît."

The maid submitted with a nod.

"You must show," Mother soon said to her son, "respect and courtesy. I'll speak to you later. For now, I think it best to leave you with her yourself. I'll take my nap early."

Mother disappeared as Sawyer watched, her projected image pixelating and dissolving in a blink as the nurse stood to her feet with one hand resting on her protruding belly. As the nurse's eyes took hold of Sawyer, the young woman raised a hand.

"Your"—Marie-Thérèse paused as she searched for the right word—"your Mother, as you say, tells that you no like the babies."

Sawyer shook his head. "It's not that, but ..." Sawyer's sentence died as he stepped back.

Marie-Thérèse waited a few moments before she spoke with a thick accent. "You are too embarrassed. With me?"

"Mother says it's bad manners, but I can't help myself."

Marie-Thérèse motioned to at the table with a sweep of a hand that Sawyer should sit and the boy did so. "Your face grows red if we talk," the nurse said. "Either you are afraid of my belly or"—Marie-Thérèse smiled—"or you have much love. To me."

Sawyer blushed as Marie-Thérèse laughed so hard her pregnant belly shook. When he tried to speak, no words came out.

"I am sorry, Sawyer," the nurse said in her Old French accent, still giggling. "I should no tease you."

Sawyer stood mute.

"I am not ashamed," Marie-Thérèse said a moment later, "for the baby I carry. It is the way of mothers in the complete world"—the maid glanced toward the hall where Mother had stood—"that is to say, for all born of woman." She patted her belly, hands clasped and fingers joined.

Sawyer looked at her fingers clasped around the protrusion from her belly and spoke with a whisper. "Does it hurt?" the boy asked.

"Non," Marie-Thérèse said with the distinct nasal pitch of her own language. "Non. Il n'a pas fait mal. La naissance sera très difficile, mais"—the nurse paused—"Désolée. Sorry. Some of the times I speak thoughts in my own language."

"That's okay."

"What I say is ... pregnancy is difficult to the end and the ... outing hurts very much."

Sawyer averted his eyes. "I'm sorry it hurts."

"It's what I decided."

Sawyer watched as the nurse propped herself on her elbows on the table. Her belly wasn't visible, only the fullness of swollen breasts draped by a slipping blouse and a rather forced smile. Sawyer stared at the young woman's cocoa cheeks until she blinked, then turned away when the nurse spoke.

"You like to touch baby?" the nurse asked.

"I couldn't do that," Sawyer said. "No, that's not really good manners."

"My brother touch the belly of my mama. He felt her baby kick."

"I really couldn't do that," the boy repeated. "I'm sorry to bother you. I'm sorry for my bad manners ... when Gunther visited. Mother told me to apologize."

Marie-Thérèse's smiled turned sour and the gleam left her eyes as she looked at her belly. "It is fine," she said. "I am only a nurse in this house. I am sorry to be too friendly. I am no your sister."

"I suppose not," Sawyer said as he prepared to return to his bedroom, leaving Marie-Thérèse to her work.

Soon, the boy sat on his bed as his heart raced and he looked toward his open door while listening for the telltale ramping up of the VL projector. Twice, he crept to the door after hearing the nurse stirring down the hall, though each time the corridor was empty when he reached it. It wasn't long before he heard the nurse sing lullabies outside his door, as if to the child in her womb. Her voice was melodious and sweet as the pregnant woman sang not to be applauded, but to applaud. Her joy was plain.

Dodo, l'enfant do,
L'enfant dormira bien vite
Dodo, l'enfant do
L'enfant dormira bientôt.
Tout le monde est sage
Dans le voisinage
Il est l'heure d'aller dormir
Le sommeil va bientôt venir.

As Sawyer listened from his bed, his heart slowed and his sweat dried. His eyelids fell heavy and his thoughts drifted into stillness. Before the maid's stanzas were twice repeated, he lay asleep, one arm tucked beneath the pillow held close to his cheek and the other tucked against his chest.

MOTHER FLASHED lights and rang bells to get the attention of the sleeping boy as soon as dinner was ready. "Son," she announced, "wake up."

"Awww," Sawyer said as he rubbed his eyes. "What'd you want?"

Sawyer looked toward the door where Mother stood, clothed with what appeared to be a short-sleeved silk blouse and a matching skirt that hung to her knees. Her hair was rolled into a bun and her face brushed with makeup; she even wore glasses.

"Freydis called," Mother said.

"Why didn't you tell me?"

"You were sleeping."

"You should've woke me."

"Perhaps next time," Mother replied, "I will. For now, you have work to finish."

"Not that much."

"Have you finished your paper on the aristos?"

"Almost," Sawyer said. "I wrote about their origins after the Asian wars and how they brought alien ideas to our society."

""Have you dealt with their motivation?"

"They're just old-fashioned. Obstructionists. They don't like equality, but believe in blood rights. That's why they're stripped of citizenship and exiled. They don't really belong to our world."

"It sounds like you learned much."

"I figured out why they're called aristos."

"What'd you learn?"

"They're aristocrats," Sawyer said, "because they believe in rule by the few. And in the supremacy of bloodlines."

Mother said nothing.

"Anyway," the boy continued, "aristos think they should be in charge: that they should be given the first place in society."

"They don't," Mother said, "believe in equality."

Sawyer looked Mother in the face. "Are there any here?" he asked.

"Where?"

"In Napolis."

"I know none."

"Where do they live? Who are they?"

"Last year," Mother said, "four Old Believers were convicted of sedition and imprisoned, two Equals were declassed for conspiracy, and twenty others sentenced to hormonal therapy. Also, a Guardian from Napolis was exiled for parricide."

"Who'd he kill?"

"She"—Mother corrected her son—"killed her Mother and assaulted a father who tried to stop her."

"Where was she exiled?"

"A land of inequality."

"Which land?"

"I don't know."

"But why—"

"This is your paper," Mother objected, "and you need to do your own work. For now, it's time to take your dinner."

Sawyer washed his hands and face, then proceeded to the dining room where he took his usual place at the table. It wasn't long before the nurse emerged from the kitchen with a platter balanced on one hand and a vase clutched in the other, bringing sandwiches and fruit without word.

When Sawyer glanced at her, the nurse answered his smiles with blinks and bats of her eyes.

After lunch, Sawyer started on his homework since he had four books to read and two papers to write. He began with his Tahitian paper, laying out the political chronology of the contested islands following the first Chinese war and detailing the diaspora of nearly a million Old Believer refugees following the collapse of the Pacific Commonwealth of the Four Allies: Korea, Indochina, Australia, and the Philippines. What fascinated Sawyer wasn't merely their political pugnacity in the face of the Chinese onslaught, but their refusal to accommodate themselves with modern technology, especially birth control and gender equality. The Old Believers refused progressives mores and mostly followed the archaic lifestyle of the 1950s, with a few splinter groups allowing a measure of fertilization suppression after the begetting and baptism of three or four children, depending on the sect.

Sawyer also was startled by the theo-kultural basis of their society, psycho-segregation of the sexes, and civil organization by houses rather than classes. The effect was to produce a society that practiced the strictest Puritanism and allowed almost no touch before marriage while making a fetish of a kiss. Sawyer also was amazed at their unashamed indecency and could hardly look at a native photograph without seeing some cocoa-skinned girl with smooth arms, swollen breasts, and an engorged abdomen—and never a hint of embarrassment. The unsocialized and uncivilized girls almost looked proud of themselves with their flowing hair and soft limbs, though Sawyer thought their lack of muscle and mistaches made them look more like children, or even old-fashioned dolls, than real persons.

Following a short chat with Mother, Sawyer watched childhood digitals and spent an hour watching electronic memories of Mother and himself in Old California. He slept early that night.

6

MATCHES UNMADE

"Wouldn't you like to have Freydis?"

"Shut up!" Sawyer was red-faced and loud as he scowled at his friend's coarse jesting.

Gunther just laughed. "She wanted you at Festival."

"Did not."

"We," Gunther said, "aren't in third class anymore. You're allowed to talk about them and even want some. You can get permission, you know."

"I don't want," Sawyer said, "any part of Freydis. She's just a classmate."

"She'll be a sister soon."

Sawyer shrugged.

"And," Gunther continued, "she has the best grades in class. She can choose anyone she wants and there's not a thing you can do to stop her or to stop it. She'll be a first chooser."

Sawyer said nothing.

"Not that I disagree with your view," Gunther added, "cause hers are flatties. Get roundies. but not Heidi's. I want those myself. You can take your turn later."

Sawyer shook his head. Gunther was making no effort to be subtle or discreet, even though they stood in the main corridor surrounded by classmates and electronic censors. Now a Guardian passed, her arms muscled and hips narrow, but her breasts full and fluid. She wore fatigues and showed chin stubble. Blonde hair fell to her shoulders.

"Oooh," Gunther said. "Look at the vest on her."

Sawyer didn't need to feign his shock when he saw the Guardian quicken her pace. "You idiot," he whispered. "You can't eye Guardians."

"Why not?"

"They're the wrong age."

"Perhaps the wrong age for coupling, but not for eyeing."

"It's forbidden. Only Guardians mate Guardians. That's policy."

"And," Gunther noted, "when I'm a Guardian, I'll take her."

"By the time you make Guardian," Sawyer said, "she'll be so old she might let you."

Gunther punched Sawyer's shoulder and then they walked to philosophy class, talking about assigned readings and wondering where Cicero would lecture. Sawyer wanted to meet the Roman orator at the Forum while Gunther hoped for the baths, preferably with undressed slaves. As it was, Cicero held class on the Appian Way to discuss friendship and family among the Latins. He was less engaging in his present incarnation than in written speech and it wasn't long before both boys (along with most of their classmates) were self-slapping cheeks and prying their eyes open. Few succeeded and soon only two students remained in conversation with the Roman orator.

Heidi spoke with an air of detached affectation, as if to imitate her teacher, while Freydis chimed in with a few salient points. Both girls debated the renowned Roman senator regarding paterfamilias authority, the Augustan legislation to increase family size, and Christianization of Roman law after the triumph of Constantine. Though Cicero said little regarding later developments, he made several points as they discussed slave rebellions, mass crucifixions, and the nature of political socialization. At first uncomfortable with Cicero's justification of military and police coercion as a precondition for political association and social camaraderie, the girls eventually acknowledged that diminution of state power almost certainly loosened the bonds of association by which civilized peoples were held together, at least in a world lacking biopolitical socialization. They even admitted the state needed to defend paternal authority and familial piety from social vice and other anti-communal behaviors, though Cicero didn't object when the girls argued that all such authority must be exercised only in defense of the egalitarian ideals proposed by Plato and codified in the *Salonic Legislation of 2062*. No one else commented since they'd all dozed off.

Break came soon. Students made their way to a windowless dining room off the main corridor. As before, Gunther and Sawyer took lunch with Heidi and Freydis, this time taking a semi-private room where they were greeted by two petite Koreans, neither one taller than 150 centimeters and both graced with straight-tooth smiles and black hair trimmed at the shoulder. The hostesses showed the young Equals to a round table sitting low to the floor where all four classmates ordered from a menu as their hostesses served lunch with polite words and ready smiles. Meals were served quickly and eaten without delay.

Within an hour, the students found themselves in art class with Giorgi Vasari and Leonardo Da Vinci—who provided personal reminisces of the lives of the great artists and described the architecture and portraiture of the Italians. Michelangelo and Titian appeared for a few minutes and brought several of their best-known models. Sawyer wondered at Titian's soft-fleshed Venus while Gunther admired Michelangelo's muscle-bound nudes, especially the women. Class ended with the appearance of Botticelli and a fair-skinned Madonna. Heidi and Freydis turned their backs to the Virgin while Sawyer stared at the hologram until both mother and child faded into nothingness.

Athletics followed aesthetics—with Greek wrestling as the day's designated sport. Sawyer and Gunther walked to stadium with Heidi and Freydis, reaching the showers earlier than other students, and changed to gym clothes in an otherwise empty locker room. Since Sawyer's locker was adjacent to that of Freydis, the boy turned his back as he unlocked the steel door with a finger swipe and kicked off his shoes.

Freydis faced Sawyer even as she unbuttoned her shirt, unfastened a thin-cupped chest suppresser, and unzipped her denims. As she stood bare-chested and pants loosened, Freydis tapped the boy's shoulder, turning his head and drawing Sawyer's eyes to her own.

"You'll wrestle with me?" Freydis asked.

Sawyer said nothing.

"It's my turn to pick a partner," the girl said.

"I guess so."

"It'll be fun."

As Sawyer looked at his own bare-skinned feet, Freydis pulled her shoulders back and thrust out her chest. "We're of age now," she said.

Sawyer nodded.

"Be careful with my breasts," Freydis added. "They're sore. I think they've grown more. Can you see any change?"

Sawyer glanced at the somewhat fleshy chest of the girl and turned away without an answer. Freydis changed into athletic gear and went for warm-up laps, leaving her designated sparring partner to dress alone. The girl hadn't circled her first lap when Sawyer reached the track, careful to pace his run against hers so they wouldn't cross paths.

Twenty minutes later, class congregated on nylon wrestling mats, watching Sawyer and Freydis had squared off to wrestle in a middle ring (having been selected to spar first). As soon as the coach blew his whistle, Sawyer sprang forward, his hands circling as he took bearings of his match foe. Freydis did the same, closing the gap with shoulders forward and legs crouched as she struck first, smashing into Sawyer's chest and knocking him off balance. The boy staggered, then grabbed the girl and threw her to the mat as she dropped to his knees and drove a shoulder into her chest. Spread-eagled, Sawyer secured his opponent's wrists and pinned her legs with sufficient force to immobilize any resistance. As soon as the coach's whistle blew, Sawyer rolled aside.

"I hope I wasn't too mean," Sawyer said, just a bit breathless from exertion.

"No," Freydis said, "you fought well."

Sawyer sprang to his feet, then helped Freydis to her feet. When the girl pulled him close, the boy leaned back until she released her grip with a giggle. As Freydis walked away, Sawyer turned toward Gunther.

"You pinned her today," Gunther said almost immediately, "but she'll pin you soon enough. She'll be on top then."

"I took her easy enough," Sawyer replied with a blush.

"Easy is the word," Gunther said, "it'd be easy for you to take her since she's more into grappling than wrestling."

"Cut it out, Gunther."

"Watch me," Gunther said as he dropped his voice to a whisper, "and I'll show you how to grapple a girl."

Gunther chose Heidi for his sparring partner. When the whistle blew, they locked in combat at center ring. Within the half-minute, Heidi was face down on the matt with Gunther atop her. Gunther pinned the girl's shoulders to the ground with a forearm and wrapped his right hand around her chest, sliding it between her breasts and the mat.

"You savage," Heidi screamed, "get your hands off."

Gunther pulled his hand back as Heidi rolled away asked what he was doing. The boy said that he was wrestling.

"That's not a move," Heidi said.

"It's a great move."

"Find another partner."

"I don't think so."

"I'm not fighting you."

"You have no choice," Gunther snapped as he stepped toward Heidi, cutting the distance to an arm's length.

"Then keep your hands," Heidi said, "where the belong or I'll tell the coach."

"All right, puritan," Gunther said as his face turned red, his eyes narrowed and voice sharpened, "let's grapple. By the book."

Heidi stepped forward and Gunther lunged for her hips, driving a shoulder into his opponent's thigh and wrapping his arms around her knees. The girl fell hard, striking the back of her head on the mat, groaning as she fell and yelling as she hit. Even the give of the rubber matt didn't fully cushion the ferocity of Gunther's attack. In moments, Gunther had flipped Heidi and locked a forearm around her throat while twisting her wrist with his other hand, his face filled with anger.

"I could break either one," Gunther growled. "Submit."

When Heidi refused, Gunther twisted harder and again told the girl to surrender. Though the former tried to kick free, she managed only to inflict a jolt to her own elbow, which caused her to scream out loud.

"Let go," Heidi shouted.

"Submit," Gunther growled.

"Let go."

"Submit!"

The whistle sounded as the coach grabbed Gunther by the scruff of the neck and pulled hard, forcing the boy to release his opponent—who fell to the ground, her lip quivering. Gunther was sent to the showers with a reprimand for poor sportspersonship while Heidi reported to the coach and a father (who'd been hastily summoned) for an examination and consultations.

Eight matches were fought before class was dismissed and the students sent to the locker room. There, Freydis showered beside Sawyer and tried to initiate conversation even as Sawyer turned his back and responded only with grunts as he lathered and rinsed. As the unresponsive boy returned bare-hipped to his own locker, Freydis scrubbed her crew cut and rinsed the thin hairs under her arms.

Sawyer was gone before Freydis returned to her locker and when the bell rang, Freydis and Heidi were only partially dressed, so they straightened their lockers and exited through the narrow corridor. Though tardy for class, the pair made little effort to hurry.

It was in the hall that the two girls encountered Sawyer, standing alone with slumped shoulders and dropped chin. As they approached him, Sawyer wiped the back of a wrist across his eyes and stiffened his back.

"What's wrong?" Freydis asked.

"The fathers took Gunther."

"It's about time," Heidi snorted, "that they disciplined their miscreant son."

"Two of them," Sawyer said, "grabbed his arms and walked him to the office."

"Did they say anything?" Freydis asked.

"I heard," Sawyer said, "them mention that hormonal treatment was ordered."

"I thought as much," Heidi declared, the satisfaction in her voice obvious, "he was completely out of control."

Sawyer stared at her for several moments. "But estrogen?" he finally whispered.

"Three shots a week," Heidi said, "for three months and Gunther will grow up. Fully civilized and not so single-sexed. As the fathers say, balance is reason."

"He," Sawyer said as he dropped his chin, "won't be Gunther anymore."

"What he won't be," Heidi retorted, "is so mean and obnoxious."

"He's my friend."

"We're all friends," Freydis said, "and classmates. Equals. No favorites."

"He'll be different now. He won't be Gunther."

"Exactly," Heidi declared, "soon we'll begin to see a new man: one who's finally growing up."

"He," Sawyer said, "won't be any fun. He won't be my friend. He won't be Gunther."

"That," Heidi said with an evident smirk, "is something to thank our fathers and Guardians for."

Sawyer said nothing as he walked away.

7

THE LOST BOYS

Several weeks passed before Gunther knocked. Several light raps of the knuckle sounded and Mother opened the door to a socialized Gunther, one whose hair was combed and shirt pressed. Mother projected herself wearing linen slacks and a cotton blouse. Her hair was cut short, almost to her ears, and she greeted the visitor with a melodious tone.

"Good morning, Gunther. How are you feeling?"

"Very good, Momem," Gunther said. "Is Sawyer home?"

"Please don't address me with slang."

"I don't understand."

"Momem," Mother explained, "which is also pronounced Mamem, is an abbreviation for Mom-memory. It was used in protest by the aristos a generation back."

"I'll try to be more careful Ma ... Ms. Adams."

Mother called for Sawyer, her voice localized to his bedroom while her image projected near the front door.

Only a moment passed before Sawyer emerged from the hallway, his hair uncombed and hands unwashed. "Hey Gunther," he said with a nod.

"Want to do something?" Gunther replied as he too nodded.

"We're going outside," Sawyer announced.

"Have you eaten yet?" Mother said.

"You watched me."

"Son," Mother said, "I know you took lunch. I was asking Gunther. I couldn't ask his mother since she's napping."

"Did ..." Sawyer said before checking his question.

"She uploads every day about now," Gunther explained. "Everything's fine. And, yes, I've eaten."

Sawyer told Mother he was going outside and when she didn't object, he returned to his room for a sweatshirt. Only after the boys reached the courtyard did Sawyer raise a question. "I have to ask," he said, "does it hurt?"

"The needle's not big," Gunther replied.

"I mean afterward. Now."

"My chest is sore. They tell me the hormones give muscle ache."

"Why?"

"It's the estrogen."

"Estrogen," Sawyer said as his eyes narrowed and voice cracked, "is what girls are made of."

"Not really," Gunther said. "The fathers told me male and female consist both of estrogen and testosterone. Don't you remember health lectures? It's not just snips and snails and puppy dog tails or sugar and spice and everything nice like the old tales told, or even X-X and X-Y or other biomyths. It's a matter of balancing hormones. Balanced bodies bring human harmony. The Guardians call it social ecology."

"You aren't getting soft chest, are you?"

"No," Gunther snapped, "my muscles are sore, that's all."

When Sawyer asked if his friend intended to wear a

chest suppressor, Gunter looked away and both boys fell silent.

A few minutes later, the boys walked further into the commons area where a number of stern-faced cadets were engaged in physical training across the lawn, having been lined in rows of twenty as their Guardian directed pushups.

"You want to run laps?" Sawyer asked as he nodded toward the cadets.

"Not today," Gunther said as he looked to the grass. "I'm sore."

"How about some digitality? We could get in our non-tactile training."

"I don't know. What sport?"

"We could," Sawyer said, "hunt the Serengeti. You shot a lion last time."

"I'm not in the mood for that," Gunter said. "Let's go to the Virtual Scriptorium."

"On break?"

"Why not? I've had a hard week."

"You're joking, right?"

"I'm not."

"I'm not falling for it," Sawyer said as he pushed Gunther.

"Don't," Gunther said with a whine to his voice. "I don't want to wrestle. I'm tired."

Sawyer looked away, speaking only after a pause. "What'd they say was wrong?"

"Who?"

"The fathers. About your treatment."

"It wasn't just the fathers," Gunther said, "but the Guardians too. They diagnosed me as suffering from Dower's Syndrome."

"There's nothing wrong with you."

"I shouldn't have been so mean to Heidi. Or so coarse."

"You were wrestling."

"I was wrong."

Sawyer said nothing more.

"They tell me," Gunther added, "I was too aggressive because of hormonal imbalance."

Still Sawyer didn't speak.

"Too much testosterone," Gunther continued, "is a common problem for adolescent males."

"You sound," Sawyer said, "like a classroom digital."

"Besides," Gunther said as he dropped his voice, "if hormone treatment doesn't work, I'll never become a father. They said I was on a path to degendering or declassification."

Gunther fell silent for a time.

"They served me a writ," Sawyer finally said, "I had no ... I have no choice but to believe. To comply."

Sawyer said nothing more and after further discussion the boys agreed to attend the Amphitheater Simulacrum to watch a virtual play, though they debated fifteen minutes about which one to choose, with Sawyer pushing for an epic of King Arthur while Gunther preferred a videography about Susan B. Anthony. They compromised with a historically accurate production of *Romeo and Juliet*. The play was performed at the London Globe and the actors were Elizabethan era men (as in Shakespeare's day). The virtual audience was bawdy (throwing insults and eggs alike at the stage) and their rude behavior amused Sawyer as much as the stage itself, though Gunther found it distracting. When the play was over, Gunther decided to watch a dramatization of Margaret Sanger's life while Sawyer returned home.

. . .

Sawyer stepped into a flat flavored with the pungent aroma of spice-baked poultry. Marie-Thérèse was cooking and the taste of her labor watered his mouth. As the boy stepped into the kitchen to take a drink of juice, the nurse mixed cake batter holding a wooden spoon in one hand and a steel bowl in the other.

Seeing Sawyer's sullen expression and evident frustration as he sat at the table without word, Marie-Thérèse poured a glass of milk and served ginger cookies on Caribbean tableware.

"This will help," the nurse said.

"Can't hurt."

Marie-Thérèse cradled her belly with clasped hands. "I think it would hurt my figure," she said with a laugh.

Sawyer forced a weak smile.

"You are fine?" the nurse asked.

"I had a bad day."

"It is fine?"

"Except I'm still hungry," Sawyer said. "When do we eat?"

Marie-Thérèse now glanced at the oven's timer. "A dix-huit heures... I am sorry ... at the ... six o'clock."

Sawyer faked a grimace. "That's an hour from now."

"Yes?" the nurse said in the nasal pitch of her countrymen.

"I'm still hungry."

"You can wait?"

"Do I have to?"

"You would like a fruit or sandwich?"

"Please."

"If your mother does no object," the nurse said, "I will fix the plate."

The nurse took silence as consent and pulled thin-cut

beef from a sealed packet in the refrigerator and layered it with cheese and greens.

Sawyer took the sandwich (along with a glass of milk) to his room, where he ate alone. It wasn't long before he returned to the kitchen to dispose of his scraps.

Marie-Thérèse remained in the kitchen preparing dinner. "Already you are done?" the nurse asked.

"It was good," Sawyer answered. "When's dinner?"

"You must wait."

"Another sandwich?"

"This time you wait."

Sawyer threw his arms in feigned despair and left the nurse to her work. Returning to his room, the boy opened the door with one word and closed it with another. Not seeing Mother, he threw himself on his bed and buried his face into a pillow where he stayed until called to dinner.

At the dinner table, Sawyer took his place with Marie-Thérèse while Mother monitored their conversation, occasionally reminding the nurse to speak in Anglo-European. Following dinner, Sawyer worked through his homework, mainly geometry problems for Euclid and his Tahiti project (which included the drawing of a timeline and the assembling of a digitheme made of text and visual files) for Current History. He set the assignment to traditional music played on synthetic drums and even searched the sensualizer for forest smells.

After completing his homework, Sawyer took a shower, then wrapped himself in a sleeping garment and lay on his bed to wait for Mother. Not two seconds passed before she came into the room, now dressed in flannel pajamas, with her nightgown worn long and hair wrapped tight—or so it appeared.

"Is your homework done?" Mother asked.

Sawyer nodded.

"Did you do it well?" Mother said.

Sawyer nodded again.

"Did you enjoy playing with Gunther?"

Sawyer didn't nod.

"Please answer my question."

Sawyer didn't answer.

"Did you enjoy playing with Gunther?"

"I suppose."

Mother looked at her son, neither moving nor blinking as she searched his face. "Are you telling the truth?" she asked.

"What," Sawyer said as he sat up and looked away, "would I lie about?"

"Your words," Mother said, "and your tone don't match. I remember your words with the nurse."

"Don't you understand anything?" Sawyer growled as he shook his head in anger and dropped his eyes to an embroidered carpet. "Or anyone?"

Mother stepped forward. Her steps made no noise on the lush carpet, nor did she sound as she hovered across the marble. "I understand many things," she said as she glided forward, "and I understand you're angry with me, though I've done you no wrong. What troubles you?"

Sawyer only scowled.

"You must answer," Mother said, "since your fathers will insist."

Sawyer said nothing.

"Speak or you will be grounded. It's imperative we talk."

"That's not fair," Sawyer protested. "You can't ground me if I haven't done anything wrong."

"You've shown disrespect to me."

"What did I do?" Sawyer said, a little louder yet. "I didn't do anything wrong."

"You refused to talk to your mother."

"That's because you don't understand me and never have and never will."

"Perhaps you need to speak to a physician."

"Like Gunther did?"

"Gunther's illness is in remission."

Sawyer flared into open anger, his fists clenched and his jaw jutted forward. "You're all alike," he screamed as he stomped a foot, "every one of you. You don't understand me and you don't care about anything but your programs. And anyone who acts a little different gets stuck with needles and drugs and hormones. Well, I don't need any treatments and Gunther didn't need them either. You ruined him. You killed my friend. Just ground me again, because I don't care. I hate all of you."

Now Sawyer sprang toward Mother, trying to seize hold of her with both hands, but she stood still and silent—her image undisturbed as her son fell through the electronic projection and landed nearly on his face, his fall broken only by his own outstretched arms.

"I believe," Mother said in her ever passionless voice, "you need to speak with your fathers. I will schedule an appointment."

Sawyer rubbed a throbbing wrist.

8

THE FACTS OF LIFE

It didn't take long to walk to class and Sawyer made the trip faster than usual since Gunther was taking medical treatment. At first bell, the boy found himself in physics laboratory, where the wild-haired Professor Einstein reviewed mathematics equations. Though Gunther's presence was projected nearby, every effort to communicate through the pixilated person failed and the projected Gunther stared ahead without movement or response. Once it became clear normal communications had been blocked, Sawyer stopped trying to get the attention of his friend's alter ego.

Grammar was uneventful, almost boring, despite the fact that the lesson involved readings from the latest edition of *The Book of Womyn*. Sawyer's eyes fell heavy as the instructor rambled and the bored boy soon found it impossible to pay attention to her unceasing stream of words. His lack of concentration was aggravated by the fact he'd entered class expecting to hear the always colorful Samuel Clemens recite passages from *The Adventures of Huckleberry*

Finn (Clemens had reached the chapter where Huck fooled Pap and ran away from home).

During recess, Sawyer told Heidi it was a shame to trade a good story for the drolleries of doctrine, but Heidi thought him mistaken—saying she found Mark Twain as quaint as a Mississippi riverboat. The two were still disputing the point when a narrow-shouldered man with a thin beard and a soft voice signaled for Sawyer to follow him into the corridor.

"Sawyer Adams?" the man said after they were alone.

"Yes, sir," Sawyer replied to the man (who the boy immediately assessed to be one of his fathers despite the fact that man hadn't fully recognized Sawyer).

"Your mother asked that you be given special classes."

Sawyer said nothing.

"It's time," the man explained, "that you be instructed in sex education."

"I'm in the eighth class."

"I'm one of your fathers. I've reviewed who you are and what you know."

Sawyer looked at his classmates, to see if any were watching. Though none were, the boy still protested that he knew about reproduction just like everyone else.

"Not quite," the father said. "You have been given details about conceptions, birth, and child-rearing. Now you're old enough to hear the meaning of our lifestyle. The facts of life are understood best in a social context. There is more to life than the pollinations and reproductions of birds and bees."

When the father turned heel toward the main office, Sawyer followed him down the corridor past monitors displaying the mutable appearance of natural phenomena. Now, the sun set before Mount Fuji—whose snowcapped summit and cold stone seemed to fill the hall with a chill. Sawyer took little notice since he'd seen its summit so many times he no longer gave it a second look. Instead, he strained to see the restricted hall toward which they walked, for he'd never before been called to the inner office.

Following the father, Sawyer stepped through an open door into an attached corridor, beyond the watchful eyes of a beardless Guardian. From there, the pair walked down a narrow hall with papered walls that led to a locked door which the father opened by blinking twice while looking straight at its sensor.

As Sawyer entered the room, the boy heard the familiar voice of Mother and saw her image projected beside an oak table, though Mother looked faint as light flickered from her eyes and she struggled to maintain a visible presence. Sawyer observed that she was being originated by obsolete equipment nearly a decade out of use. He also saw a cart with an aluminum video projector bearing a simple glass eye aimed at a dingy screen fastened to the wall.

"Welcome, my son," Mother said with a momentary hoarseness indicating a poor connection.

Sawyer didn't reply.

The father remained standing even as he motioned for Sawyer to take a seat at the oak table. "Do you know what this is?" the father asked.

"We saw one," Sawyer replied, "during the 1950s seminar. It's a film projector."

"This is a real one. Touch it if you like."

Sawyer rubbed a finger along the steel recovery spool at the rear of the projector.

"Have you ever seen a real film?" the father asked. "I mean to say, a reel of old film."

"No."

"I'm going to show you one."

"Why?" Sawyer said as he shuffled in his chair.

"We all know," the father replied, "simulations can occur on telescreen: simulations that recreate the past but aren't from the past itself. We call them historical replications and they serve a good purpose. You're studying Greek philosophy?"

Sawyer nodded.

"We have," the father said, "no real film of Athens, so we recreate the city based on true facts."

"I know."

"But," the father asked, "what if the telescreen projected the goddess Athena or a Titan? Would you believe it real?"

"No."

"Why not?"

"I guess because the gods didn't exist ..." Sawyer answered the question with an uncertain tone.

"True," the father said, "but you can see that simulations would allow untrue recreations. We could teach otherwise or even revise the past as foreign enemies do."

"Yes."

"What I'll tell you this hour," the father continued, "is so unbelievable you'd rather swear the existence of a mythical Titan than believe what you'll see with your own eyes. Yet, these canisters before you are film. They can be edited, archived, or destroyed, but they can't be simulated. Physical truth can be deleted or destroyed, but it can't be manufactured. We can no more make a film reel than build an authentic Spanish galleon. We've gone beyond such technology and disposed of the means of making what is admittedly a simpler task. You understand?"

"You're saying," Sawyer answered, "film is hard copy. Like old paper prints and first-copies in Confederation Archives."

The father nodded. "Now," he said, "you'll see the way of

birth in the old world. Before we made babies by science and surgery."

"This," Mother added as she stepped forward, "should help answer your questions about pregnancy and aristos. When the film is finished, I'll return with a social physician."

Mother vanished, leaving Sawyer with the father and the film projector.

The father reached for a knob. "Ready?" he asked.

Sawyer said he was.

A few seconds later, the projector rumbled to life: reels spinning, lights flickering, and audio crackling. The lights darkened and a grey image slowly focused on a yellowed screen as the father manually adjusted the lens. The film's first clip showed a woman sprawled on a hospital bed, legs spread and knees bent: her face contorted from pain and genitals mutilated with a bloody lump protruding from within. Rubber-gloved hands reached for the bloodied object: the lump moved, hands grabbed, and the woman groaned. Voices (in a language unknown to Sawyer and left untranslated) sounded, some calm and others anxious. The woman flailed and her screams climaxed as hands reached between her legs to pull the bloody lump into the world.

When the lump was removed and the woman fell backward into her bed, Sawyer saw the clearly distinguishable form of a human baby. He had been looking at the back of the child's head, seeing no more than bloodstained and fluid-soaked hair. Hands reached beneath the child's shoulders and pulled it—pulled him—from the womb of the stead-mother. The woman sobbed and the doctors chattered as they raised the baby for her to see. A black cord binding the newborn to its stead-mother was severed, then the child was patted dry with a towel and placed on the breast of the sobbing woman.

Sawyer's father turned a knob and the screen froze, a little blurred and soundless. The episode had lasted only a few minutes, during which Sawyer sat silent: his breathing nearly as labored as the woman's and his face just as ashen.

"What do you think?" the father asked.

"I feel sick," Sawyer whispered, "that was gross. What went wrong?"

"Wrong?" the father said with a chuckle. "That was a perfect birth. Almost painless. And no harm done to the baby. That was what women hoped for."

"It was so ugly."

"It was raw nature. Now watch another scene much worse."

A click sounded, the film flickered, and a second clip rolled. This time, the film showed the birth of a child without limbs. Neither arm nor leg was seen on the newborn girl, only stumps slowly flailing. The afterbirth of exhausted joy so evident in the first film was replaced by anguish, wails, and frantic activity by physicians and staff. A man who likely was the trew-father to the stricken child trembled and cursed while the stead-mother sobbed and wailed. The child was set in an incubator and no one picked it up. Even the doctor hesitated to touch the monstrous image of flawed genetics, as if afraid to defile himself by something so unclean.

"Almost 150 years ago," the father explained after the clip ended, "there came a terrible wave of thalidomide babies. Born without arms and legs."

Sawyer said nothing, his face pale and heart racing. He'd never seen anything so horrible; he'd never even imagined something so repulsive could exist. Indeed, the child was more monstrous than Saint George's dragon.

Now the screen showed black-skinned natives, perhaps New Guinea aborigines, huddled with their offspring. Toothless old women with tube-like breasts stretched to loin-covered waists grinned at smooth-gummed toddlers nuzzling the breasts of plump girls. One woman nursed a jaundice-yellow baby who suckled without stopping, the child's nostrils flared as tiny fists pressed the flesh of its stead-mother's bosom. A man walked amidst the women with an unmoving and unblinking monkey slung across his back, dried blood oozed from the slack-jawed mouth of the dead animal. Women cooed, babies cried, and the hunter received accolades for the bloody monkey.

Sawyer clenched his stomach.

The film rolled.

Now the scenes followed one after another with increasing rapidity, some no more than vignettes of squalid human existence and others more painfully drawn out: Russian royalty in opulent ballrooms with sparkling chandeliers and velvet drapes; skinny Korean peasants striking into the mud of rice patties with sticks; and stout German storm troopers beating a small Jewish man. Color reels entered the fray: abandoned children pillaging the garbage heaps of San Paolo for a meal; Chinese infants swaddled tight and hung from pegs while their parents worked rice fields; Arab women in bright burkas throwing feces at a pilloried prostitute; an Indonesian father caning his thrashing son with a bamboo rod; lithe Huti warriors dancing over the fly-covered remains of Tutsi rivals; and weeping children sitting disconsolate in the slums of Sydney as they swatted flies from the dead-eyed stares of their parents' unmoved and unmoving corpses.

Sawyer fidgeted throughout the movie, perspiration clinging to his forehead and shallow pants blowing from his mouth. The blood rushed from his face as soon as the film showed the caning of a disobedient son by his Indonesian father and by the time the film showed Huti warriors kicking in the head of a fallen child, Sawyer clutched his stomach from nausea. The fly-covered bodies in Sydney were the last straw and the boy jumped to his feet shouting.

"I don't want," Sawyer cried out, "to see any more. It's too awful."

The father clicked a knob to darken the lamp. With a bent forefinger, he motioned Sawyer to follow and the two left the room. They returned down the narrow corridor to the film vault—turning left near the main entranceway into a more comfortable room with a large desk, two divans, and accompanying end tables on which were set glasses of water and finger snacks.

"Have a seat," the father said, "take a drink and get a bite to eat. You look pale. What you saw was disturbing. What you saw was terrible. What you saw is what we've organized our society to replace: nude birth, teat suckling, abandoned orphans, distraught mothers, inequality, oppression, floggings, failings, and all that went with the maison d'amour and its supposed affections. Your mother will arrive in a moment, along with a social physician, to take questions. Is there anything you need now?"

Sawyer lacked nothing, so the father departed, leaving the student to his own thoughts and apprehension.

A FEW MOMENTS LATER, there was a knock at the door as a white-jacketed Guardian stepped into the room. The Guardian's hair was cropped at the ears and her face covered with a wisp of a beard. She took a chair opposite Sawyer, reviewed a page of notes, then turned to her young patient. Though Mother also appeared in the room, only the doctor spoke.

"I'm Dr. Neuhaus," the Guardian said. "Let's chat for a few minutes."

Sawyer nodded.

The Guardian spoke a second time. "Do you believe the films?"

"They're real."

"How do you know?"

"I felt them."

"How so?"

"Like pain."

"What," the Guardian said, "struck you most about the films?"

"I was surprised," Sawyer said after a pause, "to see how unhappy life was."

"Go on."

"Well," Sawyer continued, "there were gross things about babies that made me sick to my stomach, but it was the sight of so many people crying that bothered me most. So many people crying."

"Why was that?"

"I don't know."

"Why do you suppose they were included in the montage we edited?"

Sawyer said nothing.

"Let me explain," Dr. Neuhaus said, "for this is at the core of our lifestyle and laws." She paused a moment to collect her thoughts, "The old life was merely biological. Male and female procreated naturally and cared for their own offspring. They gave little thought to the needs of others as long as they could tend their own garden like a private manor. And just as with feudal ages, only more so, bourgeois society was blood-based and exclusive. The sexual union was monocoupled and limited to bed sharing by one male and one female until separated by death. Moreover, only the conception of a man's own loins was considered his own child and no person called more than one man trew-father or one woman stead-mother. This meant, however, that the death of a trew-father or stead-mother left children orphaned. Do you know the word?"

"Yes," Sawyer said, "it means to live alone."

"Not quite," the Guardian explained as she stroked the thin down of her goatee, "it means to be without living parent. And it meant to be without help or hope."

"The orphaned died?"

"Not always," the Guardian explained. "Like today, sometimes. Remember the film of those children rummaging through public dumps?"

Sawyer said he remembered.

"Those," the Guardian said, "were orphans in San Paolo, Brazil. Though the film is old, nothing's changed. This very day you could find hundreds, even thousands, of orphans scavenging for food at the same dump. I've seen them with my own eyes."

"Why do they live like that?"

"Because," the Guardian said, "the Southern Hemisphere remains undeveloped: nature without civilization, resources without technology, humanity without progress."

"They still believe in blood?"

"Very much so," Dr. Neuhaus nodded. "Vendetta and famiglia and godparents and birth-rule and the natural family."

"Do aristos come from the Southern Hemisphere?" Sawyer asked.

Every trace of a smile vanished from the Guardian's face, her eyes steeled, brow furrowed, and bearded jaw jutted. She answered the question with barely suppressed scorn.

"Not entirely," the Guardian said. "While it's true that primitive peoples are aristos who make family rather than equality the purpose of the state, those people are backward tribes who pose no serious threat to anyone but themselves. Indeed, they provide us with raw materials and labor such as wheat, coffee, iron, oil, ovaries, nurses, and other commodities—which is a benefit to them and a necessity to us. But the aristos you speak of come from within. They are rebels raised among us who reject what they've been given and forsake what they've been taught. They're Equals and Guardians who value their own blood over the ideals that underpin our egalitarianism. They're betrayers unable to live by our ideals."

"Why?"

"They're aristocrats," the Guardian explained, "who seek a king. It's their will love be parceled as a birthright, that citizenship be generated by genetics and obligation be blood-born."

"Plato," Sawyer said, "teaches equality is the birthright of every person and every person wants it. Don't we all want the same?"

"You'll remember," the Guardian said, "that Plato's best pupil didn't accept equality. Never forget that raw nature isn't a direct conduit to the perfect ideal."

Sawyer returned to the issue of the aristocrats. "But where?" he asked. "Where are the unequals?"

"Everywhere. They're dispersed throughout the Confederation. Unfortunately, there are Equals who favor inequality and Guardians who forsake the state. Theirs is the desire to rebirth the old world, a life of blood and birth and orphans and outcasts. Some are spies and traitors."

Sawyer fidgeted. "Like the film?"

"Like the film," the Guardian answered, "for their aims are low. They'd put themselves and their kin in charge of everyone else. To trample equality underfoot and raise themselves above all."

"I still don't understand why they'd want such misery."

"That's the mystery humanity always faces. Why Attila? Why Hitler? Why Mao or al-Saud? Why the murder of every man, woman, and child in Kinshasa? Why the veiling of wives and the hatred of orphans? Why the enslavement of Korea or the sack of Hong Kong? Some express their diseased passions without restraint or balance or self-discipline. All we can say is such people must be stopped."

Sawyer nodded.

"The public crèche," the Guardian continued, "is the nursery of equality. Only there can every citizen be treated the same: without favoritism or particularity. The universal ideal of impartiality is the milk that nourishes life. All share father and mother and sister and brother. Equality for everyone in the class."

"But," Sawyer asked after a pause "don't we have our own mothers and sisters and brothers? And fathers and nurses too?"

"Not ours alone," the Guardian said. "Crèche nurses rotate from cradle to cradle as often as they can without stunting the maturation of a child. Brothers and sisters, too, are exchanged until we've grown into Equals. Fathers belong to neighborhoods, not to houses, and mothers ... well, each child has her own mother, but each Mother is universal in her sympathies. Every mother receives her existence from the one La Belle Grand-Mère whose thoughts infuse her own. She isn't isolated by gene or particularized by circumstance or situation and her desire isn't for the fruit of her womb alone, but for every son and daughter and sister and brother born to the state. Her love is complete and unbroken as she watches over children from crib to commencement. La Belle Grand-Mère is the grandmother who favors our children, gives substance to our mothers, and provides guidance to our fathers. She governs nursery and school alike."

"I've," Sawyer said, "never seen a nursery."

"Would you care to?"

"I suppose."

"Tomorrow," the Guardian said, "you'll visit the crèche."

9

WHERE BABIES COME FROM

Sawyer slept late, having been excused absence for his field trip, and was brushing his teeth when Mother announced a father's arrival. Once he finished flossing, Sawyer hurried to a gatehouse along a granite wall, where a grey-uniformed Guardian with rosy cheeks and sinewy biceps stood guard and confirmed the boy's authorization to exit the compound. Soon, the boy found himself seated in a state vehicle beside a soft-chested father with a shaved beard and thin lips. The father passed a boxed lunch without word, then drove toward Napolis Southeast along the eastern slopes of the Shenandoah Range—passing only a few vehicles as the pair motored past fading signs attesting to abandoned towns and forgotten battlefields. The drive wasn't long and it was only midmorning when they arrived at an unscalable brick wall that marked the perimeter of the birth city. As the father passed clearances, Sawyer put his lunch scraps in a garbage box.

Napolis Southeast was a contained city, lacking both borough and suburb. It included 120 massive Hôtels des Enfants positioned along three sides of a hollow square set around a large commons—with administration buildings, storage facilities, and guest quarters on the fourth side. Each Hôtel des Enfants covered a city block and stood six stories high. A brick wall eight meters high, ten kilometers long, and secured with razor wire cloistered the birth community while tactically placed surveillance cameras kept watch over the cleared fields beyond the ramparts. Because it was forbidden to enter the city except through the east gate or a single underground port, uniformed Guardians (mostly newly commissioned subalterns) monitored entry points and patrolled the grounds. All carried radios and many cradled rifles.

Sawyer and the father were passed through the main gate after showing identification bracelets, then directed to a reception center where they were given an itinerary and an escort: a young Guardian tasked with briefing visitors and who did his job without noticeable enthusiasm. The Guardian walked Sawyer and the father to the nearest building and scanned their identification badges. Following this final check, both visitors were authorized to roam as they pleased. When the Guardian suggested they visit one of the hospital's dozen crèches, Sawyer and the father agreed to do so and soon the small entourage entered a fourth-floor rectangular ward filled with rows of monitored cribs. The Guardian waved toward hundreds of open-walled nurseries—each with three cradles, two rocking chairs, a changing table, and two couches—and spoke with a hushed voice.

"Here," the Guardian declared, "are the cradles of our civilization: the womb of equality."

Sawyer stood speechless as he surveyed row after row of cradles and children. He'd never before seen a real baby and now he saw hundreds upon hundreds.

"There are a thousand infants on this floor alone," the Guardian continued, "newborns who take little space. They require only a table for swaddling and a chair for rocking. There are three nurses for every two children, with another pair held in reserve: eating, sleeping, or relaxing. No child need cry too long, though it's our prescription to let babies cry a little to learn patience since socio-psychologists doubt the utility of spoiling babies. Much has been learned since Spockean myths prevailed a hundred years ago, most of it based on neurosociology and social impact modeling."

Sawyer surveyed the ward. The nearest station was quiet and comfortable and a dark-skinned nurse held a light-skinned baby near her breast. The baby fed from a bottle as the nurse sang a lullaby. Little fingers clenched at her chest much like the photo Sawyer kept at home, tearing at the nurse's blue frock. The teenaged boy watched as the child was suckled, burped, and bedded, then watched a second nurse rediaper a baby—who cried out several subdued sobs before falling asleep and being gingerly returned to its crib, after which its nurse fell into a lounge chair and closed her eyes too. A third nurse left the duty station after her replacement took from her another screaming baby, soothing the child with gentle words. Sawyer couldn't identify the language, though he guessed a west African dialect.

Looking down the ward, Sawyer saw scores of nurses tending rows of stations. The wide aisle between stations extended so far that he couldn't see where it ended, nor count the cribs and couches. At first, Sawyer thought the babies numbered in the hundreds, but quickly realized there were literally thousands of infants and turned to his guide.

"Where do they come from?" Sawyer asked.

"From Post-Gestational, the birth dispensary," the

Guardian looked at Sawyer before continuing, "Napolis is divided into five components. You parked at Services and Support. The classes are: Post-Gestational, Natal, Post-Natal, and Pre-Toddler. Post-Gestational is where nurses give birth and babies are held for the first few days, except for uniques and unequalables sent to the Apothetae for recycling. This ward is Natal and these babies will stay until they're moved to Post-Natal at three months. Generally, they're moved to Pre-Toddler by seven months."

"Where do, ahh," Sawyer paused before continuing, "t-toddlers, that's it. Where do toddlers live?"

"Graduates," the Guardian said, "go to Lebenhaus East from two years to Preschool. You know the rest: State School and Lycurgan Gymnasium."

"How many," Sawyer said, "Hôtels des Enfants exist in the Confederation?"

"Maybe a hundred or so. At each level, I mean."

"That's close enough," the father said with a nod, "maybe a few more."

"How many children are there?" Sawyer asked.

"The exact number is classified," the Guardian said, "under *The State Family Secrets Act.* What's important to know is there's room enough for every Equal to be raised at state expense in full equality. There are aliens who don't attend our schools, but that's a matter of birth and citizenship."

"Are there," Sawyer asked, "more schools for older children since they're in them longer?"

"Very perceptive," the Guardian replied. "Remember, though, that nurses don't share quarters with older children who need more room. It's all been very carefully calculated according to socio-neurological research. Nurses live in the same room with natals: five nurses rotating for feeding and cradling for each class of three children. Our aim is twofold. First, we provide care and attachment to each child. Second, we don't allow children to become monomaternal or socially isolated. Our children learn from cradle to grave that love and life are shared qualities: a social existence."

"Older babies," Sawyer said, "are arranged like this too?"

"Certainly not," the Guardian said with a laugh. "Each age has its own needs. This ward aims to monitor development and to sort days from nights. At Postnate, the requirement is to nourish children physically and emotionally as they grow: ten babies per class with six nurses to each section. Communal living. It doesn't take up much room and teaches the value of sharing from the earliest age. It's the same with Pretoddlers, except that they have more playroom and require only five nurses for every ten babies. We wean infants early."

"From milk?" Sawyer said.

"Both the physical breast," the Guardian said, "and maternal spoiling. No child needs undivided care seven days per week. Historians note the capacity of old regime women to produce ten or as many as twenty children evidences that truth."

"Tell that to my mother," Sawyer said with a grimace. "She doesn't divide her attention by twenty or even two children. It's all centered on me."

Though both adults laughed, Sawyer's face remained unsmiling as his mood suddenly turned somber. "You said," he asked with a hushed voice, "that some children are recycled?"

The Guardian answered in a matter of fact tone, neither embarrassed nor offended.

"Though most of the sorting," the Guardian said, "takes place at germination, a few mistakes and mutations slip through. That's why every child is tested prenatal and assessed postnatal before the Lesche: so that a jury of Physician Guardians can confer citizenship to the qualified and assign an inheritance. It doesn't take more than an hour or two to run full genetic scans. A few post-natals—less than a single percent, as you know—are taken to the Apothetae for disposal."

"After the Lesche, they're brought here?"

"Exactly," the Guardian said. "Once the board concurs, they're awarded full citizenship rights and primary care benefits. That's when their citizenship transponder is implanted in an ear."

"Was I brought here?" Sawyer asked. "I mean, to this type of ward."

"You should've been," the Guardian said. "Most children from the central coastal region spend their infancy here in Napolis or at Point Napolis. What does your certification say?"

"This place," Sawyer said, "I think. At least that's what Mother told me."

"I can find your bed. Follow me. We'll see if you can remember it."

The Guardian didn't laugh at his own joke and neither did Sawyer as he watched the Guardian key commands into a nursing station before sweeping Sawyer's security badge across its plasma eye.

"Step around," the Guardian said after a moment. "Maybe we can find on the floor plan exactly where you were cradled."

Sawyer moved into a small three-sided cubicle, where he watched a display screen flicker and the Guardian observed the upload was slow.

"There'll be a diagram shortly," the Guardian said a

moment before an error code blinked. "What's this? Sweep your badge again."

This time the error message didn't appear. Rather, a three-dimensioned seal appeared. A toneless voice sounded as the screen view rotated.

"Permission granted," the toneless voice declared, "to proceed."

Now the father turned to the Guardian. "What's this about?" the father asked.

"I don't know," the Guardian said as he looked at Sawyer. "Must be a storage error. You were born here, right?"

"Yes."

"I've never seen this before," the Guardian said, "swipe your band. Let's find out what's wrong. Something's out of file."

Sawyer's eyes were fixed on the screen as its pixels flashed into immediate focus and he saw the words *State Adoption Security Act* flash as he read his name, date of birth, and place of birth.

"Wha ..." Sawyer began to speak.

Before the boy's question was completed, the Guardian slammed the reset switch hard and the screen went blank, immediately followed by a reboot.

"Sealed records," the Guardian said as he turned to the father. "We'll need written permission to open them."

"Password?" the father asked.

"Surprisingly enough," the Guardian said, "it was accessible. But I can tell you a mistake's been made in the security protocol. That was privy information and we shouldn't have been able to access it so easily. Someone tampered the seal."

The Guardian turned to Sawyer. "What," he asked, "did you see?"

Sawyer said nothing.

"What'd you read on that screen?" the Guardian said.

"I ... I saw my name."

"What else?"

"The *SASA* emblem."

"What else?"

"Nothing."

"Nothing and ... ?"

"Nothing," Sawyer insisted. "I tell you. There wasn't time."

The father joined the conversation, her voice sharp. "You know it's against the law to read classified *SASA* material?"

Sawyer nodded.

"This is trouble," the Guardian said, "for all of us, if we opened that file."

The father stepped into the cubicle and pressed Sawyer's shoulder. "What," she said, "did you read?"

Sawyer said nothing and the father spoke again, her tone terse as she turned toward the Guardian. "What if," the father said, "he didn't read anything? Do you have access to the files? Legally?"

"I do," the Guardian said. "That's how I entered the system. But I thought—"

"Sawyer," the father interrupted, "what'd you read?"

"Only the title and name."

"No information?"

"None."

"Tell me," the father said as she turned again toward the Guardian, "how this file was accessed. Tell me why no laws have been broken. I don't want to lose my equal rights. You don't either."

"This," the Guardian explained, "is what I think; there was a computer malfunction and his files were unlocked.

For some reason, the computer opened *SASA* files, so we rebooted. Isn't that true?"

"It's true," the father said.

"Probably some kind of badge malfunction," the Guardian continued. "I've seen the codes bring up the wrong child."

"We'll encode," the father said, "a new badge before we leave, and then destroy the defective one."

"Precisely," the Guardian said. "We don't even know whether the files were classified, do we?"

Both adults looked to Sawyer.

"I didn't see anything," the boy said.

"Nothing at all?" the father asked.

"Just my name, I already told you."

"You do know," the Guardian said, "everyone has a *SASA* file. I've helped to create the papers for half the children in this room. You're nothing special for having one."

"I know."

"But," the Guardian said, "they are secret since they include the most private details of every citizen's life. It takes a subpoena to read them. Even your own."

Sawyer nodded.

"What you saw," the Guardian concluded, "was a mistake. Some kind of security breach I'll report as soon as I can. Fortunately, we didn't lay eyes on state secrets. Right?"

Sawyer nodded and the others soon relaxed.

The rest of the afternoon was uneventful. Sawyer visited every level of the nursery, seeing more cribs, strollers, and rattles than he ever wished to lay eyes on. A kaleidoscope of skin tones, hair shades, and eye colors greeted the visitors on every floor—along with thousands of children who laughed, cried, and slept. Sawyer was invited to touch several babies to feel their soft skin and was made to cradle one in a rocking chair. By afternoon, he and the father were wearied and decided to return even home before the cafeteria served dinner, though not before exchanging the malfunctioning bracelet for a replacement. During the return trip, Sawyer napped in the sedan's back seat.

Mother greeted her son's return through the front door, though Sawyer quickly requested permission to retire. When Mother didn't object, he changed to evening clothes, removed his homework from the locked cabinet, and stared long at the hard-copy notes of the people of Oceania. Afterward, he also reviewed the photo of himself in Old California: the one with he and Mother at a whitewashed chapel. The boy looked long at his mother's joy and closed his eyes as he wondered whether the photo was real, wondering if any mother could ever have experienced such bliss.

Sawyer didn't sleep much that night.

10

DOUBTING MOTHER'S LOVE

Though the following day was open schedule, Sawyer rose early and unlocked his hutch with a spoken password, removing a stack of notes scribbled for his Tahiti assignment. The boy studied with unprecedented vigor and reviewed every photo with pursed lips and squinted eyes as he examined time-frozen faces, sometimes looking into a mirror to compare his own features with those of a native. Sawyer downloaded supplemental material from the Universal Scriptorium and worked ever harder and faster as morning progressed, continuing without breakfast or break alike. Dismissing Mother's rejoinders, the boy remained at his desk even as his vigor faded, though Mother didn't push the point too hard since she wasn't programmed to resist early completion of class assignments. Her patience wore thin only when she prepared to rest her eyes. Only then did she dim the bedroom's lights and shutter its windows until Sawyer agreed to take lunch.

As Mother faded away, Sawyer went to the kitchen, where Marie-Thérèse smiled to see him.

"Bonjour," the nurse said. "I mean, good day."

"Bonjour, Marie-Thérèse."

"Do you wish lunch?" the nurse asked.

"Just a snack," Sawyer answered.

"A sandwich?"

"And a glass of milk."

"Have seat, if you please."

"I'll eat in my room."

"No, no, no," Marie-Thérèse said as she wagged a forefinger. "You eat at table."

"I'm not hungry."

"I put food," Marie-Thérèse said, "on table and you eat. With good manners."

When Sawyer objected, the nurse cut him short. "You will take lunch with me," she said with a firm courtesy that permitted no dissent before fetching a tray of flatbread already rolled into sandwiches, along with wedges of fruit and slices of cake. There was iced tea and milk to drink.

Sawyer's eyes brightened. "That," he said, "looks good."

"I said," Marie-Thérèse replied, "to you it is good to eat lunch with me."

Marie-Thérèse took a chair across the table from Sawyer and ate two finger sandwiches before the boy finished his first, though it was only when she reached for a third that Sawyer shook his head.

"You're hungry?" the boy asked.

"I am too much hungry," the nurse said. "My baby grows."

Sawyer's laugh turned to a confusion. "Your baby?" he said in a hushed tone.

"It was," Marie-Thérèse said as she lowered her voice, "wrong word. I mean to say, l'enfant, the baby."

Both looked around for a reprimand, but Mother remained undisturbed in her repose.

"My English," the nurse said, "is bad. You forgive?"

Sawyer took a grape from the tray. "Are there seeds?"

"No seeds."

"You swallowed a seed," Sawyer said with a smile.

"It is too big to be grape," the nurse replied.

"Maybe a watermelon?"

"Only baby," Marie-Thérèse replied as she patted her belly.

"Do you like," Sawyer's face grew sober as he spoke, "being that way?"

"This is the first," Marie-Thérèse. "Before my baby I was vierge ... Virgin as you say. Now I do not know what I become."

"Do you ... like it?" Sawyer asked.

Marie-Thérèse winced.

"I mean," Sawyer corrected himself, "I mean, being pregnant."

Marie-Thérèse's voice grew quiet and her face still as every trace of laughter faded. "You remember," she said, "I was much ill when I came?"

"Yes."

"And my legs hurt?"

"You rubbed them all the time."

"And sometimes I am very worried."

Sawyer nodded.

"I do not like being pregnant," Marie-Thérèse declared, "like my sister did."

Sawyer listened as the nurse explained.

"For my people," Marie-Thérèse said, "this is the way from hunger. It will make them live. From this day, we will no go hungry. Not our children also."

"Will you do it again?"

"Not for your people," Marie-Thérèse answered with

tears forming in her eyes and a choke to her voice. "Only for myself, no more for money. Already I love ... it is très difficile."

As Marie-Thérèse excused herself and hurried to her room, Sawyer picked over his plate for a few minutes before returning to his desk to finish his research. It was only after Sawyer sat down that Mother rose from her repose to greet him.

"Good afternoon, son."

"Good afternoon, Mother."

"I see you ate lunch."

"I did."

"I see the nurse is upset," Mother said. "Did you say something to her?"

"I didn't say anything uncivil," Sawyer said. "She isn't feeling well. We talked awhile."

"That is what she said."

As Sawyer closed his book, Mother asked what he'd eaten.

"Two sandwiches and a dessert," the boy replied.

"Now," Mother said, "you may finish your homework. You should complete it soon."

"Yes."

"When is the assignment due?"

"In a couple weeks."

"I'm glad you're so far ahead."

"Can I be left alone?"

"Yes, son."

Mother's voice fell silent and Sawyer returned to his paper and pulled from his cabinet a photograph of a woman —her belly swollen with new life—clothed in a white summer dress that hung to her knees as she stood before a whitewashed cottage. Sawyer didn't turn from the photo as before, but scoured it in earnest, staring at every object for signs of date and place, but finding none. The cottage's style probably hadn't changed for a century, nor had the girl's dress changed with fashion. She could have been so dressed before the early World Wars or to this day. The same was true with her shoes and her satchel. It was only in her hair that Sawyer found a mark of time. Though it fell untrimmed and loose just as island women had fashioned for many generations, a pink ribbon had been woven into its dark strands according to a passing style when Sawyer was very young.

Sawyer held the photo up to light as he looked at the swelling of the young woman's cheeks and the heaviness that draped her hips. He saw both of her hands clasped beneath the young woman's belly, as if to cradle the growing life, and pressed his forearm against the table to compare the cocoa tone of his own skin to that of the native. They weren't dissimilar. Sawyer shut his book and returned his notes to the desk, he heard a voice.

"Sawyer," Mother said.

Sawyer spun in his swiveled chair, somewhat startled by the stealth of Mother's approach and the suddenness of her appearance.

"Yes?"

"May we talk?"

"I suppose."

"Do you wish to sit?"

"I'll stand."

"As you wish."

Mother wore a flowered skirt (white and red roses on pink silk), her arms unveiled through a sleeveless white blouse and her black hair falling to the shoulders. Streaks of grey hair conferred a hint of gravitas and experience.

Sawyer stared at her and said nothing

"What's troubling you, son?" Mother asked after a time, her voice more hollow than empathetic.

"Nothing."

"You seem quiet."

"Just bored."

"You never do homework on free day."

"I was bored. That's all."

"Why?"

"Gunther won't play."

"Why not?" Mother asked. "His therapy continues to progress and his mother says he's available today."

"Gunther is gone."

"His mother says he's home right now."

"I mean," Sawyer said, "he's changed."

"Please explain."

"He just wants to play with Heidi and Freydis."

"That's not wrong."

"He doesn't like to do our things any more."

"People change," Mother said, "and Gunther may change even more. You too will grow up."

"I will," Sawyer said, his voice hushed, "or the fathers will make me. And the Guardians."

"What did you think of Napolis?" Mother asked without pause, switching subjects, seemingly without thought or effort.

Sawyer said nothing.

"What do you think of Napolis?" Mother asked.

Sawyer whispered one terse word. "Interesting."

"How so?"

"There were so many babies."

"Yes, so many. Do you like babies?"

"Have you forgotten I'd never seen one before?"

Mother spoke in a higher pitch than before, a noticeable feminine rise to her voice. “Babies,” she said, “are so tiny.”

“Did,” Sawyer said as he twitched a little, “you ever want one? I mean, a baby.”

Mother’s face displayed no emotion. “I can’t bear a baby. I’m a mother, not a nurse. It’s for hard copiers like Marie-Thérèse to give birth. It’s for my kind to raise children after they have attained reason. Hers is the body; mine is the mind.”

“What is your mind?” Sawyer asked. “You’ve never said what you think about babies and nurses?”

“I think of them very little,” Mother said. “Only when you ask such questions.”

“What do you think of them now?”

“Nothing.”

“Tell me your thoughts about babies,” Sawyer said.

“I have many memories of babies,” Mother said. “Which ones will you hear?”

"Just the Hôtel des Enfants.”

“What about it?”

“The babies,” Sawyer said, “cry after their nurses lay them down. Do you think the babies miss their nurses?”

“Until they sleep.”

“No,” Sawyer pressed his point. “I mean, do the babies miss one nurse when she is replaced by another? Permanently.”

“Why would you ask such a question?”

“Because I don’t remember my nurse.”

“You had,” Mother said, “many nurses: Belinda, Carmen, Susyn, Marcus, Michel, Nola, Francois, Abdul, Desmond, Christophe, Moham, Yuri, Hazel, Khun Mae, Carloman, Hai, Joseph the Male, Joseph the Female, and Anastasia. I remember them all.”

"Will I see them again?" Sawyer asked.

"You have no need," Mother explained. "Your life is filled with classmates and friends and sisters and brothers—all of whom friend you—and also your fathers and mother. And I will never leave you nor forsake you, but will be at your side through all your days, remembering your likes and dislikes, your needs and preferences, what you love best and what you don't. As you age, so will I."

"Mother," Sawyer whispered, "I have a question."

"Ask it."

"Do you care for me?"

Mother took a long processing pause. "Yes," she eventually said, "I care for you."

"How?"

"I provide everything necessary for your life: food, clothing, shelter, connectivity. When you're cold, I raise the temperature and when you're warm, I lower it. You seldom notice and never ask. Indeed, I can read the temperature of your goose pimples even before you feel the cold. I ensure your favorite foods are stocked in the pantry and prepared by Marie-Thérèse. I send your laundry to the cleaner and have it returned. It's I who connect you with the Gymnasium and schedule your medical appointments. I read stories to you in the evening and converse with you during the daytime, both to share your joy and console your sorrow. When you need transportation, I order it. When you want entertainment, I arrange it. If you need medical attention, I provide it, sometimes in this very house. And I'm your link to the communal family and your interface with La Belle Grand-Mère, your fathers, and the Guardians. Nearly every minute of every day I am with you, except for my short naps, which give me rest while I receive directives from the fathers and allow you a moment of true independence so you may mature. Surely you can see I care for you?"

After a long pause, Sawyer asked whether there was anything more to love than what Mother had listed.

"What more can there be?" Mother asked.

Sawyer's eyes showed tears. "Tell me," the boy whispered, "what love is."

"I've told you before."

"What if I were gone?"

"Where you go, I'll be. I'll never leave you."

"I mean to say if I died. What would you do?"

"I'd cease to be," Mother said, "since I'm your mother. I have no other son just as you have no other mother. After your death, the fathers will erase my memory."

"You don't seem sad."

"You're not dead and I'm not subject to sadness over my own devirtualization. I don't consider hypothetical situations. That's why I'm able to be objective and disinterested in your welfare."

"More like uninterested."

"I follow directions," Mother said, "from the fathers, without regard for myself. Disinterested is the correct word for my love."

"Will you be sad when I die?"

Mother looked Sawyer in the face and put hands to her hips as she replied with a firm voice. "I'll plan your commemoration rites."

"I don't care about my funeral," the boy snapped. "I want to know if you'll miss me."

"It'd be unfortunate for anything to happen to you, which is why I watch over you day and night. Fear not, for I will be with you always, except for naps and blackouts."

"That's not the point."

"Your safety is my concern."

"But," Sawyer asked as his fists clenched and jaw tightened, "you don't really care about me."

Mother stepped toward her son. "I love you and I watch over you every day."

"So," Sawyer said with scorn in his voice, "do the nurses at the crèche, but they leave. It's just a job."

"This," Mother said, "isn't a job to me. I'm your mother and you're my existence. Without you, I am nothing at all."

"But you don't care. Not really."

"You're becoming upset. Try to control your emotions."

"You don't care for me," Sawyer screamed. "You can't care for me because you can't even care for yourself. You wouldn't think about me for one minute if I was gone. You can't love anyone at all."

"Love," Mother replied, "is not a matter of emotions and hormones, but of reason and society."

"That," Sawyer said as he glared at his mother, "isn't so clear for flesh and blood."

Mother didn't grow angry; she never did. "What's clear," she announced, "is that you're too upset to talk. You may stay in your room to settle yourself. Good night."

The room's shutters closed, its doors locked, and Mother vanished as Sawyer fell to his bed and wept.

11

UNIVERSAL IDEALS AND REAL THINGS

Sawyer ignored his mother the next morning, despite her efforts to generate conversation. When her entreaties fell on deaf ears, Mother faced the dilemma of with restricting her moody son or tolerating his sullenness, at least for the moment. After soliciting the fathers for advice, Mother chose the latter and sent Sawyer to class. Despite her forbearance, Sawyer remained withdrawn throughout the morning as his friends chatted: Gunther making inoffensive jokes, Heidi studying, and Freydis flirting. Even lunch didn't end Sawyer's moodiness.

Not until he and Gunther finished lunch and were returning to class did Sawyer make his first quip of the day.

"Give," Sawyer said with a smirk, "your mother any viruses lately?"

"Never again," Gunther said, without bothering to pinch his earphone. "My father checks on me every week and I'm under strict orders, I told you."

"Oh."

"He's not a soft woman."

"Oh."

"Besides that," Gunther said, "I don't have much use for childish antics any more. It's time I grow up. We're not as young as before."

"Are you afraid?" Sawyer asked.

"It's more than being afraid," Gunther explained. "It's time to reboot my life. To stop breaking regulations. If I want to be a father, or even a Guardian, I have to follow the rules."

"The rules," Sawyer said, "were always there."

"Well," Gunther said, "I just don't feel like breaking them. Before I did and now I don't. I can't tell you why. Maybe it's fear and maybe it's good sense."

"Maybe it's the hormones."

Gunther shrugged.

It was then the boys reached the classroom and took their assigned seats. Soon, the dusky still of the chamber radiated the glory of Greece: the burning chariot of Apollo circumnavigating the unclouded heavens, the frothy kiss of Aphrodite lapping the rock-strewn coasts, and the martial pomp of Ares chiseled into the bronze-clad chests of spear-carrying hoplites drilling near the city's walls. As Plato materialized from the cybervoid, his pupils absorbed the sights, sounds, and scents of a long-passed world: from the salted wind of the seacoast to the scented olive blooms of a spring day. The philosopher's hair and beard were curled, his shoulders strong and his skin smooth as polished marble. Indeed, he resembled a late Roman bust of himself and spoke without emotion as he engaged his students.

"Are you," Plato asked, "ready to review politics?"

Several students nodded.

"What," Plato asked as he pointed to hoplites inching forward in a tight phalanx of arms-locked men (shields left and swords right of each soldier), "is the purpose of these men?"

Heidi raised her hand. "They're warriors."

"What's the purpose of war?" Plato asked.

"To secure the good of the state," Heidi answered.

"And what's the good of the state?"

No one answered, not even Heidi.

"Let me," the philosopher said, "rephrase my question. What does war accomplish?"

A blond-haired boy with blue eyes stood. "War," the boy said, "allows the state to survive. We fought China to keep the enemy from defeating our interests and allies in the Pacific."

"Is it," Plato said, "because they speak another language or live on the far side of the sea that we fight our enemy?"

No one answered.

"Do we simply fight to survive, like wild animals hunted by predators?"

Still the students remained silent.

"Why," Plato said with deliberate and enunciated words, "not simply surrender to the Heavenly Laws like the Japanese did? Or accept Sharia like the Bulgarians? Why not submit to foreign government?"

"What?" Heidi objected with a loud guffaw. "They're tyrants and brutes and they don't even let women govern. I'd rather die than bear the burden of burkas and binding and babies."

"So," Plato said, "it's not simply the fact of having a state that matters, not only the survival of the political order that counts. You also believe it's a certain kind of society that should survive. And we fight for that style of life?"

Several heads nodded.

"Remind me," the philosopher said, "of the attributes of the ideal state."

Heidi raised her hand. "Equality."

"And?"

"Justice."

"And?"

"Freedom?"

"But," Plato asked, "what's the reality that stands behind these phrases? Behind such slogans?"

Plato turned toward Sawyer. "Look," the philosopher said, "at the soldiers. Tell me what you see."

Sawyer stared several seconds. "I see," he said, "a hundred men, each one dressed the same and ready for war. They look alike and march in step."

"Very perceptive," Plato said. "What's their task?"

"They train for battle."

"Why will they fight?"

"To protect the state."

"Which state?"

"Athens."

"Which Athens?"

"Your Athens?"

"No," Plato answered, "these men come before me. They're the hoplites of Pericles—the men who made Greece glorious."

Plato looked to his students. "As individuals, what do they fight for?"

The first student answered without raising his hand for permission and others followed his lead.

"Riches."

"Glory."

"Honor."

"Power."

"Friendship."

Plato stirred, raising an open-palmed hand to reclaim his podium. "Good," he said, looking again at Sawyer, "but as a phalanx, what do they fight for? Who moves them?"

"Their commander," Sawyer answered.

"What does he fight for?"

"His rulers."

"And why do the rulers command war?"'

"For the good of the state."

"For personal riches and glory?" Plato asked.

"Not ideally," Sawyer said, "but for everyone's good."

"The good of all," Plato said, "the universal good, the supreme good, the true end of war. Not to fight for plunder, nor for the glory of one's house, but for the equality and justice that belong to every citizen in equal measure."

Now the philosopher pointed toward the troops. "The phalanx," he lectured, "is a perfect image of equality. Every soldier receives the same ration of bread and oil and the same task is set before each soldier. Every man can replace a fallen compatriot and no one is given more than a single share of the glory of victory or faces greater risk than his compatriots. None stand for the good of lineage or the fame of name. This is why we fight and what we live for in our ideal state: the perfect equality of all citizens. This is what we believe to—"

"Athens had nobles," Sawyer stood to his feet as he interrupted his teacher, "and Sparta had kings."

Plato raised his arms toward the heavens. "I speak of the ideal state proposed by Socrates, not of Athens or Corinth or Sparta as they existed in history."

"I'm confused," Sawyer said as he swept a hand across the projected horizon, "is this real or not?"

"You," Plato now explained, "look on the beauty of

Athens and smell the aroma of Greece, but I speak of that which underpins physical reality, which provides the form from which substance is forged—though with rusting iron—to make a world. It's this mold into which you are cast and from which you yourselves are formed as citizens."

Sawyer sat down.

"We spoke in an earlier session," Plato continued, "of households. Today we speak of war. But the real discussion doesn't change. It's a question of equality. Unless all citizens share in public duties, there will be private differences between them. I would have my Athenian friends muster their daughters into the phalanx to ensure their equal rights and to guarantee just treatment."

Heidi raised her hand.

"Speak, sister Heidi," Plato said.

"This is why our sisters serve as Guardians?"

"The very reason," Plato replied. "The state fights for equality by means of equality. No difference is justified by birth or nature or race or gender. All serve the state and all are served by the state."

Two women with muscular arms and hard thighs ran toward the students. Neither wore a tunic. Their bodies were unshaven, their hair both unkempt and uncut. When they stopped to catch breath, the students saw that both women possessed the black eyes and olive skin of the Greeks, stood lean and statuesque, and showed similar sharp cheekbones and angled noses. They also had the same narrow shoulders and thin arms. Indeed, the women were born of the same blood. The younger one, whose hips remained narrow and breasts firm, spoke first.

"You told him," the young woman asked, "to come back with his sword raised in victory or strapped on his shield for burial?"

"I won't have a coward for a son," the older woman, whose breasts were stretched and hips widened, explained. "Our family won't bear the disgrace. I'd strangle him with my own hands."

"Nor would I have one for a brother."

"To raise such a son," the older woman said, "would be ruin for our family and for the state."

As the women jogged toward the horizon and disappeared, Plato rematerialized. "Who were these women?" the philosopher asked.

"Laconians," Heidi said as she answered without raising her hand.

"Yes," Plato said, "Spartan women. Someone explain their significance."

Adrian raised his hand and answered that the women represented the Spartan codes of state loyalty and military strength through which that warlike city inspired Plato's gender egalitarianism, defeated the Persian empire, and dominated Greece. Plato commended his answer and asked for other thoughts.

"Well," Sawyer said, "maybe they wrestled naked like men and were merciless to men who ran from battle, but they didn't train for war or serve as kings and commanders."

"Do you understand why not?" Plato asked.

Sawyer shrugged.

"It's because," Plato said, "pure nature is unequal. It takes striving for the universal ideal to establish equality, even in the best of circumstances. Spartan women were the most equal of the ancient world, but they too lived more through sons rather than the state and were physically too weak to bear armor. Neither did their men raise babies or the Spartan state attain perfect equality as we have. Sparta was the beginning of what we aspire to, but pure equality of citizenship wasn't perfectly realized in Laconia for the simple reason that nature hadn't been domesticated—at least not human nature. Indeed, our evolution, our breeding, remained raw and unrefined."

Sawyer stood as he spoke. "If Sparta ... if your own ideal state remained unequal, how can its inequality become our ideal?"

"Spartans," the philosopher said, "closed the ranks between man and woman as best they could. Women and men aspired to the same universal ideal: a state born of equality rather than bile and blood; of philosophy rather than biology."

"Still," Sawyer protested, "their women didn't fight. They weren't made kings and, to tell the truth, I don't think they were very philosophical."

"True enough," Plato said, "but they wrestled nude like men, praised prowess rather than pleasure, and subordinated their affections to the state. They accomplished much with little. Today, we understand that children need their own mothers and biology is destiny; we also have applied the skill of statecraft and science to remake men and women through digital and hormonal socialization. We reshape impure nature by the ideals of our own republic and thereby engineer a more perfect equality."

Sawyer sat down.

Heidi stood. "So you believe," she asked, "we should always aim for equality? To remake changeable life into the form of unchangeable ideals?"

"This," Plato explained as he lifted his eyes toward the heavens, "is the reason I wrote *The Republic*. To show men and women how to attain universal equality and truth."

"And the Greeks followed your ideals?"

"Many," Plato said, "aspired to universal truth and

believed that they served the state in equality of citizenship."

"Alexander didn't serve the state," Sawyer said out loud.

Plato froze, his eyes lifeless and face paralyzed. When he again moved, he spoke with long pauses.

"Alexander the Great ... was not Greek ... he was a Macedonian ... who betrayed Greece ... He was not taught by me or by my master Socrates, but by Aristotle the naturalist philosopher who betrayed all men and women by grounding politics in the transitory, changing world and in the base pleasures shared with beasts and birds and creeping things. Aristotle understood human nature and state interest from bed and birth and scarcely looked to the heavens at all. He knew not where man might soar, but only the horizon where the ideal is mired to earth, where clay and death and mortal passion corrupt life and existence. Speak not of this man, nor of his student who mistook himself for a god and imperial plunder and royal glory for the public good."

The class fell silent as Plato flickered, then faded from sight. The dusk-like void of an empty classroom returned and the students rose from their benches after their calls to Master Plato went unheeded. Following a short discussion regarding protocol, the majority voted to proceed to early lunch and did so. Only a single student remained behind.

INDEED, as his compatriots filed from the room, Sawyer pretended to fumble with his books until the hall emptied, then called out.

"Can I speak," Sawyer now said with a loud voice, "to Aristotle? Is Aristotle here?"

Within seconds, an old Greek cloaked in a faded tunic

and graced by a greyed beard appeared before the boy as the room transformed into a great forest lorded by towering oaks. It was autumn and blood-red leaves fluttered to the earth at the whisper of the wind. Squirrels scampered about the forest floor, their cheeks stuffed with acorns, and birds chirped from the canopy of the forest.

Aristotle spoke. "Greetings, my son."

"Greetings, Aristotle."

Aristotle bent his neck with a slight bow and asked why he had been summoned. Sawyer asked if the philosopher would answer questions and Aristotle agreed to do so.

"Master Aristotle," Sawyer said after a pause, "Plato taught today about war. Last week he spoke of women."

"He spoke of his ideal republic?"

"Yes."

"My teacher," Aristotle said, "was a visionary. He dreamed great visions and tried to bring the very heavens to earth."

"You disapprove?"

Aristotle swept his arm across the facade of the forest and a squirrel startled by the suddenness of his movement scampered up a tree and a blackbird frightened by the squirrel took wing with a loud caw.

"We are not," Aristotle declared, "in the heavens. We live on earth. These animals, the trees, your own flesh and blood are born of humor and even humanity."

Sawyer didn't wait for permission to respond. "Plato spoke—he still speaks—of an ideal realm," the boy said. "Of a world of pure thought and form. Of that which gives shape to everything we see."

Aristotle walked to an oak tree projected several meters away and picked up an acorn. "What do you see?" he asked.

"An acorn."

"I see an oak tree, lofty and laden heavy with nutty fruit."

"Someday. Possibly."

"I see a potential oak actualized over time from this small seed."

Sawyer listened.

"Let me simplify," Aristotle said. "It's the world of forms that matters to Plato: the realm of ideas, ideals, and conceptual thought, you might say. I don't deny there exists a transcendent realm—a universal that governs nature. But what I declare is the ideal is realized in the world around us: in our states and houses and bodies. And not only in ours, but in those of every animal. How else can we exist?"

"We exist," Sawyer replied, "because the Guardians will it. They're the makers of humankind."

"No," Aristotle objected, "your Guardians are no more than shepherds and caretakers of the flock. Human nature is real and it's they who must tend its needs."

"I don't understand."

"The human household," Aristotle said as he raised his hand, "is real. It rises from the division of nature into male and female and their reunion at the nuptial couch. Passion and friendship lead man to woman and woman to man until desire is spent and seed implanted. Children are born and farms founded. Households gather into villages and villages organize into states. Government is established and armies mustered, all of this originating from the natural desire of men to lay with women. This is the way for birds in their nests, gophers in their holes, and people in their villages."

"But," Sawyer said, "we have neither stead-mother nor village and our children are born by the will of the fathers and raised by electronic mothers as the Guardians decide."

"Your Guardians," Aristotle said a little louder than before, "have created a laboratory: conceptions without passion and infants without mothers. They have tried to uproot every good impulse and every natural affection, though even they've been forced to plant conceptions in surrogates and bring human touch to child rearing. And to what end has this all been done?"

"We're Equals."

"Yes," Aristotle replied, "every child equally unknown and equally unloved. Without families or father or sisters or brothers or mothers."

"But we're all brothers and sisters."

"No," Aristotle said. "There's not one true brother or sister among you."

"We love like brothers and sisters."

"How can you love those you know not?"

"Our love is shared for everyone."

"These are no more than passing acquaintances and wisps of wind," Aristotle said as looked straight at Sawyer. "Who feels affection for a nameless crowd?"

"That's not fair," Sawyer answered. "We have our class-mates and bedfriends. And we never worry about being orphaned."

A squirrel raced for a nearby tree, its mouth gorged with acorns. Aristotle and Sawyer watched as the small animal (its every movement hurried and nervous) disappeared into a tree hollow.

Aristotle pointed to the spot. "That mother," the philoso-pher said, "takes nuts to her young whom she tends and for whom she scampers and frets."

Sawyer said nothing.

"Better," Aristotle continued, "to live a few years as the

whelp of some small beast than to live long as an unloved son."

"I don't think," Sawyer said as his shoulders slumped, "I understand what you mean."

"A mother's love isn't for understanding, but for feeling. To suckle milk from her breasts as a babe, to know her kisses as a boy, and to enjoy her warmth even as a man: this is to exist beyond biology and to be loved beyond necessity."

Aristotle paused to watch another squirrel running up a tree, taking a walnut into a hollow where she hid her nest.

"Master Aristotle," Sawyer said, "tell me more about a mother's love."

"The poets," Aristotle said, "tell us that the love of mother for her child can be neither defined nor explained, only known. They speak of a desire more powerful than passion and affection more tender than friendship."

"Your histories," Sawyer interrupted, "tell of parents who were cruel and of children mistreated after their parents died."

"Even in your world," Aristotle said, "friends part and passions fade. While it's true children in my world sometimes were born to bad parents, it was also true every child was free to grow up to become a good father or a loving mother. That's a joy no man or woman born into your world will ever know."

"Being a parent was a joy?" Sawyer said with an uncertain tone to his voice.

"And," Aristotle explained with a nod of his head, "a sorrow too, since love isn't always blessed. You spoke of orphans, but the parentless suffered less than the childless, especially those whose children were taken in an untimely manner."

"You mean stead-mothers suffered?"

"Few recovered the loss of a child. Most mourned until they themselves were buried."

Sawyer shrugged. "Mother says she'd cease to exist if I died," he said, "but I don't think she'd even suffer for one second."

"Just," Aristotle said as he raised his right hand, "as she feels no great joy at your existence."

Sawyer stared at his shoes and spoke only after a long pause. "Mother," he whispered, "has never sung me a lullaby."

Aristotle didn't reply and Sawyer fell silent.

After a time, the philosopher asked if there were other questions and when Sawyer said not, Aristotle vanished, leaving the young student in an empty chamber. Only after Sawyer called a moment later for Aristotle to return did forest refill the room, with the philosopher projected just a couple meters away.

"Master Aristotle," Sawyer said, this time his eyes locked on the virtual philosopher, "I have one more question."

"Ask."

Sawyer dropped his eyes and his chin and spoke with a hushed voice. "If a stead-mother gave her child up or lost him when he was born, did she miss him for a short or long time?"

"Women often grieved lost sons or daughters for their entire lives."

"But," Sawyer said, " if she never knew her son, how could she love him?"

"She carried him nine months in belly and heart as part of her very self. Love was begotten when the child was conceived. That's why mothers love their children from the womb while children learn to return love only as they grow up."

"But she couldn't find him, could she?" Sawyer asked. "I mean, if they were separated by thousands of kilometers?"

"Haven't," Aristotle answered, "you read our histories and myths? Don't they tell of sons lost and then found? Of gods returning lost children in answer to the prayers of grieving parents? In the old ordering, as you call it, the very face and form of a child confirmed parentage. While mothers might know without doubt who fathered the child in their womb, many fathers feared betrayal. Such men could confirm parentage by observation, judging as illegitimate that child whose flesh and face did not resemble their own. Such offspring might be sent away and their mothers condemned as unfaithful."

Sawyer grimaced. "She was punished? And her child?"

"Sometimes," Aristotle said, "but that doesn't concern us. What you also must remember is the inverse of the equation; if bastards may be discovered by dissimilarity, then parents can recognize lost children by likeness to themselves and their kin. Plato was mistaken to imagine parent and child might be separated while living in the same city. If they're physically close, recognition and favoritism born of kinship will come. If any state wishes to disestablish the order of nature, the two must be kept from each other. As far as possible."

"Tahiti," Sawyer said aloud, almost without forethought, "is halfway around the world."

Aristotle faded with the forest.

12

MOTHER'S DAY

When final bell rang, Sawyer sprinted home and went straight to his room, where he unlocked his hutch and arranged its contents on the desk: clipped articles, historical images, and an outdated map. Mother appeared in the room without sound, though her voice was loud enough.

"Sawyer," Mother said.

Sawyer jumped. "Don't scare me."

"Is that homework?"

"My Tahiti project."

"When's it due?"

"Next month."

Mother calculated in a blink. "That's my memory as well," she said. "Why so much effort today?"

"I don't know."

"You've never worked so diligently before."

"Guess I want a good mark."

Several seconds passed while Mother considered his words. "Do you," she eventually said, "have questions for me?"

"Not for you."

"Very good," Mother replied, "Marie-Thérèse will serve dinner in twenty minutes. Please remember to wash."

Mother disappeared with her instructions and Sawyer returned to his work. Twenty minutes later, the boy found himself sitting beside the nurse. Though they talked little, they made eye contact and Marie-Thérèse smiled when she caught Sawyer eyeing her belly.

Sawyer blushed.

After dinner, Sawyer watched Marie-Thérèse wash dishes for a moment, then reviewed digitals—spending an hour watching the news, being interested mostly in Confederation naval movements between the Philippines and Old Australia. Indeed, it was reported that the Alliance of Oceania Islands had reaffirmed its neutrality and was sending ambassadors to Brussels and Beijing. Sawyer watched war images flicker across the screen until the news recycled and the boy returned to his room to work.

After a time, Marie-Thérèse brought cake and milk: treats for which Sawyer expressed his gratitude by returning the glass and plate to the kitchen.

As the boy rinsed the dirty dishes, the nurse tapped his arm. "That is kind," Marie-Thérèse said.

Sawyer dropped his eyes. "Dinner was good," the boy said. "It's always good. Since you came. Dessert too."

"It is my job."

Mother appeared in the kitchen, her hair set in a tight-wrapped bun and her eyes hidden behind glasses. "Marie-Thérèse," she said, "have you anything to do beside fraternize—"

At that very moment Mother's words died on her lips, along with every appliance in the flat as the room went dark.

A thin line of emergency lights penetrated the darkness as emergency settings opened the shutters.

"What," Marie-Thérèse said with a gasp, "is the wrong?"

"It's blackout," Sawyer said.

"I did not know they come here."

"Not often."

"How long?" the nurse asked.

"Every year or two," Sawyer replied.

"I mean," Marie-Thérèse said as she shook her head, "how long to last?"

Sawyer looked out a window where he saw that darkness had blanketed the neighborhood. After a moment, he faced the nurse. "I don't know," the boy said, "an hour or two. Maybe more. Maybe not."

"What do we do?"

"Wait."

"I cannot finish work if there are no lights."

"Anyway, your machines won't work."

"Oh no," Marie-Thérèse replied. "It is necessary for me to do the clothings."

"And I have homework," Sawyer said, "but we'll both wait till the light returns. Batteries are on emergency power and Mother won't awaken till she's safe from surges. All of the appliances are down too."

A few minutes later, Sawyer and Marie-Thérèse went to the living room (where a picture window faced the courtyard) and sat on the sofa in near dark, separated by a single cushion. An unaccustomed silence fell on the room since there was neither the omnipresent backdrop of white noise nor the faint whisper of Mother's teleprojectors. Quiet was as deep as the dark and the pair found themselves in a room graced neither by the artificial light of civilization nor the ever-distracting noise of human sociability.

While Marie-Thérèse neither moved nor spoke, Sawyer tapped his fingers against a lamp table and bumped his knees together as he fussed and fidgeted. Only when he started to rock his whole body did the nurse press a hand to his shoulder.

"You are nervous?" Marie-Thérèse asked.

"Just bored."

"You need to be ... how do they say ... occupied?"

"I don't like to sit still."

"It is the way of your people. They are très impatients."

"You don't get bored?"

"Boredom," the nurse said, "is to your people. To the rich."

"You don't mind just sitting here? With all your work to do?"

"If I do not get into trouble to sit with you."

"You won't," Sawyer said. "Mother can't hear or see anyone or anything during a blackout. What she doesn't know won't hurt you."

Marie-Thérèse rested her right hand on her belly. "There," she whispered, "is much time to work. I am content to sit with baby."

"It's hard to imagine a baby in there," Sawyer said as he looked at the nurse's swollen abdomen.

Marie-Thérèse took the boy's hand and laid it on her belly. "Baby will no hurt you," she said.

For a moment, Sawyer kept his hand where it had been placed. Only after he felt a quiver did he startle and pull back.

"You can no feel him so much now," the nurse said, "but soon you will. Then I let you feel my baby kick."

"Your baby?" Sawyer said. "You called the baby yours."

Marie-Thérèse scanned the shadows. "My baby," she said after a pause, "I am his mother. I love my baby."

Silence returned.

Outside, darkness prevailed and even the cold radiance of the moon frequently was cloaked by the ethereal mist of broken clouds that eclipsed its pale reflection. When Sawyer spoke after several minutes, his voice was a mere whisper in the dark.

"You love your baby?" Sawyer asked.

"I do."

"How," Sawyer said, "can you love someone you don't know? What kind of love can that be?"

"I can no explain," Marie-Thérèse said.

"You can't say what love is?"

"I only can love."

"Then how can you give it away?"

"I do not want to."

"Then why?"

"I have no"—the nurse paused—"I have no choice."

Sawyer pressed his point. "Will they let you see him after the birth? Or hold him?"

"No."

"Ever?"

"No."

"Not one time?"

Marie-Thérèse shook her head.

"What would it hurt?" Sawyer said. "Nurses hold babies all the time. What would it hurt?"

Marie-Therese whispered her reply. "They say this would make questions. I mean, after babies grow up."

"I suppose," Sawyer said. "I guess people might want to know if they were held by a trew-moth ... like the photo."

Sawyer fell silent.

When the nurse asked what was wrong, the boy told her he was just thinking, so she dropped the matter. Only after a long while did he speak.

"Don't," Sawyer said, "you want to keep the baby?"

Marie-Thérèse's voice broke, almost in a sob. "I came to make money for my family," she said. "It is nec ... necessary. My country is poor and beaucoup d'enfants ... I am sorry, many children, I mean to say, go hungry. Some die. A woman who makes baby for your people is paid much. More than women earn in their lives. With this money I marry and make my family."

"With no money," the nurse continued after a short pause, "it is necessary that I make no family. No marriage. No baby. I must live to alone. Toujours. Always."

Sawyer's voice quieted. "But," he said, "this your child. How can you give it away?"

Marie-Thérèse answered with a whisper, her voice choking and eyes tearing till she wiped them with her fingers.

"I would take the baby home," the nurse said, "if I could. If I had choice. Even if I have no money. But my child belongs to your people. He is boy and was ... conceived, is that the word? Yes?"

Sawyer said it was.

"He is conceived," the nurse continued, "from eggs of your girls and seed of your men. I carry the baby of others. He is not my flesh, but I am home for his body."

"I never thought about that."

"I do," the nurse continued, "each day. I carry the baby who is no mine, but I would take him home if they would give. He is in me."

"Can't you just leave?"

"No," Marie-Thérèse said after a long pause, "my child

belongs to the people of yours. I go when I choose, but they will remove the baby before I leave to home. He is the property of Confederation."

"They would move it—"

"Him."

"They would move him to another nurse?" Sawyer asked.

"If they do so," Marie-Thérèse answered, "I would leave. But this can no be. Baby would die."

"You can't sneak away?"

"No," Marie-Thérèse said. "If I am caught, they let baby die, and if I return to my people without money, also the baby will die."

"And you won't let him die?"

"His life depends to me. I made choice."

Sawyer and the nurse fell quiet except for a single sob that echoed in the dark.

More silence followed and neither spoke until Sawyer broke the silence after several minutes.

"Is it," Sawyer said, "hard after you give birth?"

Marie-Thérèse nodded as the clouds broke and a glint of moonlight showed the wet shine of her face. "Oui," she said. "The women are very sad."

"From the pain?"

"They take the babies by the surgery. Sometimes the women can no make others. Also, there is the pain of the memoi ... the memory."

"Then why do they do it?"

"It is the only way to make babies. Our country is no like yours. As I say, we are no rich. There is no much food. They pay me in gold, so I marry when I go home to make my own baby. It is ... we call prix-mama ... mother-price."

Sawyer's voice remained a whisper, barely distinguished

from the sob of the nurse. Their conversation was so still Mother's sensors couldn't have amplified their whispers.

"Will," the boy asked, "you forget this baby soon?"

"No," Marie-Thérèse said. "I will no forget. Never."

Sawyer said nothing.

"In my city," Marie-Thérèse continued, her voice trailing almost to nothing, "there is hill ... a mountain ... where many women throw themselves."

Sawyer wrinkled his brow. "I don't understand."

"I mean to say," Marie-Thérèse explained, "la ... the women kill themselves for the babies they can no love."

"Like you?"

"Yes, women who have done what I do. Some can no endure the memory."

"They can't bear the memory?"

"Many. Too many."

Silence returned while Sawyer considered for a few moments what she'd said. Only then did he speak.

"My mother left me," the boy whispered.

"She'll be back soon."

"No," Sawyer said. "Mother is not my mother. She's not even a person. Only a program. A projection. My mother is real and comes from Tahiti. I don't know anything else about her except I'm of her body. She was a real mother. A stead-mother."

Marie-Thérèse's answer was so soft Sawyer leaned even closer to hear her reply. Their noses almost touched.

"How do you know?"

"I saw my files at the hospital."

"You must tell to no one," the nurse said. "It is très dangereux to know things."

"I know."

Marie-Thérèse no longer weighed her words. Though

her voice remained a whisper, her words came quick as she took advantage of this unguarded moment when Mother remained offline.

"Sawyer," Marie-Thérèse said, "I ask question and you answer. When we have time. Alone."

Sawyer nodded his consent.

"Do you think," the nurse continued, "to the mother who born you?"

"Sometimes."

"What you think?"

"I want to know what she looks like. What she is like."

"Why?"

"She's my stead-mother."

"Would you go to her?"

"Yes."

"You fear danger?" Marie-Thérèse asked.

"What danger?" Sawyer replied.

"To leave ... home."

"No."

"You are honest?"

"Why do you ask?"

"There may be a way," the nurse said as she took Sawyer's hand, "to go to your mother."

"How?"

"Les aristos."

Sawyer sat straight up and leaned toward the nurse. "They're terrorists. And kidnappers."

"They are no terrorists. They never explode airplanes or make wars."

Sawyer looked confused. "The fathers say they are guilty. That they're subversives."

"Do you know what they do?" Marie-Thérèse said.

"No," Sawyer replied.

"They bring mothers to children. C'est tout."

Sawyer's squeezed the nurse's hand. "I thought they're aristocrats who want to rule by their blood."

Marie-Thérèse laughed. "They say this?"

Sawyer nodded.

"It is no true," the nurse said. "They are not wicked men. Or women."

"How do you know about the aristos?"

"I ... I know men who are aristos. And women also."

"Are you one?"

"No ask questions. C'est trouble."

"Can," Sawyer said as he pressed his point, "you take me to my stead-mother?"

"I do not know."

"Can you try?"

"You must have much patience."

"How?" Sawyer said with a curt voice.

"You must wait," the nurse explained, "until they find you."

"How?"

"I give your name," Marie-Thérèse said, "and they will find her, I mean, your mother. Maybe they search already. C'est possible."

"Then what?"

"They try to find your mother."

"Will I see her?"

"It is no certain. Sometimes only letters."

"I hope I can see her."

"Une chose de plus ... One thing more," the nurse said. "A mother must risk everything, even life, to give birth, so you risk tout... no, no, all, you say. You risk all things for her."

Sawyer nodded.

"Comprenez-vous?" the nurse asked. "If you want that I

continue you must take all chances for her. You will take the chance?"

"Yes."

"If you are caught," the nurse explained, "they will send you from this country to a land like mine."

"To my stead-mother?"

"Non," Marie-Thérèse said. "I mean to say, no. You will be without home or friend or la famille. You can no turn back and not, as your people say, guess second. There is one time to decide."

"It must be better than this place."

"I have seen boys of your country without food or house. It is no good. It is bet ... bitter to them."

Sawyer nodded.

Now Marie-Thérèse pulled her hand from Sawyer's. "So," she whispered, "you must tell me what you wish ..."

It was at moment that lights flickered and then returned to full radiance and Sawyer's electronic mother revived with them, immediately showing herself to nurse and son. Marie-Thérèse turned away while Sawyer rubbed his eyes to accustom himself to the return of the artificial light. Once his eye opened, he turned to the nurse and spoke with a determined tone that allowed no misunderstanding.

"I want my mother," Sawyer said.

"I'm here, son," Mother declared, "and dark is dispersed."

Sawyer looked at maid and blinked.

Marie-Thérèse batted her eyes.

13

FATHERS KNOW BEST

It was a stern-faced father dressed in the black robe of a magistrate, her grey hair cropped close and her wrinkles unvarnished by facewash, who greeted Sawyer at the Lycurgan Gymnasium. The father stood inside the security portal and beckoned Sawyer to enter as a beep cleared his identification code. While Sawyer hesitated, a sharp wave brought compliance and the boy followed the father to the medical disposition quarters just before first bell sounded.

It took a few minutes to check in. Only then did the father explain.

"Do you know," the father asked, "why you've been brought here?"

Sawyer said he didn't.

"Do you know what this place is for?" the father said.

"Hormones?"

"And veracity detection."

"Veracity detection?"

"Yes," the father said, "we administer neuroverography examinations."

"Oh."

"You're scheduled this morning."

"Have I lied about something?"

"Not," the father said, "that we know of. Still, the Guardians have observed lapses and ambiguities in your profile, so we're reviewing your upbringing."

"What lapses?" Sawyer asked.

"Several things: a security violation at the Hôtel des Enfants, friendship with a former delinquent, and a few inopportune words recollected from your mother's memory."

"Did Mother send me here?"

"You ought to know," the father said, "that your mother does nothing without the permission of the fathers and the fathers act according to policies set by our Guardians."

"I suppose so."

The father led Sawyer to a dressing room where she handed the boy an oversized gown and told him to change. Sawyer turned his back as he did so and after slipping the robe over his head, he flung his clothes on a chair, letting one sock and both shoes fall to the floor.

"Try," the father said with a scowl, "to be less messy."

"Sorry."

The father said no more as she led her charge through a narrow hall to a dimly lit examination room where they were greeted by a Physician Guardian and a nurse who provided brief instructions while setting equipment to order. The nurse, a short man with balding hair and a weathered face, led Sawyer to a chair with adjustable sensor arms that were twisted and bent to positions a few centimeters from the boy's chest, abdomen, and back. The nurse gave the young patient a lime-colored solution to drink before leaving. Soon, a faint hum sounded across the room from an oval-shaped reader, which was larger than a bedroom cabinet and molded as smooth as marble.

Sawyer twitched.

The attending Guardian (a tall woman with red hair, green eyes, and brown skin) spoke. Her voice was practiced and smooth. "I'm going to ask you a few questions," the Guardian said. "Will you answer them truthfully?"

"I'll try."

"How do you feel about this interview?"

"It's okay."

The Guardian looked at her console. "You have," she said, "no trouble with me? Or this process?"

"I guess not," Sawyer replied.

The Guardian reviewed her readings. "Your density pattern," she said, "says otherwise."

"I'm not lying."

"Do you feel nervous?"

"Who wouldn't be?"

"Relax," the Guardian said. "This won't hurt and we aren't looking to disturb you. This is routine. Nearly every boy your age is given this test."

Sawyer dropped his head.

"Sawyer," the Guardian continued, "tell me about your trip to Napolis."

"I was sent to the nursery for a field trip."

"What'd you see?"

"Babies."

"What kind of babies?"

"Rows and rows of them."

"What'd you think of the babies?"

"They're noisy."

"Anything else?"

"They smell."

"They do," the Guardian said without a smile, "but I'm not speaking of their physical characteristics. I mean to say, what do you think of babies themselves? Of the idea of babies?"

Sawyer hesitated.

The Guardian looked to her display of digitized neuro-clusters.

"Well," Sawyer said after a minute-long silence, "I don't really think anything of them. What am I supposed to think of something I never see or hear, except once, in my whole life. It's strange to think I was at the h ..."

Sawyer paused to consider his answer before continuing. "I'm amazed to know I was a baby too."

"Stop," the Guardian said as she manipulated the clusters via a memory enhancement program. "Why did you pause?"

"I don't know."

"You're dissembling."

Sawyer said nothing.

"Why did you pause?" the Guardian asked.

"I don't know."

The Guardian raised her arm, elbow bent and palm facing forward. "It's mindful," she said, "that you tell the truth. All insubordination will be disciplined."

Sawyer looked at his knees and fidgeted with his shirt sleeve as the Guardian motioned to continue.

"The fathers," the Guardian said, "must deal with your insubordination if you refuse cooperation."

"I've nothing to hide."

"So tell what you know of your birth and how you know it."

"There's nothing to tell," Sawyer said, "but what you've told me my whole life. They say I was born in Old California and transferred to Napolis due to modernization of facilities."

"Yes," the Guardian said, "that's what they say. Do you believe what you've been told?"

"I suppose."

"You're not being truthful."

"I am too."

"That's not what the program says."

"Are you going to believe a person or a program?"

"Programs never lie. People do."

"And," Sawyer replied immediately, "programs don't know anything except what programmers tell them."

"What I need to know," the Guardian continued, "is whether you're telling me everything."

Sawyer shrugged.

"Your reticence troubles me," the Guardian said. "Tell me if you saw anything unusual?"

Sawyer didn't answer.

"What did you see?" the Guardian asked.

Sawyer remained mute, his eyes steeled and lips pursed.

The Guardian scowled. "You'll not talk?"

Sawyer stared ahead.

The Guardian took a moment to read the charts, then whispered a data request. A minute passed before she spoke out loud. "I'm locked out of the system," she said, "and don't have access to the necessary records. It requires court approval to proceed, so we'll have to wait a day or two to finish this section of the examination."

Sawyer bit his cheek as he suppressed a smirk.

"Tell me about your Mother," the Guardian continued. "She reports your affection is weak."

"My affection is weak?" Sawyer cried out as he thrashed in his seat, knocking one of the sensors so hard it crashed into the wall. “My affection is weak? She cares for me only because you’ve programmed her to do so and if you ordered otherwise, she’d forget me in a flash like any other deleted data. If I were sick, she wouldn’t worry and if I died, she wouldn’t weep. She cares no more for me than a thermostat does. To tell the truth, a thermostat is better than my mother. At least it senses warm and cold on its own.”

“What’d you expect of her?” the Guardian said with an indignant look. “Does any mother behave otherwise?”

Sawyer remained in his seat, still restrained by the well-fastened leather belts. He said nothing.

“Does any mother behave differently?” the Guardian repeated.

Sawyer shrugged.

“Speak up and answer my question.”

“Yes,” Sawyer snapped after a moment. “Some do.”

“I don’t know any,” the Guardian snapped.

Sawyer said nothing.

“Tell me of one.”

Sawyer pursed his lips, but said nothing.

“Such beliefs,” the Guardian said, “are old world myths long forgotten.”

Sawyer opened his mouth, but spoke no words.

“That,” the Guardian continued, “is what I thought. There aren’t any such mothers.”

“Marie-Thérèse,” Sawyer now shouted, “loves her baby. And she’s never seen him.”

The blood drained from the Guardian’s face. “No more,” she whispered, “than your mother loves you.”

“The nurse,” Sawyer now raised his voice, “the nurse loves her baby. For certain.

“How would you know?” the Guardian asked as she leaned forward.

"She told me," Sawyer replied. "She told me herself."

"She lied."

"She cried for her baby," Sawyer said. "I saw her tears. They were real. More real than that electronic mirage you call my mother."

Now the Guardian left the room while Sawyer remained in his seat. When the woman returned, she pushed away the remaining sensors and spoke with a sharp tone.

"Your case," the Guardian announced as she unstrapped Sawyer from the chair, "will be reviewed. You'll be taken to your mother and grounded until further notice. You're to be tested for Dower's Syndrome."

Sawyer said nothing.

"Nor will you be left alone," the Guardian said. "Wait in this office until your fathers can escort you home. Your mother will lock you down until the fathers pick you up tomorrow."

"What'd I do wrong?"

"I'm afraid," the Guardian said, "you've fallen into inegalitarian belief. We can only hope it originates from acute Dower's Syndrome, which is quite common with boys your age. Though we'll need a Doctor of Psycho-Biology to make the diagnosis certain, I'd be surprised if you're free of it."

An hour later, Sawyer was escorted to the foyer of his flat by two thin-bearded fathers who remained at the door until Mother locked it after the boy entered the flat in evident dismay. Sawyer shook his head as the door shut behind him while Mother greeted him without projected emotions or pleasantries, explaining that his fathers were angry.

Sawyer said he didn't care.

"They're investigating," Mother said, "your visit to the Hôtel des Enfants."

"Let them."

"They've scheduled appointments with your father. And the guide too."

Sawyer said nothing.

"And," Mother continued, "they'll interview you about our nurse. And her too."

"Why?"

"She violated her code of conduct."

"Wh ... how?"

"She spoke of our baby as hers and showed affection, which is strictly forbidden."

"Marie-Thérèse!" Sawyer called out as he hurried toward the kitchen.

"She won't hear."

"Marie-Thérèse!"

"She isn't here."

Sawyer spun, almost as if Mother were real. "Where is she?" the boy screamed as he turned toward the nurse's quarters.

"You won't find her there."

Sawyer hurried to the kitchen where he found a half-cooked roast steaming atop the stove. A pan of peeled potatoes sat on the counter, along with a bowl of unmixed cake ingredients and a pitcher of milk. Sawyer touched the roasting pan with a forefinger. It remained hot.

"Where is she?" Sawyer called out. "Where's Marie-Thérèse?"

"The fathers took her."

"When?"

"Ten minutes ago."

"Why?"

"She violated," Mother said, "the code of conduct. She grew possessive of the state-child carried in her womb and contributed to juvenile delinquency in you. She wasn't a good nurse. Don't regret her passing."

"I've already reprogrammed the oven," Mother continued, "if you set the roast on the center rack, you may eat within the hour. The fathers will send another nurse tomorrow. This isn't your first duty change."

Sawyer started for Mother, fists clutched and eyes teared as his whole body quivered. "What's wrong with you, Mother?" he shouted out loud.

"It's just that," Mother said, "I have no arms to make the meal, so, you must place the roast in the oven and mix the mashed potatoes yourself. I apologize for the inconvenience."

"Shut up, Mother," Sawyer screamed. "Can't you just shut up?"

Mother looked neither confused nor dismayed and spoke with a perfectly tranquil voice as she asked if Sawyer was upset. But the boy just hurried to the nurse's quarters, where he found a suitcase opened on the nurse's bed, sloppily packed with oversized dresses and undergarments. A few toiletries also had been tossed inside. A silver-banded watch and unframed photographs remained on the bed itself, along with a folded bath towel.

"Why didn't they let her pack?" Sawyer asked as he turned toward a wall.

When Mother didn't answer, Sawyer repeated his question. "I said why didn't they let her pack?"

Still, Mother didn't answer.

"Tell me," Sawyer shouted, "why she didn't pack and when's she coming back?"

Mother appeared in the room. She was dressed in a dark crème dress, her hair falling to her shoulders and her feet graced with open toe sandals.

"Marie-Thérèse is gone," Mother said, "and won't return. I'm told she'll be compensated for her lost property and her private possessions will be collected next week. She'll be compensated seven-ninths of the contracted delivery price, though not the labor bonus."

"Let me tell her goodbye."

"It isn't permitted."

"You took her away," Sawyer said, "before I could speak with her, didn't you? You didn't want me to talk to her."

"It's late now," Mother said as she pointed to the hall, "and your father says you must retire for the night. Perhaps there'll be time to talk tomorrow."

"But I ..."

The room darkened, except for a single row of running lights showing the emergency exits. Even these dimmed as Sawyer lay in his bed and cried himself to sleep.

14

FROM POUTING TO PARRICIDE

Sawyer lay quiet and still in his thoughts a long while after he woke. When Mother finally opened the blinds, the boy pulled a blanket over his head and pretended to sleep. The deception never fooled Mother.

"I know you're awake," Mother said. "It's time to tend your studies."

"It's too early," Sawyer said.

"You must prepare breakfast for yourself. Until a nurse arrives."

"I'm not getting up."

Instantly, the room sounded with the amplified noise of the Great Plains: wolves baying, coyotes howling, prairie dogs barking, and bison grunting. As hot, dry air poured from the vents, Sawyer shouted at his Mother—though she responded with an even louder cacophony of birds and beasts until the boy finally threw up his hands.

"Turn it off," Sawyer shouted as he sat up. "Just make the house quiet. I'm getting up"—the room quieted and the air cooled as Sawyer clutched his stomach—"I feel ill. I'm going back to bed."

"Are you really ill?" Mother said.

"I feel sick."

"Go," Mother said, "to the shower room and take a reading from the wall thermometer."

"I don't feel like it. It's too far."

"Then look to the corner."

Sawyer did so.

"Yes," Mother said after a few seconds, "you look ill. You may sleep another two hours."

Sawyer slipped beneath his sheets as shutters closed and lights dimmed, then slept after several minutes. When he awoke, morning nearly had passed, so the boy nibbled at a bit of stale bread and a well-ripened apple as he paced the hall, notwithstanding Mother's nagging for him to show better manners. In any case, when Sawyer returned to his room, he pulled files from his desk for sorting.

It didn't take the boy long to stack papers in separate piles. Nor did it take long to find what he searched for: the photograph of the pregnant girl at the whitewashed cottage. He pulled the image from its storage folder and placed it on the desk. With both elbows planted on the table and hands propped beneath his chin, Sawyer stared at the photo. The girl wore an old-fashioned dress and a corresponding lack of modesty. The gleam in her eye showed the girl wasn't ashamed of her pregnancy and the smile on her face suggested outright pleasure.

Sawyer brushed a finger across the young woman's distended belly, as if to touch the unborn life, though his caress didn't disturb her repose.

"Good-bye," the boy whispered, "Marie-Thérèse. Adieu."

"Sawyer," Mother said with a voice smooth as silicon.

"What?" Sawyer's reply was curt.

"You aren't to speak to the nurse."

"How can I—when—you've—taken—her—away?"

"You must speak to me with respect, not sarcasm."

"I didn't say anything wrong."

"Don't, "Mother said, "use that tone with me."

"What tone?"

"I detected sarcasm."

"You're wrong," Sawyer said with a noticeable smirk. "Maybe you should ask the fathers to reprogram your emotions."

"I have no emotions."

"Marie-Thérèse did," Sawyer snapped. "She felt for a baby she couldn't see and a son she didn't know."

Mother said nothing.

"The nurse," Sawyer said, his voice raised to an angry pitch, "was a real mother."

"I spoke," Mother said, "to your fathers about this and they assured me no one can truly love someone she can't see. They wish for you to remember it's your own household that provides clothing, food, and shelter. And your own mother is the umbilical conduit of all good things. You're not to mistake fantasy for reality, nor nightmares for dreams. These are the words of a father herself."

"The words," Sawyer snapped, "of a cold-blooded programmer."

"You've shown filial ingratitude," Mother replied a moment later, "and I've informed your fathers."

"I have no fathers."

"What does that mean?"

"I have no father or mother!" Sawyer screamed as loud as he could. "I'm an orphan!"

Mother didn't scream. "You're no orphan," she said. "You're no different than your brothers and sisters and classmates."

"You're dense as a toaster," Sawyer said as he pointed to the image on the table of the calico-dressed girl near the whitewashed church, "and you aren't my mother. My mother is a woman. Like Marie-Thérèse. I have a stead-mother."

"You're mistaken. I'm the only mother you've ever known."

"Liar!" Sawyer screamed as he continued to point a finger at the photograph, "you're just a machine! A dumb, stupid machine!"

"She's nothing to you," Mother said as she appeared in the room dressed in a blue suit with her hair pulled back and pointed to the image of the calico-dressed Tahitian girl. "Your life isn't her life and your thoughts aren't hers."

"You think you're my mother," Sawyer snarled, his lips curled and eyes drawn tight, "but the fathers don't tell you everything. Maybe they don't even know the truth. I think the Guardians hide it from everyone."

"Tell me what troubles you," Mother said as she stepped toward her son, her arms open as if to embrace him, though her hug had no grip.

Sawyer stepped back without speaking.

"I know everything," Mother said, "about you, more than a stead-mother will ever remember of her child. I can recollect every day you've lived as if it were today. I recall every meal you've taken, your tears, your smiles, and ..."

Sawyer cut her short. "Can you remember," he said, "the body that carried me? Can you remember where I was born?"

"I can," Mother replied. "You were carried in a state nurse and begotten by the will of the fathers. You were born in Napolis State Nursery."

"I wasn't born in Napolis."

"Where do you imagine you were born?"

"In Oceania."

"And why would you believe such an absurdity?"

"I saw records at the Hôtel des Enfants."

Mother fell silent while she streamed to the fathers. When she spoke, her voice was calm and words few. "You'll speak no more of this until the fathers arrive."

Sawyer stepped back, his face flush and voice angry. "They're coming?"

"You're grounded until they arrive."

"You told them?"

"I'm communicating now. My protocol is clear."

"Then you've given me to the fathers. Just like Gunther's mother."

"I'm not Gunther's mother."

"You hate me," Sawyer muttered, then louder. "You can't love, but you can hate."

"I love you as any mother does," Mother said, "but you're growing troubled these past weeks."

"You feed me," Sawyer shouted, "because you have to and you'd starve me if the fathers told you to. But you don't love me. Not really. Not like Marie-Thérèse loves her baby."

"Her baby," Mother said, "is our baby and your fathers say her love is a fantasy."

"It's no fantasy," Sawyer said as his eyes glistened.

"The fathers say so."

"They lie."

"How would you know otherwise? At your age?"

"I just know."

As Sawyer pulled back his shoulders, Mother pressed her point. "But how?" she asked. "How can you doubt our entire society based on one nurse's emotions?"

Sawyer said nothing.

"I don't understand," Mother said, "how you can be so convinced all others are wrong and you alone know truth. The fathers don't understand either. They would like to know why you believe these things."

Sawyer glared at her.

"I ask you again," Mother continued, "how you can doubt our way of life on the word of a foreign-born nurse?"

Sawyer stared as Mother waited.

"Tell me," Mother said.

Sawyer waited nearly a minute before he whispered his response.

"Because," the boy growled through clenched teeth, "because I love my stead-mother even though I've never seen her. That's how I know the nurse loves her baby."

Mother flickered and disappeared. Only her voice remained as she told Sawyer that he'd remain in the house until his fathers arrived, at which time he needed to surrender his homework files and do as told. She advised the boy that matters would proceed better if he cooperated and reminded him to feed himself while she napped.

Sawyer heard shutters lock and bolts click, then white noise. He slumped at his desk, his eyes burning and throat constricted as tears rolled down his cheek and fell to the desk—striking the breast of the Tahitian girl.

Sawyer lifted the photograph between a forefinger and thumb. "The fathers," he whispered, "will destroy you."

Grabbing the image, Sawyer stood. "They'll take you. I'll be put on hormones and"—his face now filled with blood as he grumbled out loud—"and they'll make me forget my stead-mother or not love her."

Sawyer hurried to the window and yanked at the shudders. When they held fast, he ran to the front door, but it too held firm. Now the boy moved several steps back toward the kitchen, then stopped and pumped his fist before hurrying to his room. There, Sawyer collected several of his belongings: identification bands, wallet, debit vouchers, favorite photographs, and even the Tahiti images. He hurried to the kitchen, where the pulled the temporary override switch to the hallway fire alarm, then tossed bread and apples into a food pouch. Placing the pouch near the front door, he returned to the kitchen to ignite an electric burner and lay a linen towel atop it. As the towel smoked, Sawyer carried an armload of blankets and clothes to Mother's door, then retrieved a cricket bat and returned to the stove, where the linen now smoldered. Sawyer blew once and the towel burst into flame. He hurried the burning rag to Mother's door, where one swing of the aluminum bat broke the door lock and a second knocked the door wide open.

Alarms sounded.

Mother's furniture at the room's center consisted of an oak desk on which Mother's mind, a large polymer-framed processing unit with a memory extension device, was bolted. Sawyer flung the burning cloth toward the room's curtains and looked straight at the processing unit before striking hard, showing no pity. The first blow shattered Mother's glass face and the second broke her shoulder bolts and knocked her to the floor. Another dozen blows were aimed at her brain until Mother's mind was no more than smashed silicon and carbon fragments scattered across the floor.

Mother was no more.

15

ANGRY FATHERS AND A RUNAWAY

Sawyer dragged flaming curtains across the broken fragments of Mother's mind and then piled an armful of shirts grabbed from his closet upon the fire. Soon, the room was ablaze, with alarms sounding and doors opening as the boy grabbed his belongings to flee the only home he remembered. Outside, distant fire trucks wailed as Sawyer hurried to the main gate, where he was stopped by a Guardian with close-cropped hair and a weathered face.

"Where to, brother?" the Guardian asked.

"To take a walk," Sawyer answered.

"Do you have permission?"

"Mother gave me permission."

"Your name?"

"Sawyer Adams."

"Swipe your identifier."

A buzzer sounded and the Guardian shook his head. "You don't have a pass," the Guardian said.

Sawyer pointed toward fire trucks now parking outside his flat—lights flashing, sirens sounding, and citizens congregating—as he explained to the Guardian that his mother had told him to go outside until the commotion subsided. The Guardian told Sawyer to wait while he double-checked to confirm whether the alarms had delayed transmission of maternal permission.

Sawyer didn't wait.

Indeed, as soon as the Guardian stepped into the gatehouse, the boy sprinted for the outer fence: a thirty meter dash to cover. Sawyer neither heard nor observed what occurred behind him, focusing on the exit before him and a woods beyond it. He had neither plan nor purpose, only desperation to escape what he knew to be his inevitable destruction. When the distance was down to ten meters, he ran faster. At five meters, he took a breath and looked back as he ...

Whmmpphh.

Hard force struck from behind. As arms pulled at his waist, Sawyer crumpled to the ground. Before he could get his bearings, the boy was rolled and restrained, his arms pinned behind his back by the ungiving grasp of a Guardian. Within minutes, the runaway had been handcuffed and walked to the guardhouse, where another Guardian pushed him to a chair and told the boy to wait as two compatriots watched their charge's every move. None of the Guardians provided drink, food, or a single word of comfort.

After forty minutes, a pair of fathers took depositions and spoke with a fire marshal before escorting Sawyer to their sedan. The Guardians locked the rear doors before driving their charge into the heart of the urban heights along the west bank of the Potomac and finally parked at the Apothetae (an enormous limestone pentagon-shaped complex flying Confederation banners) where they delivered the boy to a dour-faced father with broad shoulders.

Sawyer was examined before being sent to a cell not lacking comforts (it had a bed and videoprojector), but possessing neither window nor external door: only a single entrance guarded by laser alarms.

That night, Sawyer listened for footsteps—though none came to him. In fact, no one at all visited until a girlish-looking attendant with shoulder-length hair and wide hips served an early breakfast of coffee and pastries. When she wished good day in a slavic accent, Sawyer realized the girl was neither Guardian nor father, but a Eurasian migrant (likely a Slav) trained in old nursing and contracted by the Confederation as a warden. Sawyer took his meal, then returned to bed.

The Slav nurse woke Sawyer at midmorning for vital readings and told him to shower for his custodial interview in a nearby conference room. There, a doctor issued a medical clearance and subsequently excused herself as two male fathers (one with fiery red hair and the other with very dark skin) and a blonde Guardian with a somber face entered the room. The fathers took seats at the table and the Guardian stood behind them.

All three stared at Sawyer until the boy himself broke the silence.

"Now what?" Sawyer said.

The Guardian, whose cropped blonde hair was set against a black uniform with maroon insignia, replied that everything depended on Sawyer.

"Nothing depends upon me," Sawyer objected. "You're going to give me hormones whether I want them or not. You're the fathers and I'm the son. Nothing depends on me."

The red-haired father shook his head. "Our society," the father said, "is built on choice, not compulsion. You'll determine your own fate. No one will force your loyalty. No one will compel you to accept our style of life. No one is born into lifelong citizenship. You must pledge you allegiance every day. Moreover, there's no one else to decide your fate since the three of us represent Confederation equities. I speak for the fathers of Napolis District while she"—he pointed to the blonde Guardian—"represents the Agency of Medical Evaluations. Your other father speaks for the Agency of Familial Affection. What you will, shall be done, so choose well."

Sawyer straightened his shoulders. "You gave Gunther," he said, "no choice."

"You mean Gunther Stadtson," the dark-skinned father said, "your classmate?"

Sawyer nodded.

"Tell us about your friend."

"He was funny and fun and you ruined him. You killed everything I liked about him."

Both fathers looked confused.

"You gave him hormones," Sawyer explained, "for Dower's Syndrome. He softened."

"Many adolescents," the dark-skinned father said, "suffer from Dower's Syndrome. In fact, a vast majority of young males receive hormonal supplements to make up what's lacking in their own bodies."

"You killed him."

"Contrary," the dark-skinned father said. "We gave him life. He's healthier and better socialized than ever before."

"Whatever he is," Sawyer snapped, "he's not himself."

"You assume pure nature is the highest good," the father continued as Sawyer grimaced, "and thereby challenge our entire civilization."

"Not your civilization. Only what you did to my friend."

"If you disapprove," the father said, "of our prescription,

you doubt our diagnosis and medicine. And our science. You challenge our statesmen and scholars. Do you really doubt our civilization?"

"You're the fathers," Sawyer said. "I'm just a son."

"We're not here to defend our government of Gunther, are we?" the dark-skinned father said.

Sawyer rolled his eyes, but didn't interrupt.

"You've committed," the dark-skinned father declared, "a high crime against the state: parricide. The killing of your own mother."

"I didn't hurt anyone," Sawyer said. "At least no one real. She was never alive, so she didn't die. Put in a new memory chip and make her live. I pulled the plug on a machine. Like unplugging a toaster. You have backups, I suppose."

It was the blonde Guardian who answered. "The fundamental relationship," she said, "of our society is trust between mother and child. You have—"

Sawyer jumped to his feet. "Don't lecture me," he shouted, "about trust when you've lied to me my whole life. I know your lies about my birth. I know I have a steadmother, a real one of flesh and blood. You took her away and gave me a mirage."

As both fathers blushed, the Guardian continued. "You've assaulted," she said, "your mother and insulted your fathers. You're a parricide and lawfully can be declassed. *The Code of Civil Law* authorizes us to take the most drastic measures, if need be."

"So what," Sawyer said, "you'll just kill me like you did Gunther."

"You speak too freely," the Guardian said.

"You said the choice is mine."

"The choice is yours, yes, but the decision is ours."

"Just give me the hormones. Make me obedient."

"We've found," the dark-skinned father explained, "that hormones are quite effective when taken with a good will. For those who want to be cured, they work wonders. For those who prefer disobedience, even the strongest medication proves inadequate."

"For some," the red-haired father said, "the only answer is declassification."

Sawyer dropped his head.

"We've sent incorrigible children to distant lands," the dark-skinned father added, "exiled from family and state. From our family and our state."

Sawyer twitched. "What happens to them?"

"I neither know nor care," the red-haired father said. "They're not our concern after they're declassed. They've no more rights than any other unsocial or uncivil."

"Are you going to declass me?"

"Is that what you want?" the red-haired father asked.

"I don't know."

"Tell me what it is you want."

Sawyer shrugged.

"What is it you want?" the red-haired father said.

"What I want," Sawyer said, "is my mother. My stead-mother."

"You have no stead-mother."

"I've seen my birth files."

The blonde Guardian leaned forward. "What," she said, "did you see?"

"You know my files?" Sawyer asked.

"I do."

"Do you know where I was born?"

"You were born in Oceania."

"Tahiti," Sawyer clarified.

"Many children," the blonde Guardian explained, "were

born in the Undeveloped World during the years when the Chinese inflicted terrible losses on our armies in Korea and we needed to grow our population. The Undeveloped World has always provided raw materials."

Sawyer buried his face in his hands.

"We've learned better since then," the blonde Guardian continued, "and expanded our state nurseries. We now bring surrogates to our lands to ensure pure conceptions. What happened to you was an anomaly, but not a singularity. Thousands of children were imported from the Pacific, both from our need and theirs. There was famine and many pregnancies ended with the death of mother and child. We did both a favor by importing women to give birth or feeding them in their own land until the appointed day. Afterward, surrogates were paid in gold or goods, as they preferred."

Sawyer looked pale.

"It's a shameful history," the Guardian said, "but—"

"I didn't know," Sawyer interrupted, "that I was made natural. I only thought of a nurse surrogate, like Marie-Thérèse."

"You read of your adoption?"

Sawyer said he did.

"Then you knew."

"I didn't think about it," Sawyer said. "Only that a stead-mother carried me. I didn't see the files for long."

"Well," the Guardian replied, "it hardly makes a difference. One is the same as the other. Just a uterine cavity."

Sawyer glared at her.

"Don't look at me that way," the Guardian said. "You're not likely to remain Equal the way this interview is proceeding."

"She wasn't a cavity," Sawyer whispered. "She was a home."

The Guardian shook her head. "Your stead-mother gave you away," she said, "because you were nothing to her but a problem. Why should she be anything to you?"

Sawyer jumped to his feet, spraying slobber and his face flush. "You," he shouted, "don't know anything about stead-mothers or about my stead-mother or about me. You're trying to make me forget her. You want me to take medicines like Gunther so she'll go away. I won't do it. I can't do it."

"Won't," the red-haired father said as he leaned forward, "do what?"

"Where's my stuff?" Sawyer said as he sobbed a little. "I want my picture. I know it's her."

"Sawyer," the blonde Guardian said, "you have to concur for us to continue treatment. We diagnose you with Dower's Syndrome and prescribe immediate hormone treatment. You'll feel better in a few days and all of this will pass. But ... you must consent or you will be declassed."

When the blonde Guardian slid a paper and pen across the table; Sawyer tore the form in half and flung both pieces to the floor without word.

"You won't be given another chance," the blonde Guardian said. "You have until evening to consent. Otherwise, we'll be forced to declass you, just as you've asked."

"I've asked for nothing."

"Indeed?" the Guardian said. "By every action to this day you've forced our hand, almost against our will. Lies, violence, and running away from home brought you here and even now you don't see your peril. You know our laws and yet place yourself on the wrong side of them. Declassing is certain if you don't turn about."

"I don't really care what you do to me," Sawyer said,

"except for one thing: Marie-Thérèse loves a baby she's never seen and I love my stead-mother who I've never seen. And I won't forget her. You say I have a choice, then here's what I choose: no Dower's Disease, no hormones, no forgetting. I choose my stead-mother. My head hurts. Can I lay down?"

The fathers and Guardian stepped from the room. When they returned, a nurse was with them. Sawyer was remanded to the nurse's custody and led to his room—where he was provided pain relievers and served his lunch.

PART II

Aristotle, *Politics*, Books I-II; *Ethics*, Book VIII

There must be a union [of] male and female [that] the race may continue; and this is a union which is formed, not of deliberative purpose, but because [people naturally] desire to leave behind an image of themselves.

Parents love their offspring from the first moment of their being, but their offspring them only after a lapse of time, when they have attained intelligence or instinct.

Each citizen will have a thousand sons [and all alike will] be neglected. How much better it is to be a real cousin of somebody than a son after Plato's fashion!

. . .

Nor is there any way of preventing brothers and children and fathers and mothers from sometimes recognizing one another; for children are born like their parents, and they will necessarily be finding indication of their relations to one another.

16

HOMEWARD BOUND

Sawyer sat in a Volksbrummi Kaida, a windowless utility van used for prisoner transport and funerals. A gaunt-faced Guardian with grey eyes and red hair who shared the rear seat with Sawyer leaned forward to talk with a broad-shouldered and brown-eyed father and a blue-eyed and slender-armed driver—none of the Equals paying any attention to the young déclassé. As for Sawyer, while his hands remained free, his legs were secured with kevlar straps and his right earlobe was bandaged with medical tape that indicated his transponder had been removed. The boy slumped against the side window and held fast to a duffle bag filled with spare clothing, food rations, and personal effects.

Already, the sun fell from the western sky and a rubescent glow radiated from the lower heavens. Sawyer watched as the vehicle passed kilometer after kilometer of suburbs, the rows of houses fading almost as soon as they were seen. Disconcerted by the speed, the boy looked far ahead: where walled neighborhoods sat near sky-reaching towers, commuter trains moved along transit rails, and roofed plazas stood as storehouses of abundance and entertainment. Everywhere, there could be seen a smorgasbord of restaurants and malls and theaters. There were also scores of Gymnasia, each one gated and fenced, uniformly constructed of mortar and brick and government planning. Within these organized communities were raised the egalitarian ideals and persons who constituted the Western Confederation. Sawyer closed his eyes as the van sped west.

The blue-eyed driver did most of the talking to the two escorts. While Sawyer didn't pay too much attention to what she said, he did overhear stories of a vacation to the Greek coast that ended with a fatwa and death threats against nude swimmers. Both escorts were amused and a few minutes into the trip, all three Equals were laughing out loud. Only as they approached a checkpoint near the Greater Metropolitan International Airfield did the escorts temper their joviality in the interest of professional decorum.

Once identification was cleared, the van was waved through the checkpoint. Within a minute, the driver stopped at the check-in entrance for departing flights and opened the Kaida's doors. The vehicle's passengers stepped to the curb and the vehicle pulled into a nearby parking area.

"Now I'm declassed?" Sawyer asked as he entered the airport terminal.

The red-haired Guardian said the team was just doing its job and Sawyer responded by asking where they were going.

"We just escort to the aircraft," the Guardian said.

"Which flight?" Sawyer asked.

"I don't know."

Sawyer looked confused. "I'm going to b-b ..." the boy

now stuttered, took a deep breath, then continued, "I'm going to board the plane. It won't be a secret for long."

It was the brown-eyed father who shook his head. "Doesn't work quite that way."

Sawyer waited for his explanation.

"You'll be sedated," the brown-eyed father said, "before boarding. A father-nurse will accompany you on the flight, but you won't wake until you've landed."

"Then what?"

"Then," the father continued, "you'll be handed to local officials for in-processing."

"Then?"

"Then you're on your own."

"Where will I live?"

"Never been abroad."

"Will I have a house?"

"Not sure."

"What'll I eat?"

"Don't know."

Sawyer panicked. "How," the boy said with a cracking voice, "will I live?"

"Choices matter," the gaunt-faced Guardian with red hair said as Sawyer's eyes watered. "You've always known our fathers and mothers tend their children every hour and the world outside is filled with orphans."

"I thought—"

"We can say nothing," the red-haired Guardian said, "since custodians and diplomats make arrangements. What I've been told is that the Confederation rents orphanage beds for declassès. You should expect something of that sort. It brings our state no repute for its bastards to beg bread."

"But—"

The brown-eyed father motioned to Sawyer. "No time," he said, "to waste. We're due at the nurse's station."

Both escorts flanked the boy (one to each side) and pushed him along. Ascending an escalator and hurrying down a corridor lined with transit stations, they led Sawyer to a small office where Sawyer's bindings were removed, his vitals checked, and a hypodermic needle injected into his forearm. As soon as a small vial was attached to the needle and its sedative began to drip into the boy's veins, the two officials escorted Sawyer to the departure gate of Federated International Airways. Even while he moved, the boy grew drowsy, his step slower and movement clumsy. At the gate, the escorts locked elbows with the boy and pushed him through security and passenger boarding.

Ten minutes later, Sawyer was belted into a reclined seat near the rear of a quad-engine Air Coach 7105 beside a waif-like father with a leather satchel in her lap. The Guardians transferred paperwork to the nurse father, then collected a signed receipt and departed without further word.

Sawyer struggled to keep his eyes open as he looked through the double-pane window of the Air Coach, though his eyes began to blur even before the aircraft pushed from the gate—all four of its hyper-turbo engines still unturned as the waifish father secured her charge to his seat with a slip harness and attached medical electrometers to his neck and wrists. Even as the boy's eyelids grew heavy and he struggled to watch the father flip through a courtesy magazine, it wasn't long before he saw and heard no more.

Sawyer slept without dreams.

It was the screech and bump of the landing that woke Sawyer from his slumber. The first jolt stirred the sleeping boy and the second opened his eyes. The screech of burning rubber snapped him to attention, his head thrown forward as the engines reversed thrust. Sawyer looked at the father strapped in her seat and raised his window shade. As the aircraft decelerated and stopped near the end of the runway, Sawyer pressed his face to the double-pane glass, hoping to see what lay outside. As soon as he saw the wing, the boy turned to the father.

"This plane only has two engines," Sawyer said.

"We switched in Lima," the nurse-father replied.

"Where are we?"

"We're in Tahiti. An island in the neutral zone."

"Th-this th-this is Tahiti?"

"They say," the father explained, "the beaches are beautiful, though it's quite uncivilized. Rather wild and untamed. Almost a nature preserve."

"T-Tahiti. You said Tahiti?"

"Yes, yes," the father said, "you'll be taken to customs and delivered to local authorities."

"I'll live in Tahiti?" Sawyer said.

"I said so already," the father said, this time with clear irritation. "How natives live with all their children and their endless questions, I'll never understand."

Sawyer slunk back into his chair. As the aircraft rolled to a stop, its engines emitted a last whine and doors opened. The father told Sawyer to stay seated until all other passengers had deplaned and the boy did so, watching thirty men and women (most of them dark-skinned and carrying clutch bags or leather satchels) push through the aisles. Sawyer observed that some of the younger women appeared to be returning nurses, but the father just shrugged and looked away. Only after the compartment had emptied did the waifish father retrieve two bags from the overhead compartment, keeping one and handing the other to Sawyer.

"This is yours," the father said, "food, clothes, money. Don't lose the bag. It's all you have."

Sawyer pulled the luggage with a single arm since it wasn't too heavy, even for a skinny-armed boy. He followed the nurse-father to the terminal and then to a customs post where they were greeted by a wiry, middle-aged local who introduced himself in an Old French accent as Robert LeBoeuf.

An hour was spent signing protocol documents and transferring Sawyer's guardianship to the sovereign state of Tahiti. When the final signature was garnered, Sawyer and the father passed through a customs gate where the former declared his few possessions to an agent who subsequently inspected Sawyer's luggage for contraband. The search completed, the small party passed into Tahitian territory where Leoeuf led the two arrivals through a main corridor in the terminal toward a sign (posted both in Old French and Anglo-European) that directed travelers to departure gates or baggage claims.

Where the hall divided, LeBoeuf led Sawyer to the right as the father hurried toward her departure gate to the left, saying her flight was being called. Only when the father was beyond earshot did LeBoeuf grab Sawyer's shoulder to turn the boy toward himself.

"What've you been told?" LeBoeuf said. "What do you know?"

Sawyer said nothing.

"Tell me everything," LeBoeuf said. "For your own protection, and of others too."

Sawyer looked confused. "What," the boy whispered, "is going to happen?"

"I'm sorry," LeBoeuf said as he softened his tone. "That was rude. Nothing will happen to you. I just needed to find out what you've been told. I know now that nothing was said."

"Said?" Sawyer asked. "Said about what?"

"Have you eaten?"

Sawyer shook his head he hadn't.

"Good," LeBoeuf said. "I'm hungry. Let me take your baggage. You look tired."

Sawyer didn't protest as the stranger took his suitcase, but followed the man to the street, There, LeBoeuf hailed an old driver pedaling a rickshaw over concrete streets peppered with sand-filled potholes. Despite the age of the man, the rickshaw passed hundreds of pedestrians (many of them children escorting younger siblings) along sidewalks that paralleled aging roads, as well as dozens of dilapidated hotels and restaurants situated along main roads and side streets alike. The majority of the hotels and restaurants were closed, mutely testifying to an abundance of tourism and prosperity that no longer existed, and many of the remaining buildings had been cannibalized for building materials. Scores were no more than piles of rubble burned or washed out long before and never rebuilt.

Twenty minutes later, the driver was paid and a table claimed at a weathered hotel whose walls were water-stained and peeling, carpet threadbare, and broken windows partially boarded. Still, the aroma of coffee was strong and the smell of pastries inviting as a waiter dressed in bleached trousers and a cotton shirt served occupied tables and set tableware at empty ones.

Looking to his right, Sawyer stared straight at a couple who kept close to each other and paid others no heed. The dark-skinned man talked with a loud voice, his hair cropped close and his face obscured by an untrimmed beard. He wore a sleeveless shirt that revealed thick shoulders and arms whose muscle stretched hard beneath tight flesh. In contrast, the woman was as soft as the man was hard. Her bronzed arms were bare and smooth like the flesh of a child, as were her cheeks. Her hair fell to her shoulders and she often spoke with her eyes dropped to the table and arms folded across her breasts. The young woman's face was delicate and showed not the slightest shadow of a beard.

Sawyer stared a long while, until LeBoeuf broke the spell.

"Is everything okay?" LeBoeuf asked.

"I'm fine," Sawyer said.

LeBoeuf wasn't easily dismissed. "What's so interesting?" the man said.

"Just how those two are ... completely different."

"Just locals."

"No," Sawyer said as he shook his head, "I mean different kinds of people. She is so much, well, prettier than him."

"She's pretty enough," LeBoeuf replied, "he looks like a soldier. Maybe police."

"That's not what I mean," Sawyer said. "It's just they look so different."

"Oh, you mean their skin color? The local color. They're Tahitian locals, like I said. Maybe a bit of Korean in her."

"Not that," Sawyer said. "They just look ... well, so different from each other, not equal in any way. Less grown up looking, I mean. Like children."

"Now I understand," LeBoeuf said as he laughed out loud, "what troubles you. What you have here is natural man and woman—`l'homme et la femme' as we say in our tongue. None of that androgynous mix you grew up with. A paired couple probably does look odd to your eyes, at first. You'll see plenty like them from now on, but that's not why we're here."

"I've seen," Sawyer said "images of naturists before and some nurses, but never an obsolete couple together. He looks harder than in pictures and she looks softer. They aren't balanced."

"Our balance," LeBoeuf said, "isn't in one, but in many. We keep differences as nature intended."

LeBoeuf didn't elaborate further and after a time Sawyer faced his host and again spoke. "Why," the boy asked, "are we here?"

"Let me tell it to you straight. You've been kidnapped."

"Kidnapped? How? When?"

"Your orders were for Peru."

"The father said we flew to Lima."

"Yes, your escort was given replacement orders."

"For here?"

"Yes," LeBoeuf said, "for Tahiti."

"Did the Guardians change their minds?" Sawyer asked.

"They changed nothing. We did."

Sawyer looked at the stranger, studying the man's eyes in search of a clue before he asked who had kidnapped him.

"The aristos," LeBoeuf answered.

Now Sawyer hyperventilated, his breath fast and shallow and head swaying.

"Settle down," LeBoeuf said. "You won't be hurt. We're not the beasts they say."

Sawyer breathed out until he regained his composure and spoke in a whisper. "Send me," he begged with tears in his eyes, "back to Peru. I have a home there."

"A home?" LeBoeuf said as his voice rose to a shrill peak. "A home? Whatever you might find there, which would be little enough, it won't be a home. You never had a home in Napolis. You'll see that soon enough."

"How do you know about Napolis?"

LeBoeuf removed an envelope stuffed with papers from a satchel. "These are your life files," he said. "We also have your electronic dossier."

"The Guardians gave those to you?" Sawyer said.

"They were sent yesterday."

"By the state?"

"By our agents in Napolis."

"I have to go," Sawyer said as he stood. "You're with the aristos."

LeBoeuf reached across the table and pushed Sawyer to his seat, both telling him he had no other place to go and consoling the trembling exile.

"Hear me out before you panic," LeBoeuf said. "We can return you to South America, if you ask us to."

Sawyer stilled himself.

"You shouldn't despair," LeBoeuf said, "and this shouldn't come as a surprise. You told a friend you'd risk your life to find your true mother. We're taking you at your word."

Sawyer looked to either side: the café was empty, except for a fat woman who stood at a counter and the heterogeneous couple to his right. "Marie-Thérèse sent you?" he asked.

"Let's talk about you."

"Is she here? Let me see Marie-Thérèse."

"It cannot happen," LeBoeuf said. "Her country is elsewhere."

"But she's okay?"

"You don't need to worry about her."

"I'm listening," Sawyer said.

"That's better," LeBoeuf said, "I haven't time for a runaway."

"Okay."

"You want coffee?"

Sawyer shook his head as LeBoeuf called the proprietor.

"This'll take a few minutes," LeBoeuf said to Sawyer, "you need anything to eat? I'm having coffee."

"I'm hungry."

"Bread and fruit work for you?"

"And a glass of water."

As the proprietor prepared their order, LeBoeuf began to explain the situation.

17

FIRST STEPS

"You've been kidnapped," LeBoeuf said, "by aristos and I'm the kidnapper. We hope to reunite you with your natural mother."

LeBoeuf picked up his cup of coffee and sipped from it while he gauged Sawyer's reaction. When, however, Sawyer remained mute, LeBoeuf tried to stir the conversation by asking whether Sawyer was frightened.

"What's it matter?" Sawyer answered as tears welled in his eyes and he breathed fast. "I'm already here."

"That you are."

"What else," Sawyer said, "can you do to me? You've taken me from my home."

Now the proprietor set a cup of coffee before LeBoeuf. "La crème ou du sucre de canne?" the man asked.

LeBoeuf shook his head.

"Where was I?" LeBoeuf said as the proprietor walked away. "Oh, you asked what we could do to you?"

Sawyer dropped his eyes, but said nothing.

"What we can do," LeBoeuf said, "is find your mother."

Now Sawyer looked straight at LeBoeuf. “You can find her?” the boy asked, almost in a whisper.

"If she’s alive.”

Sawyer wiped his eyes with the back of his wrist. “My stead-mother?” he said.

“You don’t have a stead-mother. We call them stepmothers. You have a real mother. A natural one.”

“I have an electronic mother.”

“No,” LeBoeuf said. “You’ve lived like an orphan, just a ward of the state with unknown Guardians and loveless fathers. You never had a mother before you came here. Well, that’s not quite true. It’s better to say you’ve never known a mother before. Not a real one.”

“Who are you?” Sawyer asked. “Why are you here?”

“You shouldn’t ask,” the man said, “for my true name. Confederation spies roam this island. Some of us they turn and others they”—LeBoeuf’s sentence died on his tongue —“It’s best you know only my face and you should forget it when you can. As I said, just call me LeBoeuf.”

“How could I be kidnapped,” Sawyer asked after a pause, “when I was sent here by the fathers?”

“There are many ways to kidnap an unwanted child. Not all are outside the law.”

“You mean the people who sent me—”

“Some of them,” LeBoeuf said as he interrupted the boy’s question, “may be witting and others certainly aren’t. There are people who serve our purposes believing they conduct your state’s secret affairs and there are aristos in high offices of the Confederation itself. You spoke with our namesake in the forests of Greece.”

“Plato?”

“Not that denuded mind. His student.”

"Aristotle?"

"The Guardians," LeBoeuf said as he nodded, "remove him from cyber and we return him. He speaks for us."

"But," Sawyer objected, "the Gymnasium projected Aristotle. I mean, didn't the Confederation make him?"

"It did," LeBoeuf answered, "in response to our bidding."

"Who," Sawyer said even as he again hyperventilated, "kidnapped me?"

LeBoeuf put a finger to his own lips in an effort to settle the teenaged boy.

"The Guardians at Napolis?" Sawyer asked.

"I told you," LeBoeuf said, "it's dangerous to discuss. You should be concerned with your own journey."

"My journey? To where?"

"To your mother."

"She was in Tahiti once," Sawyer said, "but where she is, who she is, I don't know."

"We may."

"Anyway, what's it matter? Where will I live since you've taken me?"

"There are many places in the world," LeBoeuf said, "not worth living in. But we may—and I make no promise except to try—may be able to find you a real home."

"With my stead-mother?"

"With your natural mother."

"She doesn't want me. She gave me away."

"Perhaps not willingly."

Sawyer blinked.

"Many women," LeBoeuf said, "want their children back even as they give them away. Few forget."

"She'd want me?"

"Possibly."

"Why?"

"You're her son."

"I don't know her. Or where she lives."

Now LeBoeuf leaned forward. "We've found," he said, "many such mothers. Not only hundreds here, but thousands throughout the world."

"Why? Why would you?"

LeBoeuf leaned back and sipped his coffee. Only after considerable reflection did he respond. "The Confederation," the man explained, "has misunderstood Dower's Disease. They know effects better than causes and don't realize the need for a child to be loved by a true mother. We've found kisses and hugs to be better medicine than hormonal injections."

Now Sawyer looked confused.

"We have Dower's own books," LeBoeuf explained, "in their original form: the first printing. And some of his handwritten notes. Dower didn't believe in manufactured mothers. The point of his research was each child needs his own mother; one who could hold him and kiss him. Children without mothers grow up emotionally starved and often have trouble learning to give and receive love. Love is what we seek—the love of mother and child for each other. Nothing more, nothing less."

Sawyer responded with a blank look.

"You don't understand yet," the kidnapper said, "but it's simple to see. Dower proved children need to be loved as much as fed, and proved it in the 1950's by your own science. He proved the need for a mother's love is so great that children prefer a scarecrow mother to none at all. He also demonstrated that only a real mother gives the lifelong love that children need. No one can learn to love unless someone shows them how. Is that clear?"

"Not really."

"What Dower said was that material needs alone aren't enough to sustain a good life. Food, clothing, and shelter can't replace the love of a mother."

"I still don't understand."

"You don't need," LeBoeuf now explained, "to understand quite yet. Just don't run away. We'll have you with your mother soon and then you'll know that children—I mean everyone—must love and be loved. We've found lost boys like you need to experience love before they can understand it. But once you're loved, you'll grow fast, like teenagers who grow several centimeters in a few weeks."

"I don't know about that," Sawyer said. "We love in the Confederation. And we have friends and Equals."

"Desire you have," LeBoeuf scowled, "and maybe good will, but never love. It can't come from the engineering of a programmer or the touch of a stranger."

"Well," Sawyer said, "Mother took care of everything I ever wanted. She provided everything needed."

"There's more to love than comfort and convenience. There's passion and sacrifice."

Sawyer fell silent. "Where's my true mother?" the boy asked after a long pause.

"Confederation records show you were taken from Moorea."

"What's Moorea?"

"An island to the northwest of here. Just a couple hours away."

"Kidnapped?"

"Taken," the stranger said. "Women sometimes sent their children west to give them better lives. The years were hard."

"What's her name?"

"We were more concerned," LeBoeuf said, "about eating than bookkeeping in those days. Our archives are incomplete and Confederation records aren't easy to procure or decode."

"I don't understand."

"We've reunited," LeBoeuf said, "hundreds of mothers and children in Tahiti and Moorea with less information than we have of you."

"How?"

"There are memorials where mothers sans ... without children come to visit. On the island of Moorea stands le mur des fils et des filles perdus. The Wall of Lost Sons and Daughters. And there's one right here on Papeete too. The birth dates of the missing are carved into the marble and mothers leave their names and address near the birth dates."

"You have her name?"

LeBoeuf leaned forward. "You must remember," he said, "that our records are imperfectly matched to the stone. Maybe their parents died or emigrated or ... don't care. There are bad mothers. And fathers."

Sawyer winced.

"You need to realize," LeBoeuf said, "nothing is certain. There are no guarantees with a mother who's real rather than electronic. There may be sorrow or there may be joy. No one can say which. Real love can't be programmed; it must be willed."

Sawyer whispered his next question. "What's her name?"

"Several years ago," LeBoeuf said, "flowers were left at the wall in Moorea. The card gave your birth date and your mother's name. Our agents filed the information. We haven't yet obtained the samples of tissue. Maybe soon"—LeBoeuf paused, as if to remember the name—"I have the records in my office. Tomorrow we'll look for her."

"You don't remember?"

"Not for certain. First thing in the morning, we'll make plans to sail to Moorea."

Sawyer's voice grew sharp. "You don't know?"

"Patience," LeBoeuf whispered as he put a hand on Sawyer's shoulder. "Until ten minutes ago you didn't know she might be found. We've brought you here like hundreds of other orphans. And we'll return you to your family, if it pleases God. But it takes a little time. You're not the only lost child on this island."

"Let's go find her."

LeBoeuf shook his head. "Take the night to think it over and we'll go tomorrow. Also, you must remember that we can find you a home if it doesn't work with your natural mother."

Sawyer shook his head. "You don't understand," the boy said. "I think of seeing her every day. To talk to her and even ... even to hold her like a true ... a true mother. I don't want to wait."

"I've heard others say the same, but it doesn't change the fact I have plans for this evening."

"First thing tomorrow?"

"We'll take," LeBoeuf said, "our breakfast on the road. We can reach her by nightfall, if we can find a boat. Two days at most."

The answer satisfied Sawyer, so he no longer objected.

LeBoeuf paid the tab with hard currency and Sawyer followed the boy to the street, where a taxi was hailed. The driver was told to take Sawyer to a hotel where a room was registered to his name. The fare was prepaid and Sawyer jumped into a rusted Renault whose brakes screeched and windows rattled. Fifteen minutes later. Sawyer found himself in the lobby of a ramshackle hotel with a dozen rooms and a lobby restaurant with six tables. Still drowsy from the long trip and unflushed sedatives, Sawyer fell clothed into bed, closed his eyes, and dreamed.

18

NO MAN'S LAND

Boom! Boom! Boom!

The dark remained deep when three explosions sounded from the direction of the airport, quickly followed by another dozen preceded by the whine of missiles just before they reached their targets. Even as Sawyer ran to the window to look at the distant fires, the boy realized that the airport had been attacked. Jet bombers thundered overhead and emergency sirens wailed from a distance.

Boom! Boom! Boom!

Bombs exploded near the airfield—the blast flash and reverberation nearly five seconds apart.

Boom! Boom! Boom!

Another barrage struck closer—its blast and rumble separated by two seconds only.

Boom! Boom!

This time flash and thunder were nearly simultaneous. Flames shot into the sky just blocks away, high and intense.

Sawyer stepped back from the glass.

Boom! Boom! Boom!

Boom!

Now, explosions rattled the hotel, their percussion shaking windows till Sawyer thought the glass would shatter. The boy ran to a closet with his pillow and blanket to escape the barrage of missiles and thud of bombs. Indeed, hundreds of explosives fell as the city and Sawyer alike endured barrage after barrage. When bombs sounded far off, the boy breathed just a little easier and when they shook the hotel, he pulled a blanket over his head as a facade of protection. Close bursts shook his nerves and distant ones provided unfounded hope the attack was ending. The last bomb exploded before dawn.

Only when the room began to light from the new day did Sawyer emerge from the closet to take a long look out the cracked window to stare at spirals of smoke which cast a grim haze over the burning city. The room itself was undamaged, except for a few pictures fallen to the floor (now cracked or otherwise broken), so Sawyer hurried downstairs to check the lobby where he found the proprietor picking up broken bottles and glass shards.

"Do you speak Anglo-European?" Sawyer asked.

The proprietor didn't answer, so Sawyer raised his voice and asked what language the man spoke.

"Je ne parle pas anglais," the proprietor snapped as he turned around. "L'hôtel est fermé."

When Sawyer sat at a table, the shopkeeper shook his head and spoke louder yet. "Le restaurant est fermé," he said.

Sawyer shrugged.

"En anglais," the man said, pausing to make translation of his own words, "in Anglish. We close. It is good to you for leave."

The proprietor's accent was thick and his Anglo-European bad, but he'd made himself understood, so

Sawyer returned to his room, packed his belongings, and left. Outside, he found an unoccupied bench along the street and waited on it for the return of LeBoeuf. The streets were mostly deserted, the only traffic being an occasional car crammed with fleeing refugees who had lashed bundles to vehicle roofs or packed crying children and bleating and baying animals into back seats and open trunks. There also were convoys transporting bleary-eyed soldiers in the direction of the airport. Ambulances wailed, warplanes streaked overhead, and the greasy fumes of burning oil could be tasted. Sawyer shivered from a chilly breeze.

After a while, a dark-toned truck approached the hotel, then sped away. Two hours later, a soldier walked past without turning either to his left or right as he stared straight ahead: his shock displayed in his stooped shoulders and emotionless expression. The sight of the expressionless soldier so unnerved Sawyer that he tried to reenter the hotel, only to find the door locked. Unable to enter the hotel, the boy pressed his face to the glass until he saw from a wall clock that LeBoeuf was late and returned to the sidewalk bench.

ANOTHER TWO HOURS passed before Sawyer despaired. Now the boy saw civilian and military traffic less frequently and soon the only moving vehicles were trucks carrying armed soldiers or mustering militia. A police officer bicycling south shouted indiscernible words and even motioned for Sawyer to follow, but the officer didn't wait to see his orders effected (whatever they actually were). Sawyer didn't follow the man, though he realized from the fear in the officer's face that it'd be prudent to leave before night brought another attack.

To that end, Sawyer now emptied his luggage on the

street and sorted through its contents until he found a money wallet with identification cards and the photograph of himself and Mother at the whitewashed chapel in Old California, as well as the image of the pregnant Tahitian girl. He tucked the wallet into his back pocket and the plastic-wrapped photographs into a shirt pocket, then donned a jacket and stuffed its pockets with undergarments and socks. Sawyer also rolled a sweatshirt, jeans, and shoes into a wool blanket that he tied shut with shoestrings and slipped into a duffel bag used for dirty laundry. Everything else was left on the sidewalk as the boy started walking toward the airport.

Two convoys of soldiers had rolled by and Sawyer had walked a kilometer when the boy came upon a taxi parked along a side street, its driver dozing at the wheel. Sawyer rapped at the driver's window to rouse the unshaven driver until the man rubbed his eyes and rolled down his window.

"Oui, monsieur?" the driver asked.

"I need a ride to the aerodrome," Sawyer said.

The driver looked surprised. "A l'aéroport?"

"Yes."

"Non," the driver said with the nasal accent of a native, "ce n'est pas possible. L'aéroport est fermé. La guerre est près. Avez-vous une famille?"

"I don't speak," Sawyer said, "Old French. Only a few words."

When the driver raised his hands to indicate that he was as limited to his own language as the young boy was to Anglo-European, Sawyer pointed northwest. "Can I," the boy said, "get to the other island?"

The driver tried to understand, his brow furrowed and cheeks taut as the boy again pointed northwest, now motioning with his hands as if paddling a canoe.

"The island to the north and west," Sawyer said. "The i-land to the north and west."

"Je ne comprends pas."

"To the island of Moorea. I need to go to Moorea."

"Ahhh," the driver said, "Le mur des fils et des filles perdus. A l'ouest. J'ai un ami avec un bateau."

The cab driver signaled for Sawyer to get into his vehicle and Sawyer did so. They drove east until they reached a checkpoint in the far outskirts of the city—where soldiers conducted a cursory search and asked several questions. After a short delay, the taxi was waved through and its driver proceeded without word along an ill-kept coastal highway made of concrete and asphalt, much of the road no more than sand-filled potholes and weather-worn fragments flanked on both sides by abandoned houses: trees and brush obscuring many of the houses and reclaiming their lawns. Eventually the driver turned down a dirt road that led through a hamlet of twenty ramshackle bungalows, some of which lacked doors while others showed broken or boarded windows. All alike showed faded, peeled paint. Chopped wood was stacked in front yards and laundry strung between trees and poles. There were no electrical wires.

Sawyer watched as two children were chased from the front doors of a cottage by a broom-wielding matron while neighbors laughed from nearby porches. Most of the village's young, however, congregated into play groups of bare-chested children, boy and girl alike, milling along the dirt lane. Several boys who held balls and sticks paused their game as the taxi passed. Every child among them stared except for one boy who stuck out his tongue.

Near the pier, the driver parked in grass and honked his horn twice, sending a pack of half-tamed dogs scurrying away. A grey-haired man—shirtless, shoeless, and with a paunch over his unfastened belt—emerged from the closest bungalow: a large cottage with flaking brown paint.

The villager walked to the taxi as the driver rolled down his window and waited. "Bonjour, mon ami," the villager said.

The taxi driver didn't smile. "C'est très mal."

"Nous espérons partir," the villager said, "avant la nuit. Tu viens?"

"Non. Je veux voir ce qui va se passer."

"On dit," the villager said, "que les chinois arriveront tout de suite."

"Alors," the driver replied, "je combattrai."

"Alors, tu mourras."

"La mort," the taxi driver said as he forced a grim smile, "c'est la vie."

Both men fell silent and until the taxi driver nodded toward Sawyer and rekindled the conversation.

"Le garçon," the taxi driver said, "n'a pas de famille. Il est arrivé aujourd'hui. Je crois que c'est un Confédéré."

The villager eyed Sawyer before shrugging. "Et?"

"Et il n'a pas de famille. Ou de domicile. The villager waited.

"Tu peux l'amener," the driver continued, "au mur des enfants perdus?"

"Non," the villager said, "il est nécessaire que moi et ma famille partions ce soir."

"Pour l'amour de Dieu," the taxi driver said with a groan, "avant qu'il soit trop tard. Il n'a aucune chance."

"Il n'a aucune chance au monde."

"A mon ami," the driver said as he pointed toward the villager.

The driver got out of the taxi, leaving Sawyer inside while he and his compatriot stepped away to negotiate.

They talked nearly twenty minutes, casting glances toward the foreign-born boy—who looked perplexed and clearly didn't understand their language.

Eventually the driver returned to his car and looked to Sawyer before putting out his hand. "Doll-ars," the taxi driver said. "One ... hundred."

Sawyer nodded.

"A mon ami," the driver said as he pointed toward the villager.

Sawyer climbed from the taxi and reached into his pants pocket. Pulling out his wallet, he counted the required sum, leaving only forty Confederation dollars for himself. He paid the villager, then handed the remainder to the taxi driver—who kept only single note before returning the remainder.

"Pour l'essence," the taxi driver explained.

A moment later, the taxi driver wished Sawyer farewell, embraced the villager, and turned his vehicle back through the village even as the villager led Sawyer down a dirt path to a dilapidated boathouse where the man boiled breadfruit for lunch, then tapped his watch to indicate a long wait. Sawyer thought the meal bland, but still wished for a second helping as he sat in a corner listening to the squawk of gulls and roar of the surf. Occasionally, the boy looked out the window at the white-sanded beach and once saw jet aircraft fly overhead, though he didn't hear subsequent explosions. Somewhat later, Sawyer rolled his jacket as a pillow and slept.

The sun was nearly at the tree line when the villager woke Sawyer with a grunt and motioned for the boy to follow, which Sawyer did after the grim-faced man retrieved a pouch of navigation charts and a bag of tools from a desk drawer. The pair walked to a pier, where a dark-haired woman with a wrinkled face and wide hips greeted Sawyer, as did three boys huddled behind her—the woman speaking in her language and Sawyer responding in his own. The man gave instructions to what clearly was his family (each of the three boys shared his narrow face and thin lips) and led the middle child down a rickety pier missing too many planks to be safe. Following behind, his wife held their youngest boy's hand as she escorted him across the creaking planks and shouted at the oldest boy as he raced nimbly to a weather-beaten fishing boat moored at dock's end.

Sawyer lagged behind and finished crossing the ill-kept pier well after the villager and his family were aboard. Just a few minutes later, two women and three young children also arrived, bringing with them bags of food and threadbare blankets. Each of the children carried a single wooden toy in one hand and an extra pair of shoes in the other.

The boat sat low in the water, being filled with crates and tools, along with drums of fuel, jugs of water, and bags of food secured to the deck. Once the children stepped into the cabin, the villager slipped the mooring ropes to shove off and his wife started the motor of the boat. As the craft drifted from the pier, the woman reversed thrust and soon steered toward open sea where she throttled the engine to cruise speed. Indeed, the boat sailed west nearly an hour before bearing north and night was approaching by the time the craft neared a large island with rocky peaks and dark forests.

The villager pointed landward. "Moorea," he announced as the boat approached Moorea from the west and steered northeast, running parallel to the shore, maybe a kilometer out to sea. There was a break in the surf at the northwest corner of the island and the villager soon navigated through it into the shallows. After the boat slowed to a stop, the man waved at his guest, then toward a boarding ladder secured to the port quarter of the boat, speaking loud in Old French while his wife remained at the helm. It wasn't long before Sawyer found himself in chest-deep water as the boatman handed him his duffel bag and the woman idled the motor. The oldest boy tossed Sawyer a bag of dried meat and one of the village women shouted above the roar of the motor.

"Le mur est à l'est," the woman yelled as she pointed east. "Le mur des fils et des filles perdus."

Sawyer nodded as the engine revved and the Tahitians set their course for unknown waters, leaving their young castaway to fend for himself as their boat disappeared into the dark. Sawyer sloshed ashore, trembling from the wet and cold, as the boat vanished and made land as the sound of the engine faded. Immediately turning east along the shore, he hadn't walked ten minutes when his legs grew tired and his eyelids heavy. A grove of coconut trees just beyond the tide provided a suitable bed down where the boy pushed brush into a nest in which he covered himself with his wool blanket until he grew warm and the roar of the sea faded into the still of sleep.

19

THE ISLE OF LOST MOTHERS

Hunger stirred with first light and dawn bought little more than an empty belly and a stiff neck. As Sawyer shook sand from his clothes and spit salt from the night mist, the sun rose over the eastern horizon and warmed the morning—though the boy remained in a dour darkness undispelled by sunlight as he rose to a new day in which he was utterly alone in a strange land and lacking every convenience of human civilization. Without home or friend or country, there was no place to be and no one to see. There was nothing to do except search for a stead-mother he didn't know and hadn't seen, who might be dead or forever gone. And whether the woman would embrace him as a lost son or despise him as an unwanted burden remained an unanswered question and nagging concern.

The shore was lonely, excepting a flock of gulls and two pelicans satisfying their morning hunger. Sawyer watched the birds squabble over the carcass of a fish until the larger one seized it and flew inland. The boy wondered whether the pelican was a mother feeding her chicks with her own life or just another bird fighting for itself. After the pelican flew away, Sawyer rolled his blanket, stuffed dried meat into his mouth, and walked east, keeping several steps from the tide. As he moved down the beach, broken tree lines revealed inland mountains towering several hundred meters high: their jagged peaks and outcroppings of rock rising along the rim of an extinct volcano. Steep mountains covered with trees and grass streamed downward toward the shoreline and stone foundations overgrown by bush and vine testified to the force of a tsunami that had wrecked the coast of Moorea and washed to sea village and resort alike.

As Sawyer continued east, signs of current human settlement soon appeared: a fishing boat offshore, columns of smoke behind the trees, and even a native couple sitting in tall grass near a partially overgrown foundation for a beach house. The young exile made very slow progress (the sink of his step into dry sand constraining movement) and after a few minutes flipped off his shoes and walked near the lap of the waves, moving a little faster on the hard-packed sand at edge-tide. As the chill of morning passed, the boy removed his jacket and took another bite of dried meat, then another until it was gone and the wrapper tossed aside.

THIRTY MINUTES AFTER WAKING, Sawyer came to a village situated along the shore. Only one of its fifteen houses (most of them painted with prime colors long since dulled) showed signs of life, and even it showed only a wisp of smoke rising above the crumbled mortar of its stone chimney. Despite the inhospitable appearance of the village, Sawyer continued past several cottages with drawn shades and closed doors until he came to a common area: an empty field with a diamond-shaped field and a water pump painted dark red. There, the boy pumped the cast iron handle, though he could not cause any water to flow. Indeed, the device was unprimed and Sawyer didn't know how to charge it. Muttering as he tried to draw water by repetition of effort, the boy drew only attention. As the iron handle squeaked, faces peered through shades and shouts sounded. Sawyer ignored them until a barrel-chested man stepped from the nearest cottage, a faded red home with warped boards and empty window frames.

The man shouted out a sharp command. "Allez-vous-en."

When Sawyer looked at the man without word, the latter repeated his command.

"Allez-vous-en," the man shouted.

As Sawyer pointed to the pump, the villager cleared his throat, spitting into the dirt from contempt and shouting even louder. "Je dis," the man yelled, "allez-vous-en. Maintenant!"

Sawyer stepped away. "I just want," the boy called out to the angry villager, "a drink of water."

The villager gestured to show his meaning: two clenched fists pumped in the strange boy's direction. Coming from a large man with an angry face, the threat was unmistakable—though Sawyer remained at the pump, his thirst proving stronger than his fear. Only when the man stepped toward him after breaking a branch from a nearby poplar tree did the boy stand up straight. As the villager slashed his switch through the air, Sawyer backed away several steps, then hurried toward the beach until the man was out of sight. Only there did he rest beneath a palm tree as he clawed without success at the husk of a fallen coconut.

In a short time, Sawyer dropped the unbroken coconut and continued his trek east to the next village, where he encountered several women standing near a simmering kettle. Three of the women kept toddlers at their feet and two held babies as they themselves stirred wooden ladles into a cast iron pot from which the pungent stench of boiling soap wafted across the beach. The first woman to notice Sawyer was a short woman with coarse hair and a stony expression—who nudged a tall girl until both stared at the passing boy, the women speaking in whispers that the intruder couldn't understand. The girl stamped her feet, the hard-faced woman glared, and Sawyer quickened his pace. The others paid no attention, being too engrossed in steaming laundry and tending children to heed a passing mother-hunter.

Sawyer kept his pace until he came to a third village, this one better kept than the others: its cottages bright and clean. Paint wasn't peeling and windows weren't broken. Two women and a dozen children (not one of them more than five or six years) played in the grass. The children scampered away at the sight of Sawyer—who kept moving without attempting to make contact with a young woman who called to him.

A TURN south and twenty minute's walk brought another village. Here, Sawyer encountered a large group of boys playing mitt-ball in an open field. One wielded a wooden bat used to strike a leather ball which the others subsequently fielded with bare hands and rawhide gloves. As Sawyer approached, play slowed and eventually stopped altogether. The older boys shouted among themselves while younger ones barked from afar. The smallest boy sprinted for the village and the tallest trotted toward Sawyer.

"Comment vous appelez-vous?" the tall boy asked.

Sawyer said nothing.

"Vous pouvez parler?" the tall boy said.

Several boys catcalled. Two dropped their mitts and menaced forward.

Sawyer didn't respond.

Now the tall boy spoke louder, his tone insistent. "Parlez!" he commanded.

Sawyer told the tall boy that he didn't speak Old French.

"Vous êtes espion!" the tall boy shouted.

Sawyer didn't understand the meaning of the words but knew he was being accused, so he protested his innocence, his voice high-pitched and quick-breathed.

"I don't know," Sawyer said, "what you're saying. I'm looking for my mother."

Now, one of the younger boys spoke: a dark-faced child with thin shoulders and a swayed back. "Vous habitez avec quelle famille?" the swayed-back boy asked.

"I don't understand your language," Sawyer answered.

The village boys heard enough. Several moved to striking range even as Sawyer backed away. They were joined by a mob of younger brothers and friends standing behind them.

"Il est d'Opuncho," someone shouted from the mob of boys. "Il est du village d'Anton."

The dark faced boy with thin shoulders and a swayed back picked up a stone. Others followed his lead even as Sawyer inched backward as he scanned his foes for threats.

The first stone whizzed past Sawyer's head only a meter off target and the second kicked dust at his feet. The third and fourth stones also missed. It was the fifth stone, thrown by the swayed-back boy, that flew straight toward Sawyer's head.

Wham!

Sawyer twisted right, but the stone struck above his left

ear as pain throbbed and blood spurted from a finger-length gash near his temple. He yelped as his knees buckled, but quickly regained his balance, picking up with his right hand the very stone that struck him and with his left hand an even larger one—and firing the former toward the swayed-back boy. Sawyer's throw was so hard and accurate that the boy dove face into dirt to avoid being struck between the eyes, eating a mouthful of grass and tearing his lip. Before the others could react, Sawyer raised his arm, the larger stone posed to throw.

The island boys backed away since few had stones in hand and none was willing to test whether Sawyer's aim had been very good or just lucky.

His foes momentarily cowed, Sawyer backed away until he was out of range, then slipped the large stone into a pants pocket and hurried down the road near the village. Only after he had cleared the area and slowed to a walk did he press a hand to his head only to realize his hair was sticky and matted from coagulated blood. Even as Sawyer massaged the wound, blocking torn flesh from the sting of air and the throb of movement, he frequently looked back to ensure he wasn't being followed.

After a couple minutes, Sawyer turned down the shore of an inlet and soon saw the gang of boys (now returned to their mitt ball) across the small bay he had circumnavigated. Slipping behind a line of trees, he remained behind cover as he picked up his pace despite being far beyond throwing range. Only after he was beyond the sight of the boys did Sawyer's strength flag, his legs slowing and shoulders sagging as the sun burned and baked his every step. Blood and sweat seeped from his forehead and his throat parched. The sea breeze died and he warmed fast. When he arrived at the shore of the main beach, the boy continued east, now moving sluggish and slow.

Dropping his eyes as he walked, Sawyer didn't notice a woman who was coming toward him until she nearly was upon him, his attention finally awakened by her loud and labored breathing. The two had walked straight at each other without paying much attention and were only a few steps apart when each looked up and noticed the other. Neither one spoke out loud, woman and boy alike casting no more than furtive glances in the direction of a stranger.

The woman wasn't young. Maybe forty years old, she was a local with cocoa skin and waist-length hair streaked with grey: her face wrinkled, her eyes bloodshot, and her teeth protruding and stained. For her part, the woman glanced at Sawyer several times before she finally broke eye contact and hurried away. Sawyer stared as the woman moved west, leaving shallow tracks that would be washed away before the sun rose again—then sighed and remembered her no more.

Now a flock of gulls squawked overhead and Sawyer watched them as a second woman appeared, at first little more than a mirage where the sun's rays met the sand's glint. As the second woman approached, she became more concrete and visible, appearing somewhat younger than the previous woman. She was no more than thirty-five years old, her hair and skin were lighter than other islanders, and she bore the drawn eyes of a Korean. This woman wore a coarse cloth dress and walked with cautious steps, her sandaled feet stepping only where her eyes directed them and her gaze focused on the sand. When she heard Sawyer's steps, she looked up and opened her mouth as if to speak, but said nothing.

As Sawyer subsequently slowed, so did the woman, her

eyes tightening as she wiped away tears. When Sawyer slowed to a halt, she too stood still as she eyed the boy just a few steps away, her lip quivering and hands trembling. Neither woman nor boy spoke for a long while, but stood in mute bewilderment. Only when a gull cried overhead and the woman looked away was the spell broken. Only then did Sawyer drop his eyes and the woman continue west.

Neither one looked back.

Now a fishing boat appeared in the sea, the rumble of its diesel motor a welcome relief from the stillness of the shore. Sawyer watched as the craft propelled itself toward the western horizon. As its noise faded with distance, Sawyer turned his eyes east. It was then that he saw the wall.

THE REMEMBRANCE WALL was separated from the sand of the shoreline by a patch of grass, through which a narrow trail had been trampled. Standing head high, the memorial was a conglomeration of natural stone and shaped slab now cemented together without apparent symmetry—the union of mortar and stone as seemingly haphazard as organic life; here, two bricks were plastered together with crumbling mortar; there, a large stone was propped against a small one; a few steps away, an ornate slab rose from the ground. For thirty meters, stones were stacked shoulder high, with weather-worn letters and numbers etched into each one: some of the markers now crusted with sea salt and others showing the remorse and regret of heavy hearts and rough hands. Sun-baked bouquets withered on the ground: peace offerings presented to lost children, but never received.

Sawyer's own hands sweated as he approached.

The first marker was a brick into which someone had scratched four disfigured letters. The shallow-cut lines of the letters were softened by the weather and it wouldn't be too many years before they'd fade beyond recognition. Sawyer read them.

F-i-l-s.

It was a son who was mourned.

An adjoining stone, not brick but flat limestone with chiseled letters, gave only the date of a child born (or dead) a decade before Sawyer's own birth.

11-9-2070.

While the first two stones included no more than names and dates, the third (a piece of chiseled granite set near the ground) was inscribed with a child's name and day of birth or death, as well as the stead-mother's village.

Jeannette, une fille d'Nicole et d'Anton de Maçon, 2063.

Sawyer continued to survey the long wall: which included several hundred stone markers and scores of withered bouquets laying on the ground like funeral flowers. Moving to his right, the boy reached the wall's edge and started back, checking each marker for his own name or birth date, or anything that might provide a clue to his stead-mother. Most stones were chiseled in Old French and proved undecipherable, even though Sawyer recognized *fils* as son and *fille* as daughter. Indeed, the boy found nothing of note during the first hour's search, nor the second, and continued his search until every brick was checked and every stone, if possible, turned for clues. After the wall was searched front and back, he began a second check—which soon grew frantic as he circled, almost ran, around the wall in a desperate search for signs of his mother. Despite slowing for neither food nor drink nor a sprinkling of rain, the boy's efforts grew increasingly desperate.

Only the coming of dusk and a consequent inability to read the inscriptions slowed Sawyer down. Faded names difficult to read during the day became impossible to see in the deepening shadows as weathered chiseling altogether disappeared in the dark so that the wall itself became mute and unfeeling, its granite dark and brick unspeaking. His efforts rendered futile, Sawyer turned his back to the wall and walked to the sea, where he splashed his face and washed his hands. Afterward, he licked droplets of water from the undersides of palm fronds before stumbling to the wall for sleep.

Occasional drops of rain and more frequent chills came with the night as strong sea breezes cooled the evening and brought goose pimples. Sawyer lay down at the base of the wall on the inland side, then drew in his elbows and bent his legs until he had pulled knee and elbow alike to his chest. In this crouch, he wrapped a wool blanket around his body and tucked spare clothes beneath his head as a pillow. Even so, his neck ached and his teeth soon chattered from the night chill after the temperature dropped noticeably. He also grew increasingly hungry every hour and soon despaired of sleep. It wasn't long before he wept.

Tears fell for an hour, streaking Sawyer's cheeks until his eyes were swollen and his throat parched. Even dehydrated, the boy shed dry tears until he was reduced to burning eyes and a gasping throat. Minute after minute, hour after hour, he trembled from cold and sorrow, and even the moon cast a cold pallor over his grief whenever the clouds parted and no longer obscured what little light the deep heavens shared. For his part, Sawyer didn't try to build a bed or warm himself, but lay on the cold ground shivering and weeping without respite. Indeed, dawn wasn't more than a couple hours away when the boy finally fell asleep, his sorrow spent and exhaustion so complete so that he slept like a newborn baby oblivious to the labor and life around him.

The last pangs of night already had contracted and delivered the birth of a new day when Sawyer stirred from his fetal crouch to the loud cry of a woman's voice.

"Mon fils, comment allez-vous?" the woman's voice called to the sleeping boy.

Sawyer jumped to his feet and looked around, rubbing his eyes and seeing that a woman stood on the seaward side of the wall, her bare feet leaving tracks in the tide-drenched sand. A long trail of footprints stretched from the east in an unbroken trek.

"Garçon, comment allez-vous?" the woman said as she pointed to the wall and made yet another statement that Sawyer couldn't comprehend. "Vous pouvez parler?"

"I don't know what you are saying," Sawyer said loud and slow. "I don't speak French."

"You speak English?" the woman asked with an Old French accent.

Sawyer was surprised and took a moment to reply. "Anglo-European, not Old English."

"They are close."

Sawyer nodded.

"Bonjour," the woman said as she eyed the lost boy. "I am called Madame Jeannette Bonmaison."

Sand stuck to Sawyer's clothes and salt to his hair. His eyes were bloodshot, lips cracked, and he shivered even in the warmth of morning. His hair was clotted with matted blood and he held his eyes on a rumpled blanket at his feet for several seconds. Only then did he look at the woman, though still without speaking a word.

"You need to sleep?" Madame Bonmaison soon asked. "Or to eat?"

"I don't know," Sawyer replied.

"You will know if you are tired or hungry."

"I don't know."

"You will come," the woman said with the shake of a finger, "you come with me."

"I'll stay here."

"You are lost?"

"I'm not lost. I know where I am."

"You have family?"

"I hope my stead-mother is here."

The woman looked around. "Which village?" she asked.

"I don't know."

"She is where?"

Sawyer's eyes glistened.

"Where is your mother?" the woman said.

"I-I don't know. She's gone."

"What direction?"

"What?"

"How long? When?"

Sawyer looked to the wall. Only after a long pause did he answer. "When I was a baby."

The woman looked at the stone wall. "You came to find her?" she asked.

"Yes."

"You did?"

"Not yet."

"Well," the woman said in a tone not to be dismissed, "as I say, you come with me. Pour l'amour de Dieu, venez."

The woman handed Sawyer a water flask, then motioned for him to follow, and the boy did as he was told.

20

NEXT OF KIN

A squadron of high-flying bombers streaked through the clouds as Sawyer followed the woman inland. The boy counted thirty contrails and frequently slowed to listen for exploding bombs until the woman chided him.

"Why do you stop?" the woman asked.

"The war," Sawyer replied.

"It is terrible, but we hurry."

Moving east, inland, and parallel to the coast, the pair followed a winding trail through grass and brush until they came to a village of two dozen cottages set around a whitewashed chapel graced with a bell tower that rose heavenward over nearby palm trees and impenetrable clusters of bamboo. Perhaps a dozen children played in front of a it, chasing each other in a game of catch-as-catch-can, while several teenagers watched from a distance.

Now Madame Bonmaison called toward the children and teenagers. "Marie," she shouted, "Nicole. Jeannette."

Three teenaged girls immediately broke away from their friends and hurried toward their mother as she turned a cheek to receive their kisses. The oldest girl, a blossoming adolescent whose breasts were fuller and hips wider than those of a Guardian, eyed the strange boy. The young woman's skin was cocoa, her dark hair was tied in a ponytail, and she wore a calico dress to her knees. Her feet were bare.

"Qui est ce garçon?" the young woman asked.

"C'est un étranger," Madame Bonmaison said. "Il n'a pas de famille."

"Je m'apppelle Marie," the young woman said as she curtseyed.

"This is my daughter," Madame Bonmaison announced, "and she tells you her name is Marie."

"I'm Sawyer."

"Il s'appelle Sawyer," Madame Bonmaison said as she looked at her daughter.

"Saw-yer?" the ponytailed girl said as she looked straight at the strange boy.

Sawyer nodded.

"Her sisters are Nicole," the woman continued as a skinny-armed teenager with crooked teeth and thick hair bowed. This girl had not fully matured. Though her breasts were swelled and hips rounded, her arms and legs remained thin. She wore a beige dress, plain and dirty, and her hair was dark.

"Je m'appelle Nicole," the dark-haired girl said.

Sawyer nodded.

"Et," the woman continued, "ma petite, my baby, Jeannette."

The youngest of the girls, only a little taller than Sawyer himself, blushed. She was flat-chested, narrow-hipped, and wore the same cut of calico as the older of her sisters.

"Maman," the youngest girl said with a gentle rejoinder before she faced Sawyer and curtseyed. "Je m'appelle," she whispered, "Jeannette."

As Sawyer blushed and the girl turned away, Madame Bonmaison covered a smile with an open hand and the older girls giggled.

"Sawyer," Madame Bonmaison said, "do you need anything? Food?"

"I'm hungry," the boy said.

"Jeannette," Madame Bonmaison said, "will bring to bathe. After you clean, I will have dinner."

Instructions were passed in brusque nasal words that Sawyer couldn't understand and a moment later all three girls set themselves to task. The older girls walked to a nearby house (a particularly small cottage painted blue) while their younger sister led Sawyer to a water station outside the village. There, Jeannette primed a hand pump and drew fresh water into a clean pail from which Sawyer drank before setting the bucket to the ground. Next, Jeannette pulled a towel from a clothesline and led her guest to a three-sided and roofless stall where she pointed to a rope and motioned for Sawyer to pull it before she stepped behind the stall's wood planks that provided privacy for its sole occupant.

Sawyer stared at a rust-stained pipe without comprehending its use.

After a few minutes, the girl called to Sawyer, a slight tremble to her voice. "Saw-yer?"

"Yes?"

"Savez-vous," Jeannette asked, "prendre une douche?"

"I don't know what you're saying."

"Vous avez besoin d'aide?"

When Sawyer repeated he didn't understand, Jeannette knocked three times on the stall's wall, then circled back to the opening, her eyes dropped to her feet until she confirmed that the boy remain dressed by observing that his ankles remained covered with pants.

"Vous ne savez pas prendre une douche," Jeannette said with a giggle. "Je vous dirai comment le faire."

Jeannette's wordless instructions were explicit. Raising a single hand and counting her fingers, she showed Sawyer how he should enter the stall, draw water by pull cord, scrub himself using a bar of homemade soap set on a shelf beside the showerhead, then dry himself with the clean towel hanging from a metal hook.

Sawyer affirmed his understanding with a nod and began to undress, quickly removing his shirt and reaching for his belt.

"Eeeeehh."

The girl's high-pitched scream pierced the air as Jeannette covered her eyes, turned her back, and darted behind cover of the screen. When her sisters shouted from nearby, the girl yelled back an agitated answer, even as she giggled. In any event, it wasn't long before Sawyer emerged from the stall, his clothes sticky wet and hair disheveled by towel drying, Still. his face shined and he walked with a fresh step.

"Ça va bien?" Jeannette asked after she finally suppressed her laughter.

"I still don't speak Old French," Sawyer said with a smile.

Jeannette led Sawyer home—where Madame Bonmaison had set a table with clean linen and fresh fruit, along with garden greens and salted fish. As the middle-aged woman watched the boy eat, her daughters moved to the front porch and chatted until Sawyer's plate was empty.

. . .

After Madame Bonmaison cleared the table, she summoned her oldest daughter to clean the chipped ceramic plates while she herself served fruit juice in polished coconut shells, giving one to Sawyer and keeping a second for herself.

While Sawyer gulped his drink, Madame Bonmaison sipped her own. “We must talk,” she said.

Sawyer nodded.

“You came only to the wall?” the woman asked.

“I,” Sawyer replied, “was looking for my name—or my mother’s.”

“When did you come to … I mean, the big island?”

“Two days ago.”

“You know you can never return?”

Sawyer looked away.

“There is war,” Madame Bonmaison continued, “on the main island and you cannot go there.”

Only after a long pause did Sawyer respond. “It doesn’t really matter,” he said. “I was exiled from the Confederation. A kidnapper said my stead-mother was close, but he left me when the city was bombed.”

Madame Bonmaison waited while Sawyer collected his thoughts.

“He never gave me his real name,” Sawyer explained, “or hers.”

“He knew your mother?”

“He thought she lived on this island.”

“How did he know?”

“I think from the wall,” Sawyer explained, “but I don’t know the details.”

Now it was the woman who carefully considered her reply. “I cannot speak for my husband,” she said, “but I would have you stay with us.”

Sawyer's chin dropped and his eyes teared up. "You," the boy said, "aren't my stead-mother."

The woman lay a finger on Sawyer's wrist. "Our village," she said, "has many sons and daughters who came from afar."

"I've met," Sawyer answered with a whisper as he turned his face away, "some villagers already. I don't belong."

"You are wrong, my son," Madame Bonmaison said. "Some of the children who played at the church arrived from your country. Some came like you."

Sawyer tapped the wound on his temple. "Plato," he said, "taught that each state cares only for its own. Not for strangers. Aristotle said it too."

"I do not know," Madame Bonmaison said, "these people or why they say this, but have we not treated you well? Do you not drink our water and eat our food?"

"You can't care for me, not really. I'm not your son."

"Must I hate," the woman said, "the son of the other woman to love my child?"

Sawyer shrugged.

Madame Bonmaison took Sawyer's hand. Though the boy tried to draw away, she wouldn't let go and Sawyer found himself locked in the woman's grip as she told him to answer. When Sawyer remained silent, Madame Bonmaison stared into his eyes and spoke with a measured calm, her tone unbending and unwavering.

"You must learn," Madame Bonmaison said, "Nicole was not born from my body, but of my friend. Her father disappeared from fishing and her mother died of tumor the next year. I have made Nicole my daughter. No different than my own flesh."

Sawyer looked surprised. "Why?" he asked.

The woman looked behind her shoulder. "You saw our church?" she said.

Sawyer nodded.

"We are children of God. All of us. No matter our parents."

"No one believes that any longer."

"I do."

"No one else does."

"Nicole," the woman said as her eyes flashed, "believes it."

Sawyer fell silent.

When the boy spoke, he changed the subject. "How," he asked, "did you learn Anglo-European?"

"I lived in the Confederation."

"Where?"

"Metrofornia. The Angels District."

Sawyer looked up. "On the coast?"

"Inland. I was a nurse."

Sawyer's mouth dropped open and eyes opened wide as his voice brought accusation. "You were a stead-mother?" he asked. "You gave away your child?"

"I was surrogate nurse," Madame Bonmaison said. "It was my job to tend babies."

"Nurses carry babies."

"Some watch cradles."

"That's what you did?"

"Yes, for seven years. To earn money to marry. To build this house."

"Marie-Thérèse—she was my nurse—said the woman of your world must sell their babies to—"

Madame Bonmaison didn't let Sawyer finish. "Not always," she said. "Many give up their children to earn the money to marry, but some are able to work only."

"Like you?"

The woman lowered her voice. Her words were quiet and faded almost before they reached Sawyer's ears. "I have no regrets," she said.

"Others do?"

The woman nodded.

"Like my stead-mother?" Sawyer asked.

"I am sorry for you. And for her."

The conversation wound down and Sawyer relaxed the rest of the day, alternating between a palm-leaf mattress indoors and a lawn chair outside. The girls often passed near, speaking in their own tongue as they carried laundry or moved water. The older two spoke freely to the newcomer, their voices at ease and eyes friendly, but their younger sister was more reticent as she greeted the strange boy with little more than glances and blushes. For his part, Sawyer averted his eyes whenever he noticed the youngest girl looking toward him.

It was evening when a stout man whose nose was pointed like that of his oldest daughter returned home. He was brown-skinned, grey-haired, and thick-armed; and dressed in dirt-covered denims worn nearly threadbare. His teeth were stained yellow and his hands hardened with calluses. He greeted Sawyer with little more than raised eyebrows and spoke with words that sounded like grunts, then called for his wife—who led him by the hand to a separate room where they talked twenty minutes.

When the couple emerged, the man was more relaxed, his face friendly and voice calm.

"Nicole, prépare un lit pour ce garçon," the man said. "Pour une seule nuit."

"You," his wife now interpreted as she looked at Sawyer, "will stay tonight, but then you must go—"

Sawyer dropped his chin nearly to his chest and his shoulders sagged.

"Sawyer," Madame Bonmaison said, "we do not want to send you away. My husband is glad I brought you. It is only that we have three daughters and a small house. It is not proper for you to stay. Not for long."

"I'm old enough," Sawyer said as his eyes misted a little, "to sleep with sisters."

"They are not," Madame Bonmaison sounded curt, "your sisters and you do not sleep with them. Also, you must not undress before them. It is sin. Our ways are not those of your Confederation. We are believers."

"Where," Sawyer answered with a whisper, "can I go?"

"Mon mari," the woman began before correcting herself, "I mean to say, my husband, says you will live with his sister."

"Who's that?"

"She is a widow who lives in the forest. With the old women."

"She doesn't know me."

"It doesn't matter," Madame Bonmaison said. "She will take you."

"Why?" Sawyer asked.

"Because she is kind and she wants her own child—"

"I'm not her child," Sawyer interrupted.

"No," Madame Bonmaison said, "but my husband says you remind him of his brother. He died many years ago."

"I'm not his brother."

"No, he died long ago. But Monique will be pleased with the resemblance."

Sawyer's voice sounded flat. "I don't want to be remembered for someone else."

Madame Bonmaison touched Sawyer's wrist and spoke

in an almost inaudible voice. “What choice,” she whispered, “do you have?”

Sawyer shrugged.

“Where else can you go?”

“Nowhere.”

“Tomorrow,” Madame Bonmaison said, “I will take you to Monique.”

21

ARE YOU MY MOTHER?

It was past noon when Nicole and Jeannette led Sawyer along an ill-kept path choked with vines and tree limbs. The trail wasn't too steep or difficult, even if it had fallen into disrepair, and by midafternoon the teenagers reached their destination: a hamlet with several dilapidated cottages painted in muted tones, adorned with crude shutters and roofs patched with grass thatching. A walking path bisecting the hamlet was flanked on either side by mango groves from which monkeys chattered. Feral cats prowled near the houses.

On reaching the hamlet, Nicole ran to the nearest cottage as a grey-haired woman stepped from its front door to greet her with a long embrace and short kiss. As Jeannette followed her sister's lead, an elderly woman stared at the boy from the front window of a nearby house and a second from her garden. Sawyer watched from afar until the girls motioned for him to come and he did as told while Monique read a note composed on pressed papaya.

Sawyer looked at the woman for a moment, observing that she was beyond her youth: breasts sagged, hips spread, and dark hair clipped at the shoulders. She wore dirt-stained cotton that covered her arms to the elbow and legs to the ankle to protect her cocoa skin. Her eyes were circled with exhaustion and her face already furrowed with wrinkles. When she was done reading, the woman looked at Sawyer without word or movement, as if stunned, and spoke only after a long pause.

"Bonjour," the woman whispered.

Sawyer said hello.

"C'est vrai," the woman said after a pause. "Vous ressemblez à mon frère."

Sawyer said nothing.

Nicole introduced Sawyer to Monique—who greeted the boy, then spoke a long while with her niece. Eventually, it was the middle-aged woman who placed her hand on Sawyer's shoulder and closed her eyes as she blessed the boy, then motioned for him to wait while she stepped into her cottage. There, she retrieved a wood-framed photo faded from age and stained in one corner, though the faces of two children (a year or two younger than Sawyer himself) remained recognizable.

The woman pointed to the photo of the girl and tapped her breast. "Moi"—now she pointed at the other child—"et mon frère. Vous ressemblez à lui."

"He looks a little like me," Sawyer whispered as he tapped the photograph with one forefinger and his chest with the other. "That boy looks like me."

The woman nodded, a faint smile to her lips as she pointed both at Sawyer and the faded photo. "Je dis que vous ressemblez à mon frère," she said as she nodded her head and stared at the photograph. Even when a niece tugged her arm, the woman didn't respond.

Now Sawyer looked to Nicole and pointed at the photo. "Nicole," he whispered, "who's the boy?"

"C'est mon oncle."

"I don't understand," Sawyer said. "I can't understand what you say."

Touching the faded face of the photographed boy, Nicole gestured to share thoughts words couldn't.

"Lui," Nicole said.

"Louis?"

"Non. Lui. L-ui."

"We?" Sawyer asked.

"Non," the woman said. "L-ui. Ui. Ui."

Sawyer looked at the image a long while. "He?"

"C'est de ma famille ..."

"Oh, il ... I mean, he's family."

"Oui, oui," Nicole said as she tried to explain herself. "Il fait partie de la famille de mon papa et de ma tante. Mon papa et"—the girl pointed at the dark-haired woman—"ma tante."

"She's the family of your papa and your tante?" Sawyer repeated the word just as he heard it. "What's a tante?"

Nicole pointed to Monique. "C'est ma tante—Monique."

"Oh," Sawyer said, "your mother said she's the sister of your father. Your aunt. Aunt sounds like tante."

Nicole shrugged. She spoke no more Anglo-European than Sawyer did Old French.

Monique cut the translations short with a command and motioned for both nieces to follow as she led all three teenagers to her cottage, where they sat at a wood table with three round legs and a square one.

Indeed, the cottage wasn't large, being little more than a single living room with an attached kitchen and separated bedroom. It possessed no conveniences and even its toilet was an outdoor privy which spilled raw sewage into an open ditch. Likewise, the interior walls were painted with a peeling beige paint, though they appeared darker since all curtains were drawn. A lamp stinking of kerosene provided a bit of light and warmth and a large cross of wood was hung over an end table. Otherwise, the room was sparse and unadorned. Floor planks cut from palm logs were partially covered with a braided rug.

Soon enough, Monique set a basket of fruit and bread before the three teenagers, who quickly reduced the food to rinds and seeds. Sawyer showed such hunger that he ate a banana from his right hand and a mango from his left. Nicole and Jeannette showed better manners, though they squabbled over the last bit of bread until a sharp word from their aunt cut their dispute short and a blushing Nicole released her grip. Also red-faced, Jeannette broke the bread into two pieces and gave the larger portion to her sister. Their aunt embraced both girls and pointed to Sawyer, who waited for Nicole to interpret what she said, if possible.

"Vous resterez ici," Nicole said as she pointed to the interior of the cottage and to Monique, "avec ma tante."

"I rest with her?" Sawyer asked.

"Je crois que vous comprenez," Nicole said as she shrugged her shoulders.

Now Monique looked to her nieces and pointed to the door. "Il est tard," she said. "Vous devez vous dépêcher à la maison."

As Jeannette stepped toward the door, Nicole took Sawyer's hand and spoke. "Nous devons partir maintenant. Bonne chance."

When Sawyer stood to follow, Monique stopped him with a hand to his shoulder. "C'est ici votre maison," she said.

Sawyer motioned that he'd go with the girls.

"Non, non, non," Monique replied, each word softer than the one before. "Vous resterez ici. Avec moi."

"Non, non, non," Monique replied, each word softer than the one before. "Vous resterez ici. Avec moi."

Monique pointed to her own cottage floor and Sawyer stopped as the girls waved a final adieu to their aunt and newly adopted cousin before hurrying down the main path back to their village.

NOT LONG AFTER the girls disappeared into the forest, an elderly woman emerged from a thicket and motioned for Monique and Sawyer to follow her uphill to a small clearing located a hundred meters away and where there were stacks of cordwood and rows of vegetables. Once there, the elderly woman piled cord in Sawyer's arms until his back bent, then pointed for the boy to return downhill. Monique grabbed an armful of kindling as Sawyer staggered ahead.

It wasn't, however, the weight of wood that stopped Sawyer in his tracks as soon as he turned back toward the path, but a poorly maintained chapel with its front door missing and paint long since faded. The instant that Sawyer saw the unmistakable shape of the building, he froze: for the building resembled the Old California building in Sawyer's baby picture. A bell tower built with dark wood was attached to a whitewashed chapel with a dark cross that was nailed above its main entrance. Palm groves stood to either side of the chapel and a square-shaped stone served as some type of memorial near the main entrance. Even as the elderly woman walked to her house without looking back, Sawyer first slowed and soon stopped, causing Monique almost to run into him.

"Êtes-vous blessé?" Monique asked as she looked around to determine what was so interesting.

Sawyer stared at the church without word.

"Qu'est-ce qu'il y a?" Monique's eyes finally turned to where Sawyer stared. "Il y a un problème avec l'église?"

"I don't understand," Sawyer said. "I only heard the word prob-lem."

The woman pointed at the church. "L'église," she asked, "il y a un problème?"

"The church?" Sawyer said. "No, there's no problem. No problem. I've seen one like it in a photograph."

"Ahhh, une photo," Monique said as she nodded. "J'ai une photo dans ma petite maison."

Sawyer picked up the wood and continued down the path, all the while staring at the whitewashed church until he could see it no longer: its bell tower, large cross, and stone memorial suggesting to the boy that this was much like the place where he was photographed with Mother. Sawyer wondered how two places so far apart could appear so alike and resolved to question Madame Bonmaison when he was able.

Ten minutes later, the boy stacked cord on the old woman's porch and returned for a second load, then another, frequently lingering near the small chapel. Following Monique's direction, he worked another hour and stopped only when called home to take salted bread and bitter root tea flavored with lemon peelings. Soon enough, the boy finished a pitcher of tea and two small loaves of bread, and even gleaned the crumbs from his shirt for a finger snack. When Monique asked a question in Old French, Sawyer said he was full, whatever she was offering.

Then Sawyer looked over the hamlet.

The aunt's cottage wasn't the worst kept. One elderly woman lived in an unpainted shanty (its windows broken and front door covered only with thatched grass) with smoke rising from a crumbling stone chimney and an endless procession of cats moving through a hole in the grass door, some coming and others going. The cottage's only inhabitant stared with a doleful look at the newly arrived boy for several minutes before disappearing into the company of her animals. An adjacent cottage was little more than crumbling walls and appeared altogether abandoned since not even cats came from it. It sat forty meters from the trail and what once had been its front yard now was overgrown with grass and brush. Additional houses stood on either side, though Sawyer was unable to determine whether or not they remained inhabited. Twenty meters from the trail was a dilapidated log cabin (made from palm trees) with smoke wafting from its open windows. Sawyer could see no other cottages.

As Sawyer looked around, Monique moved close. Grasping his chin, she turned the boy's head to examine his eyes, cheeks, nose, and mouth. Only then did she pronounce judgment.

"Oui," Monique said with a quiet voice.

"Vous ressemblez à mon frère."

"I don't know what you are saying," Sawyer said. "I don't speak Old French."

"Vous ressemblez," Monique said, each word deliberately ennunciated, "à mon frère. Sur la photo."

"The photo?"

"J'adorais mon frère. Avant la guerre."

Monique looked at Sawyer. When the boy broke eye contact, she still stared, and when he dropped his eyes to the ground, she didn't. After a few minutes, she pointed to a vase with one hand and to Sawyer's throat with the other, evidently asking whether he was thirsty.

Sawyer nodded and watched the woman walk to her cottage. As Monique returned, the boy saw that though her forehead was furrowed from years of scratching a living in the soil, she appeared kind.

Monique offered the boy a drink from a ceramic vase and cups. "J'ai du thé," she said.

"You remind me of my mother," Sawyer said. "Only nicer."

"Je ne vous comprends pas."

Sawyer slowed his words and used gestures to make himself understood. "You look like Mother. I mean, you resemble her my mother in the Confederation."

"Je ressemble à votre mère?"

"Mare?"

"Non, non, mè-re. Le mot pour maman."

"Mama? Is mother mère?"

"Oui."

Sawyer took a drink of the tea and the woman did too. After they quenched their thirst, Sawyer again spoke.

"You remind me of my mother," the boy said, "except your face is more wrinkled and your shoulders sag. But your face is like hers and your skin's like mine."

Monique didn't reply. She didn't seem to understand. Rather, she motioned for Sawyer to follow and he did so. After collecting firewood and taking it into the cottage, he sat on the floor as Monique kindled a fire in a small fireplace. Only after it was burning did Monique speak, her voice cracking and hands trembling.

"Je suis une mère," Monique whispered, "et j'ai donné mon enfant à la Confédération Occidentale."

Sawyer shook his head to show he didn't understand.

Monique whispered as she tapped her breast. "Je suis," she said, "une mère."

"You have a mother?"

"Je suis ... suis une maman. Moi."

Monique pointed to herself and cradled an imaginary babe in her arms.

"You're a mother?"

"Je suis une mère, mais mon enfant est parti."

"Your infant parted? Where?"

Tears filled the woman's face. "Mon enfant," Monique continued as she pointed at Sawyer with a single trembling finger, "est un des enfants perdus, comme vous. Mon enfant est comme vous."

Sawyer said nothing.

"Mon enfant," the woman said as she burst into open tears, her face contorted and lip quivering, "a quatorze ans. On l'appelle Antoine."

As she spoke, Monique pointed at Sawyer and raised her hand at his head to show someone his height and age.

Sawyer's eyes welled with tears as he understood Monique's words and responded with a question. "Are you," he said with a whisper, "my mother?"

22

MOTHER AND CHILD REUNION

Monique looked at Sawyer's face until the boy repeated his question after several seconds. "Are you my mother?"

"Je ne sais pas."

"Your face," Sawyer observed, "is like hers and your skin. You're even the same size, except you're older."

Monique shrugged.

Now Sawyer spoke with quick words, his voice excited and trembling as he said he'd show what he meant and searched his duffle for his photographs. Tossing aside the picture of the Tahitian girl, he found the one of Mother holding him in front of the chapel in Old California and showed it to the woman.

"Here's my mother," Sawyer explained. "She looks like you a little, but she's just electronic."

"Eeehhh!"

Monique's scream startled Sawyer. "Wh-wh-what?" the boy said.

"C'est moi ... et mon enfant."

"Moi? I-it's you?"

"Moi et mon fils."

"Fees?"

Monique clasped her hands as if to cradle an imaginary infant.

"You and your baby?" Sawyer said. "Your son?"

"Bébé," Monique said, now speaking loud and fast as she pointed to the child in the photograph—at Sawyer himself. "Voilà mon enfant!"

Sawyer froze.

"Attendez un moment," Monique said before hurrying to her bedroom and quickly returning with a faded photograph that she placed beside Sawyer's image.

Now it was Sawyer's turn to be surprised. "Huhh?" he said. "It's the same picture."

"Oui. Les deux photos sont les mêmes. Exactement. C'est moi"—Monique said as she touched the woman standing before the chapel, then herself, and finally the picture of the baby—"C'est mon enfant. Mon bébé. Un fils."

Sawyer looked at Monique several seconds, his brow furrowed and eyes squinted as he pointed to the child. "That's me?" he said. That's Sawyer?"

The woman's lip quivered, her eyes filled with tears, and a pause followed as she struggled to understand thoughts beyond words.

Sawyer interrupted her quiet, his voice sounding increasingly confident in his conclusions. "Mother," the boy said, "never hugged me. She can't. But this mother held me. I thought it was a mirage. I never thought before. I don't understand. I don't ..."

Monique pulled Sawyer close and though he turned his face as she drew near, her arms wrapped behind his head so the boy couldn't wiggle free as she embraced him and wept loud and unembarrassed while Sawyer stood mute, his cheeks baptized by his mother's tears and his hair soon sticky from her sorrow and snot.

"Je suis désolée, mon fils," Monique sobbed. "Désolée. Désolée. Désolée."

"You're my stead-mother," Sawyer said. "My true mother."

Tears also streamed down the boy's face and both mother and son wept. At first they wept in an unmoving embrace, then dropped to the floor and cried until both were utterly wearied: sobbing and shaking until they had exhausted their grief. Sawyer hugged his mother so hard and so long that his arms ached and her back bruised. They sobbed and smiled as shadows lengthened and the day cooled, separating neither to eat nor drink nor anything else, but laying as close as modesty permitted while they held fast to each other.

At dusk, Monique lay quilts and pillows on the floor so that mother and son remained close enough to speak soft to each other. There, the two lay still for some time, occasionally laughing or speaking, but each one also withdrawing into unshared remembrances. As the night grew darker, Sawyer's eyes closed and he soon slept. When, however, Monique quietly slipped from his embrace to fetch water and bread, her son stirred and followed to watch as she filled a vase from the well. Monique then pointed to a woodpile: a gesture her son took as a command to fetch wood and Sawyer did as told. Soon a fire burned and the cottage warmed as Monique served water flavored with pineapple squeezings from coconut shells, along with bread and dried cheese. Mother and son broke bread while they ate a wordless dinner. When they were finished, they sat near the fire as Monique kissed her son profusely, allowing only a few centimeters of separation. For a long while, Sawyer fidgeted, tossed, and groaned until Monique swaddled him fast with a tucked blanket and kissed his forehead with the corner of her mouth. Thereafter, the boy grew drowsy as the fired burned down, the moon passed, and the forest awoke. Monique also slept quiet for a time, a smile on her face as fulfilled dreams comforted her and a new day approached. Morning found the mother singing soft lullabies to her son while he slumbered.

Boom! Boom! Boom!

Sawyer jumped to his feet and hurried to the front door, where he saw low-flying bombers streaking toward the main island: the blood red sun of the Heavenly Socialist Empire under each wing. The bombers shook the cottage like a tempest, knocking pictures from the wall and shaking dishes from shelves. A ceramic teapot fell and was smashed to bits. Indeed, the roar deafened Sawyer and Monique not only to each other, but to their own thoughts. Only after the planes passed could Sawyer speak.

"The Chinese are here," the boy said.

Monique pulled Sawyer inside and shut the front door.

"Il n'y a aucune raison de t'inquiéter," she said. "Ils ne peuvent pas nous faire mal."

When Sawyer didn't reply, Monique hugged him until his panic passed and they sat to the floor, now sitting side-by-side. Almost at that moment, a knock sounded and Madame Bonmaison stepped into the cottage, cutting off every attempt Monique made to speak and gesturing almost frantically to her sister-in-law. Indeed, Madame Bonmaison overrode every interruption with abrupt answers and only when she finished speaking to her sister-in-law did she interpret for Sawyer.

"I told her war will come soon," Madame Bonmaison told Sawyer, "and we must leave this night, before the armies come. It is said the Confederation is sending ships and planes. Maybe tonight or tomorrow."

Sawyer protested. "They wouldn't do—"

"My husband," Madame Bonmaison said in a tone that didn't allow discussion, "says they will invade our country, maybe this island."

"How would—"

"He knows such things. There is no time to argue. Last night he spoke of the attacks. You heard the aeroplanes?"

Now Monique directed Madame Bonmaison's attention to Sawyer with points and gestures and displayed the twin photographs as her sister-in-law stood in disbelief, almost unable to comprehend what she herself saw. It took Monique several minutes to convince Madame Bonmaison that it was true, and even then only after the latter studied Sawyer front and back. Only then did she cry out.

"Que Dieu soit loué. C'est vrai," Madame Bonmaison said. "We prayed many years for you and your mother mourned so often. She tells me she slept near you last night. I tell you the truth: this is the first time she slept a full night since she lost you. Monique reminds me to tell you she didn't sell you. She sent you because you were sick and she could not care for you. She was afraid that you would die. She is so sorry she let you go and asks you to forgive her sin. She says should have trusted God to save you."

"I," Sawyer said as he dropped his eyes. "I ... tell stead-mother that ..."

"Do you," Madame Bonmaison asked, "forgive her?"

Sawyer nodded as he leaned into Monique's arms and wept even as Madame Bonmaison watched in silence, until a distant explosion brought with it a return of her worries.

"I must go," Madame Bonmaison said. "You will return to our village by nightfall. We must leave soon to reach our destination. Bring with you what is necessary: tools, seed, clothes, and food. My husband says he must leave if you are late. Our boat will be packed. Jeannette and Nicole will help you carry your items to the dock. Do you understand?"

Sawyer nodded.

"Do you have questions?" Madame Bonmaison asked.

"Ask," Sawyer said, "my stead-mother what I should call her?"

"Stead-mother is not good," Madame Bonmaison answered. "Call her maman. It is our custom for a new son."

Sawyer said he would even as Monique said something the boy didn't understand.

"Your maman has a question," Madame Bonmaison said. "Did you have a mother in the Confederation?"

Sawyer looked into his mother's dark eyes and wrinkled face, studying her stooped shoulders, crooked teeth, and weathered skin even as he remembered the unblemished and brilliant beauty of his electronic mother.

"No," the boy said, "I was raised by the state."

"Ahhhh. An orphan?"

"Yes. I was alone."

Madame Bonmaison interpreted as she filled a burlap bag with kitchen utensils, vegetables, and grain seed from the pantry. Only when she was finished did she kiss Sawyer's cheek, which the boy accepted with a blush, and watch as Monique tended her child.

"Mon fils, tu es très timide," Monique said.

"Il a besoin d'un peu d'affection," Madame Bonmaison said. "Il deviendra plus affectueux avec une mère, avec de l'amour. Comme une plante qui a besoin du soleil"—she turned to Sawyer—"I told your mother love will do you much good. You are like a plant that needs sunshine. Soon you will hug me, then you will love a girl like my daughters."

Sawyer blushed.

"It is good," Madame Bonmaison said, "the men on this island marry young."

Madame Bonmaison now listened to her sister-in-law for several minutes before translating. "Your mother," she eventually explained, "speaks that you are shy, like her brother. She says your father was shy too."

The blood drained from Sawyer's flush face and he turned pale. He spoke in a hoarse whisper. "My trew-father?"

Madame Bonmaison laughed. "We do not make babies from ... how do you say ... oh, that is it: test tubes. We make them from"—the woman now blushed—"from men, I say, and love."

"Did," Sawyer asked, "the trew-father look like me too?"

"You resemble his size, " Madame Bonmaison said, "but le visage ... the face resembles your uncle. When he was young."

"Do you have a picture?"

"You are the only photo of your papa. He was from our village and I can remember him when he was a boy. He married your mother when he was grown, He disappeared in the fishing boat."

Madame Bonmaison asked a question of her sister-in-law, who answered without much deliberation. "He disappeared," she then interpreted for Sawyer, "in the fishing boat two months after he married your mother. Some say the boat was sunk by the Chinese; others say a sea storm or pirates. Your mother could not care for you when war came after you were born, for she had no money or house. And her famille—I mean to say, family—had no money.

Also, you must learn that your mother and father were cousins."

"Cousins?"

"Like you and Jeannette."

"Cousins married?"

"Oui," the woman said, "it is not ... forbade. I mean, it is not against les Eçritures. Against the writing, the Bible."

"I really had a trew-father," Sawyer said, his voice almost cracking.

"I do not know this word. I mean, trew-father," Madame Bonmaison said. "You have a father. He was nice boy. Timide. Like you. I think you say the word shy."

Monique spoke several sentences in her own tongue.

"Your mother wants to say," Madame Bonmaison interpreted, "she wanted to keep you, but she had no food. There were days she did not eat. The war was close and you needed le ... the medicine. Your mother could not let you die, so she sent you to the West. Your mother says she could not let you die. Her milk was dried."

"Her milk?"

"From the breast," Madame Bonmaison said. "Do they tell you about the babies in the Confederation?"

"I s-su ... suckled from her?"

"It is the way of babies."

Sawyer stood wide-eyed.

"Aussi ... also," Madame Bonmaison continued, "she must tell your name."

"It's Sawyer."

"No," Madame Bonmaison said. "The name your father gave you."

Monique held Sawyer's hand as she leaned forward and spoke words he'd never heard. Her voice was soft and her breath. "Ton nom est Antoine. Antoine Louis Manaakitia."

"Your name is Antoine Louis Manaakitia," Madame Bonmaison said a little louder.

"My true name?"

"Yes, your birth name."

Sawyer bowed a little. "It's good."

Monique's eyes filled with tears and she said something to her sister-in-law.

"Your maman," Madame Bonmaison said, "wants to know if you understood what she did."

Sawyer's eyes teared. "Tell her I understand. Tell my mother that—"

"No," Madame Bonmaison interrupted. "I will tell her that you understand, but we must finish la conversation later. You must prepare departure. I mean, to depart."

Sawyer fell silent as his aunt provided final instructions.

"As I said already," the woman said, "you must be at the boat by dark. Mon mari ... my husband says it will take all night to go to the other place and it is too much dangerous to travel by the day."

"What," Sawyer said, "of the photo? Why did she have the same photo as me?"

Madame Bonmaison turned to Monique and asked a long question. After receiving an even longer answer, the former looked at Sawyer and spoke.

"When the agent came to get," Madame Bonmaison said, "I mean, to take you, they made the photograph. He said it was necessary to have the photos of Monique. He gave one photo to your maman as a remembrance."

Madame Bonmaison embraced her nephew with a parting kiss before hurrying away. Sawyer threw himself into the breast of his mother who held her tight, again weeping for everything once lost and now found. He felt the stroke of a mother's finger across his wet cheek drying his sadness with her touch, and the soft of her breast cradle his bony shoulders. He knew the embrace of her arms and the warm press of her kiss to his cheek. He fell silent and still as his mother spoke words whose meaning he knew even without translation.

"Mon fils, je t'aime."

"I love you, my mother," Sawyer replied. "I love you too."

Monique's eyes shut and her lips pursed as she suppressed her sobs. It took her several minutes to regain her composure, but as soon as she did so, calm came on mother and son alike and both fell silent and still.

War interrupted their peace as a series of explosions, maybe a dozen, sounded from the skies. As Sawyer watched, a dozen missiles streaked from the horizon toward a flight of bombers. Several aircraft plummeted to earth, their final descents marked by smoky spirals.

Monique clutched her son's hand and pointed toward the village where her brother and his family lived, saying something the boy understood only by her anxiousness and tone.

"Yes," Sawyer said. "It's time to find our new home."

23

KISS AND KIN

It was past noon when Monique and Sawyer reached the Bonmaison cottage. Most of the hamlet's homes were abandoned, their doors boarded and windows shuttered. Sawyer's cousins sat in tall grass where Marie braided Nichole's hair into French twists while Jeannette watched cross-legged from afar. Upon seeing Monique and Sawyer, Jeannette hurried to greet her aunt with a kiss.

"Tante Monique," the girl cried as she hugged her aunt, " je suis si heureuse de vous voir. J'avais peur que vous n'arriviez pas à temps. Ma mère a dit que vous seriez ici, mais j'avais toujours peur."

Nicole and Marie also greeted Monique with kisses to the cheek and the older woman returned the courtesy. When Sawyer nodded his greetings, Marie and Nicole each wished him well as Jeannette dropped her eyes and blushed. All three girls then led the new arrivals to the beach while explaining the situation to the best of their ability. Sawyer, though, said nothing and it was clear that whatever the girls had intended to share hadn't been understood.

At the beach, Madame Bonmaison roasted fowl over hot coals as her husband cleaned his boat with a brine solution and a palm-leaf broom. The family's most valuable possessions were stacked on the pier: household utensils and garden tools, piles of clothing, rolls of twine, bags of seed, crates of food, boxes of books, and personal effects like combs and soap. After scouring the worst grime, Monsieur Bonmaison repacked storage holds and rinsed himself in seawater before taking lunch—during which he ate double portions of fowl and breadfruit, then left what remained for the four children. When grace was recited, Sawyer looked confused, so his mother gently pushed the boy's head forward and shut his eyes with her fingers.

Following lunch, Madame Bonmaison told Sawyer and the girls to fetch a cask of water from the house. It took the four of them nearly thirty minutes to complete the task and they were soaked from sweat when they finally arrived at the pier. Following his discovery of a leak along the rim of the cask, Monsieur Bonmaison sent the teenagers back to the well with empty buckets, which they filled and returned to top off the barrel. After the barrel was sealed shut and lashed down, Monsieur Bonmaison declared the boat ready to depart, except for collection a few final household goods.

Now there was little to do but wait, so the three adults returned home, followed by Marie and Nicole. This left Sawyer and Jeannette alone at the beach—where Jeannette pulled her skirt to her knees and waded into the water as Sawyer fed table scraps to gulls. Once his breadfruit scraps were gone, the boy sat down along the pier as his cousin splashed close by. It wasn't long before Jeannette worked her way to the pier, cloaking her movement with stops and starts as she approached Sawyer.

"Je peux m'asseoir ici?" the girl asked.

Sawyer didn't understand her words, but he knew their intent and nodded as Jeannette sat beside him, a meter away with her hands folded in her lap and eyes seaward. Jeannette's dark hair was tied in a long ponytail with a strip of white linen that matched her blouse and her eyes showed the gentle sweep of a Korean. Her skin was the cocoa shade of a Polynesian and her teeth straight. Her back was unbent and her shoulders square. Whenever she looked at Sawyer, she blushed. When she tried to talk, Sawyer didn't understand and conversation didn't ensue.

After several minutes, Jeannette walked to her father's boat and fetched a jug of water and a sheet of flat bread which she shared with Sawyer, except bits and crumbs tossed to the gulls now flocking from every direction. Sawyer tore his portion into beak-sized morsels for the gulls —who greedily ate before squawking for more. Even after the bread was gone, the birds continued their disturbance, so Jeannette started for home and Sawyer walked at her side.

With every step, Sawyer grew less concerned to keep his distance. Twice, he brushed Jeannette's hand with his own and both times Jeannette excused herself in Old French. When they reached the village, Jeannette took Sawyer into the whitewashed chapel through an unlocked door. Rows of worn wooden pews were lined before pulpit and choir, with enough floor space to seat perhaps twenty children in the front. Afternoon light streamed into the interior and an oversized book with two pieces of crossed wood glued to its cracked leather cover was chained to the lectern upon which it was set. Sawyer looked at one of its first pages.

Et l'homme dit:
Voici cette fois celle qui est
os de mes os et chair de ma chair!

on l'appellera femme,
parce qu'elle a été prise de l` homme.
C'est pourquoi l'homme quittera
son père et sa mère,
et s'attachera à sa femme,
et ils deviendront une seule chair.

"I don't understand," Sawyer said as he sat beside Jeannette in a faded pew, "what this book is for."

Jeannette said nothing and Sawyer fell silent as light warmed the couple's cheeks. As solitude stirred their souls, the girl clasped her hands and bowed her head.

When Sawyer asked what Jeannette was doing, the girl put a finger to her lips and closed her eyes so that Sawyer realized she was praying and waited until the girl finished before speaking.

"Why did you pray?" Sawyer said.

"J'ai prié," Jeannette said, "pour vous, Sawyer, que vous connaîtrez Dieu et la bonne vie."

"I don't know," Sawyer said, "what you prayed for and I don't even know how your prayers work, but I hope you get it. This is a nice place and I think it's good here."

Now Sawyer walked to a window and Jeannette followed. They looked outside and watched Nicole walk home from across the street—where two neighboring families had gathered, along with their household possessions.

"Your sisters and mother are outside," Sawyer said. "We should go."

"Nous devrions nous en aller," Jeannette said, "puisque ma mère et mes soeurs me cherchent sans doute."

The cousins left the chapel and hurried to a house near Jeannette's own home where three households of neighbors now had assembled: five parents and eight children who dragged burlap bags and backpacks. The families loitered at the Bonmaison cottage as adieux were said and a pair of boys (maybe in their twenties) embraced Jeannette's sisters. The men of the families were loud, their voices bombastic and bitter as they lamented exile from homes they had built with their own hands. Since their anger couldn't strike bombers and missiles high above, it fell on their families: a wife who talked too much or a child who dawdled.

Soon enough, the gathering refugees harnessed burlap backpacks to their shoulders and tugged at leashes tied to goats and hogs. They even brought chickens with legs lashed together and beaks taped shut. At the last minute, the oldest man among them went into the chapel and returned with the book Jeannette had revealed to Sawyer, much to everyone's delight. Then the two families departed —the village now utterly deserted except for the Bonmaison family.

Nicole and Marie sobbed long after the neighbors left and Sawyer understood that they wept for the young men. He was saddened for the sorrow of his cousins and wondered whether couplings were desired. He also wondered what it'd be like to make a traditional marriage and glanced at Jeannette. A little while later, Sawyer found an unoccupied chair on the front porch and sat down, now staring at the house the boys had left: its windows boarded and door closed. The home was dead now, no matter what resurrection a new season might bring. The seeds of life were scattered to the winds and the house was secured for an unknown family.

Boom! Boom! Boom!

Explosions sounded above the island. Sawyer jumped to his feet and Jeannette hurried to him. Another dozen explosions thundered as a flight of three bombers streaked across the stratosphere. Thin contrails followed the aircraft and a moment later the rumble of rockets sounded from afar as corkscrew trails of smoke and vapor rose from the seas west of Tahiti and arched heavenward toward the intruders. Two bursts flashed and thunder rumbled after a delay of several seconds as one distant aircraft blew up and a second spiraled to earth in flames. As a single parachute opened, the third bomber continued its course.

Sawyer and Jeannette watched the ethereal contrail of combat until their mothers ran from the cottage and chided the children (in a mix of Anglo-European and Old French) for lack of focus, telling them to return to their chores. A few minutes later, Sawyer slung a bag of rice seed over his shoulder and marched toward the pier while Jeannette followed with a roll of calico fabric held against her chest. Sawyer slowed until the girl walked beside him, his maneuver not nearly as coy as he supposed. Both mothers followed with bags of prepared food, as well as nods and whispers. Even war couldn't suppress their amusement.

Thirty minutes later, the Bonmaison family returned home and waited for night to come—sitting near a collection of pots and pans, burlap bags filled with food, and a frayed wicker chair. Monsieur Bonmaison worked on the front window, which he pried loose (glass and frame alike) before muttering a few words to his wife, who explained to Sawyer that her husband needed the boy to hold glass in place while he forced open the trim. Sawyer did as told and an hour later the two successfully had secured four windowpanes in padded crates and were drinking water from carved cups as Sawyer's aunt explained to Sawyer that glass was one of the island's more valuable resources. It was used not only for windows and housing, but also for cutting cloth and starting fires, with even broken glass considered a marketable commodity. The family carried the crates to the boat and secured them to cabin mattresses before returning home to eat broiled breadfruit and banana pudding. Afterward, Monique tidied dishes, including those to be left behind, while Madame Bonmaison swept floors.

Monsieur Bonmaison let the women work a few minutes longer before muttering several words that evoked no response. A moment later, he complained about something, though neither woman gave any indication that she was completing her efforts. Only when the man growled out sharp commands to his daughters did his wife put her makeshift broom into a corner and Monique drape her wet towel over an old chair.

"Mon mari," Madame Bonmaison told Sawyer, "I mean to say, my husband says it is time to depart. We will leave one hour after the sun is settled"—she took a breath and opened her eyes wide to stem the tears—"I am so sorry. This is our house. And we must go. My husband says it is fine. We will go to a place far from the war, where there are many of our people. There is land to farm, sea to fish, and God's faith too."

The family walked to the pier and then to the sole boat, *Le Contentement*, still lashed to it. The Bonmaison's fishing boat was equipped with a small cabin, tight sleeping quarters, several equipment bins, and even fish holds. Pikes, nets, and bait buckets were roped to the deck, along with homespun life preservers and a bloodstained cleaning table that stunk despite having been washed down. When Sawyer and the girls stepped aboard, the craft already sat low in the water as it bobbed in its moorings, each of its holds filled with the stocks of life: food, seed, tools, clothing, blankets, and dishes, along with salted fish and dried vegetables. Barrels of water were lashed to the mainmast and drums of diesel fuel were bound to the deck—the fuel's fumes nearly as pungent as the dead fish.

As her sisters hurried from the open deck into the cabin, Jeannette nodded toward the bloodstained cleaning table and crinkled her nose. "Ça pue," she said.

"Yea," Sawyer said, "it's pretty disgusting."

Jeannette walked to the stern and looked seaward. Sawyer followed her with his eyes, but not his feet. When the girl turned back, Sawyer blushed.

"Venez ici," Jeannette said with a wave of her fingers.

Now Sawyer inched toward Jeannette, looking seaward with his hands in pocket, though he stopped at arm's reach. "It's dark out there," he said. "I can't see anything at all."

Jeannette didn't reply with words, but extended her hand and slid toward the boy. Sawyer hesitated before opening his fingers, so Jeannette pried them open with a gentle tug and took the boy's hand. When Sawyer squeezed her fingers, Jeannette kissed his cheek. Both blushed, then looked seaward until they heard footsteps that caused Sawyer to pull his hand away and looked to where his mother and aunt now stood.

Monique looked on her son and niece with a smile. "C'est bon," she said. "Mon fils, il est nécessaire de finir une dernière tâche avant de partir."

"Your mother," Madame Bonmaison interpreted, "wishes to show you a memorial before we leave. We will not return to this island."

Monique talked several minutes with her brother and his wife as Sawyer waited for clarification.

"Mon frère," Monique soon said, "dit que nous partirons à 22h. Il fera complètement nuit et nous aurons beaucoup de temps en pleine mer. Nous arriverons à notre nouvelle maison demain, à midi. Nous aurons assez de gazole pour le voyage et même pour faire de la pêche et puis on fera le plein après être arrivés. Tout le monde doit rester ensemble jusqu'à notre départ."

"The war," Madame Bonmaison interpreted, "will be here tomorrow. We must leave tonight since it will be safer in the dark. We will arrive at our new home tomorrow. We must stay close until we go."

Monique took Sawyer's hand and pointed to the darkened beach. "Nous," she said, "devons le visiter."

Sawyer didn't reply.

"Nous," Madame Bonmaison repeated, "devons visiter le mémorial à ton père."

Sawyer raised his eyebrows to show he didn't understand.

"Ton père," Monique said a little louder.

Yet a third time the boy lifted his eyes. This time, he openly declared that he didn't understand what was being said.

"She wishes," Madame Bonmaison explained, "to show you the stone wall of your father."

"The stone wall?"

"A memorial."

"A grave?" Sawyer said. "You said he disappeared."

"Not the grave," Madame Bonmaison explained, "but the memorial. There is memorial for men lost at sea. The name of your father is written there."

A flight of bombers roared directly overhead, near enough that Sawyer now yelled to be heard. "Is it close?"

Madame Bonmaison waited for the noise to subside before she explained that it was half a kilometer to the site.

When Sawyer pointed to the bombers overhead and asked if there was enough time, the woman spoke with her husband.

"You have a few hours," Madame Bonmaison soon explained. "Hurry down the beach and see the memorial before we leave. There will not be another chance."

Sawyer looked to his aunt for a moment, then started toward his mother as she hurried down the pier toward trail. After a moment, he heard Jeannette call from behind.

"A Dieu," the young girl said, her farewell more a blessing than a sloughed formality.

When Sawyer and Jeannette exchanged glances, Madame Bonmaison nudged her husband while Nicole threw mock kisses as Jeannette blushed and Sawyer hurried to catch his mother.

24

A TRUE FATHER, HERE AND GONE

A new moon left the beach a dark place, so Sawyer walked closer to Monique. Following a series of distant explosions and several minutes of trudging in sand, Monique removed her shoes and slung them over her shoulder. Sawyer did the same and the pair soon hurried through the sand until they reached a sharp turn, then a trail leading inland. Their eyes adjusted to the dark as they cut between palm trees to a memorial which resembled the remembrance for lost children (though much smaller). Monique walked to a small stone that jutted out and touched the chiseled letters that memorialized her deceased husband.

"Ton père," Monique said, "était un très bon homme. C'est pourquoi je t'ai appelé Antoine."

Sawyer didn't speak.

"Il a été perdu," Monique said with a sob as she looked at her son. "Lorsque tu étais bébé. Je regrette que tu ne l'aies jamais connu, mais nous serons ensemble dans le ciel de Dieu."

Monique kissed the stone, then spoke to it, "Tu me manqueras, mon mari gentil."

Sawyer remained silent.

"Antoine," Monique said as she straightened up and addressed the stone wall, "voilà ton fils. Il s'appelle Sawyer."

"Dis adieu à ton père," Monique said as she turned to Sawyer. "Nous devons partir."

Sawyer still said nothing, so his mother stretched her son's hand to touch the inscribed stone before she herself stepped away from the wall to indicate that it was time to depart.

"Goodbye my," Sawyer said as he began to weep a little, "goodbye my trew-father. I miss you. I know now I miss you too."

Monique wiped tears from her eyes and turned toward the trail. In a few moments, both mother and son reached palm trees near the shore and were about to step from the shadows on to open beach when Sawyer cupped a hand over his mother's mouth and pulled her to the ground, now pointing seaward and whispering with a choked voice.

"Soldiers."

Monique didn't need to be told what she too had seen: several dark figures rising from the waves who now waded through shoulder-deep water with rifles held high. Each step brought the invaders closer to the beach and their mission.

Sawyer pointed toward the forest. "We can't," he whispered, "cross the beach."

Monique tugged hard at Sawyer's hand, then crawled back toward the memorial as fast as she could. Sawyer followed through the dark, both mother and child careful to keep their heads low and movement quiet. When they reached a bend in the trail behind tall brush, Sawyer raised his head for a quick look and spied dozens of soldiers now removing wetsuits and opening equipment bags. Keeping low, the boy moved away and told his mother to follow.

Crawling put distance from the soldiers as Sawyer and Monique moved slow and kept low, using brush and tree to conceal their movement. Only after the refugees had passed numerous trees did Sawyer stand to a low crouch and motion for his mother to hurry. Now, the pair moved noticeably faster and soon came to a hamlet of six cottages where they knocked at doors to no avail. Lights were out and fires unlit in what appeared to be a deserted village, so they followed the trail further west—moving fast to make up lost time. Neither mother nor son talked and even their breathing was so constrained as to be almost silent. Eventually, the path turned north, cutting across the lower slopes of the volcanic mountain and bringing them full circle to the Bonmaison's own village. There, they paused for several minutes to listen for trackers and watch for signs of invaders. Because the trail to the beach was partially exposed, the refugees crouched and crawled as they again moved toward the sea: small stones and shards of pumice occasionally cutting into flesh until their knees were torn raw and cheeks tear-soaked. Despite the pain, neither one slowed their pace.

As they neared the beach, Sawyer stuck his head from behind a cluster of mango trees and whispered to his mother. "It looks clear," the boy said.

Monique looked around. "Il n'y a personne?" she said with a whisper. "Tu es sûr?"

Both looked for movement, then Monique pointed toward the pier where her brother's boat was moored. It was dark and they couldn't see whether the boat remained docked.

"Au bateau," Monique whispered.

"We're really late," Sawyer responded.

Monique and Sawyer now hurried toward the landing, stopping only when they approached the pier—where Monique gasped and Sawyer nearly collapsed, staggering before securing his balance and turning to his mother. Neither loved one nor boat could be seen.

"It's gone," Sawyer said. "They're gone."

"Ils s'en sont allés," Monique said. "Ils sont en mer."

"They didn't," Sawyer said as his pitch rose and voice sharpened, "wait for us."

Monique took her son's hand to comfort him. "C'est bon," she said. "C'est bon."

"They left," Sawyer said. "They left. Why'd they leave?"

"Nous," Monique said as she pulled Sawyer's arm, "devons partir."

The boy didn't budge.

"Mon fils," Monique said as she turned her son's face toward her own, "c'est dangereux ici. Il faut sortir d'ici."

"Maybe," Sawyer said as he squinted and pointed into the dark, "they're coming back."

"Non," Monique answered with a firm tone. "Ils ne reviennent pas. Nous devons nous en aller."

"They'll come back," Sawyer said as he crossed his arms. "We just have to wait."

"Saw-yer," Monique replied with a sharp tone, struggling to keep her voice low, "nous devons partir. Ils s'en sont allés et c'est très dangereux ici. Nous devons aller à l'intérieur."

When Sawyer still wouldn't budge, his mother grabbed his hand, both mother and child wincing as torn flesh mingled with shredded skin. Monique then half-dragged her son to the forest where they could move more discreetly through dark and danger. Once again, the pair tried to keep noise down as they pushed through brush and bumped into trees, sometimes listening for pursuers after stepping on sticks or splashing puddles. Sawyer twice whispered that he heard shouting and the pair once backtracked after hearing unknown persons ahead of them. They moved so slow and deliberate that they didn't reach Monique's cottage for hours and when they finally arrived every nearby house had been abandoned: doors left open and chimneys smokeless. Even the cats were gone. Monique and Sawyer stumbled into their house and fell to the floor exhausted.

It wasn't long before they slept.

MOTHER AND SON awoke at dawn to the loud crying of an unhappy baby and rose to watch a young Polynesian and his pregnant wife lead three children uphill, the hard-pressed parents using leather leashes to move a bleating goat and two reticent ewes and firm swats to motivate their fussing children. The couple's baby cried from hunger or filth (Sawyer wasn't sure which) while two older boys whined, complained, and dug their heels. Step by step, the parents fought their way uphill. Soon, they were gone and quiet returned. Monique and Sawyer rested several hours more, until hunger stirred them from their slumber.

Lunch consisted of dried fish and shriveled fruit. When Monique struck a match to cook some eggs, Sawyer blew it out and explained smoke would draw attention. Monique misunderstood his point and restacked kindling until her son pushed it away and pointed to the sky as he sounded an explosion. Now Monique gave up the idea of cooking and instead prepared a cold lunch before retrieving a small book from her bag to read passages from it. Already Sawyer knew to close his eyes when the blessing was prayed and his mother showed her pleasure with a kiss to her son's cheek.

After eating, mother and son took another long rest and it was midafternoon when Sawyer opened his eyes. Monique had piled all remaining tools, seeds, blankets, and cooking pans on the kitchen table—along with her prayer book, two flasks of water, dried fruits and vegetables, and strips of salted hog stacked beside the blankets. Now she sewed squares of canvas into crude rucksacks with shoulder straps and bamboo framing. Sawyer was content to watch her work through the afternoon since there was nothing else to do.

A hard rain fell at dusk and chilled the air. Despite wrapping himself in wool blankets, Sawyer still shivered and it wasn't long before Monique lit a fire over the boy's objections—though only after draping a curtain over the cottage's sole window. This time the boy didn't protest, not only because he was cold, but also because the dark of night obscured any chimney smoke. Monique kept the fire small, using twigs to ignite dried palm branches, and the flames burned only a few centimeters high. Even small, the fire took the worst chill from the night air as mother and son huddled near flickering flames which cast shadows against the walls in ever-shifting shades and shapes. But the formless shadows were mere diversions and Sawyer looked to the real presence of his mother for comfort even as the fire burned down, reclining on her shoulder as she hugged him in turn. After a time, the boy poked the fire with a stick and lay down to sleep after pulling a single blanket to his shoulders.

Monique fluffed a feather pillow for her son, then lay on the floor and watched him by the dim light of glowing coals. When the room chilled, she blew into the fire with her own breath and threw small sticks on it. As the flames burned a little higher and hotter, Monique pushed a damp log near the flames, which steamed much and burned slow. Then she lay to the floor and watched her son sleep until her own eyes grew heavy. Though its flames never rose more than a few centimeters, the log burned to ash before morning.

Mother and son slept late. Even the distant din of war didn't disturb their rest.

25

PARADISE LOST

Monique woke late in the morning and soft-stepped outside to draw water before scavenging the pantry for breakfast, finding several fruit preserves and a stale loaf of bread. When she called to Sawyer, the boy remained groggy, so she pointed him back to the grass-filled mattress, where he closed his eyes not long after his mother covered him with a quilt. After a time, Monique took a place on the floor beside her child and both soon slept.

It was late afternoon when afterburners rattled the cottage and Monique jumped to her feet and ran to the window. Though the jet already was a distant roar by the time the woman saw it, she remained outside to search the skies for threats. Sawyer joined her right away.

"I liked Jeannette," the boy said after a few minutes. "She was nice."

"Ahhh," Monique said, "la petite Jeannette. Elle est très belle et tu l'adores, je crois."

"I could live my life," Sawyer said, "with this family ... with our family. My whole life."

"Cette petite Jeannette," Monique said, "est très adorable."

Another flight of bombers roared overhead. This time the walls shook so hard that a braided wreath of dried flowers fell to the floor and water sloshed from the top of a wood-carved pitcher.

"They're close," the boy said as he nestled against his mother.

Monique hugged her son so hard he almost struggled to breathe. When yet another bomber streaked overhead and emitted a roar like a mechanical belch, Sawyer turned pale, shouting that the planes were firing cannon as Monique shook her head to show she didn't understand.

"Je ne comprends pas," Monique whispered.

The mechanical belch sounded again as the aircraft circled directly overhead, its roar sounding so loud that a window shattered and plaster cracked. Explosions echoed downhill and Sawyer peeked out the front door toward oily smoke rising above the tree line. Something had blown up. The boy turned back to the cottage, but had taken only a few steps before the loud belch sounded a third time. Now, the canon was so close its blasts deafened Sawyer to his own thoughts as he saw a two-seated bomber bank to its left and disappear behind a screen of treetops, its engines screaming as it hunted prey.

"We have to leave," Sawyer said.

"Il faut sortir d'ici. La guerre s'approche," Monique said as she waved for Sawyer to come inside. There, they hurried to pack blankets, food, and tools into makeshift rucksacks. A few minutes later, they began the uphill trek. Because their arms were full and loads heavy, the pair moved slow and often stopped to rest even as explosions grew closer, jets roared over treetops, and sharp bursts of rifle fire crackled behind them. As they moved to high ground, both mother and son remained careful to keep beneath the cover of the forest canopy.

It was noon when the Monique and Sawyer trudged into a mango grove near the summit. Well-hidden, they surveyed the island, seeing around them a panoply of destruction. To the north was the beach from which *Le Contentement* departed and where the small village where the Bonmaison family had lived now burned. To the distant east were columns of black smoke spiraling toward the heavens. Across the waters, the indistinct shadow that was Tahiti was obscured by a haze of smoke that hung like a storm cloud. Only Moorea's interior highlands seem unaffected by war and it was to these that mother and son looked as they took a quick meal of dry bread and water. After eating, Sawyer touched his mother's wrist and pointed inland toward the forest and hills beyond the south slope on which they stood.

"We need to leave," Sawyer said as he stood. "They'll find us here."

Monique nodded and soon the pair collected their belongings and moved down a path where trees were sparser and houses closer. They threaded through brush so that they measured movement in meters rather than kilometers and further slowed their pace by hiding beneath trees whenever they heard aircraft approach. Indeed, the two refugees moved so cautiously that afternoon was nearly spent when they reached a tiny village of two dozen thatched huts. As they approached the village, a reeking stench first turned Monique's nose, and then Sawyer's.

There was no pattern to the massacre: three children lay in a heap, their heads broken and bloodied. A man and woman lay arm in arm a few meters away, with an unmoving baby cradled between them. A dead goat lay beside the shattered bodies of three children and a pair of sheep grazed on blood-soaked grass a few meters away. Not far away, an elderly couple lay an arm's length apart: the man's chest torn open and the woman's back blackened by coagulated blood. Everyone else lay alone, some close to the village and others nearer the forest.

Sawyer's knees buckled and Monique grabbed her son's shoulder to provide support.

"Why?" the boy asked.

Monique said nothing as tears ran down her cheek.

"These aren't soldiers," Sawyer said.

Monique dropped her eyes.

Sawyer cried out a second time. "Why?" he said. "These aren't soldiers."

Monique fell to her knees and clasped her hands in prayer. "Ah, Dieu," she called out to the heavens, "protège-moi et mon fils de cette atrocité. Permets-moi de vivre avec mon fils, que tu m'as rendu, ou laisse-moi mourir avec lui."

A bomber flew above the ocean, the shrill whine of its engines drawing their attention.

"They're coming," Sawyer cried out.

Monique prayed more fervently.

"Don't you understand?" Sawyer said in a voice equally loud and panicked. "We have to leave."

Now Mother stopped praying and looked in terror toward the heavens. "L'avion?"

"The aircraft will see us. We must go."

Sawyer and Monique watched the skies as they hurried around the corpses, moving fast until the village houses, the corpses, and the stench were left far behind. They worked through the brush more slowly and even when the sun stretched their shadows, they remained well uphill. When Monique sat on a fallen tree to rest, Sawyer shimmied up a palm tree to look south into the hills and forests of the interior, but saw nothing of note. As the boy climbed down the tree, Monique divided fruit and cheese from a burlap bag into unequal portions and gave the larger share to Sawyer—who offered to return a bit of cheese until his mother scolded him with a cross word.

"Mange!" Monique commanded.

"Thanks," Sawyer said as he pulled back his hand. "I mean, merci."

"Très bien," Monique said. "Tu seres celui qui peut m'enseigner à parler."

Sawyer said nothing.

"Au moins dans ta langue."

As mother and son ate, explosions sounded atop the hill, not far from the place where they had stood at noon, soon followed by a long burst of automatic weapons fire, then another. A moment later, pistol shots sounded.

Sawyer jumped to his feet. "That's c-closer."

"Nous devons nous cacher."

Monique stuffed food and blankets into her knapsack and moved downhill into the undergrowth where the brush remained dense. On several occasions, Sawyer let out a yelp and once Monique groaned when a thorn lodged in her breast. Both stumbled and sweated until they reached the valley, and with it a stream that brought water from the interior hills. It was nearly dark as the pair searched for a hiding place and Monique found a patch of dry ground beneath a clutch of breadfruit trees. There, the woman pulled a burlap cloth from her knapsack and Sawyer did the same (though his own blanket was wool) as they prepared to make camp.

After matting down a patch of grass, Monique spread her canvas across the grass and draped Sawyer's cotton blanket atop the canvas: with grass piled to the sides like a nest. Monique then lay on her side, face toward the brush, while Sawyer slept on his back. A nearby bird's cry sounded from the forest and distant explosions punctured the night. Clouds obscured the moon and a breeze stirred the treetops. Sawyer got goose pimples.

"As-tu froid?" Monique rubbed Sawyer's s arm, patting goose pimples on his arms. "Tu as froid."

Sawyer shivered. "It's cold."

Monique doubled the blanket over Sawyer, careful to tuck the sides to prevent escape of warmth. "Je n'ai pas froid," she said. "Il fait très chaud."

Sawyer pulled his mother's forehead close to his face and kissed her cheek. "It's like I've been born again," he said. "Born into a new life. A real one."

Tears filled Monique's eyes and her chin quivered as she stroked Sawyer's cheeks and prayed a blessing. Covered with warmth and guarded by care, Sawyer slept without stirring despite the hard of the ground and nearby rumble of war. Monique also slept well, being more than content to be near her son despite having no blanket to warm her in the chill of night. Even dew didn't disturb their slumber.

26

THE COMING OF GUARDIANS

Gunfire heralded morning. First light brought renewed fighting as aerial gunships swept the forest with cannon. Startled by the shooting, Sawyer sprang to his feet and said they needed to leave even as rifle fire, a quick successions of single shots rather than an indiscriminate spray of automatic weapons, sounded uphill. Three pistol shots rang out, then silence. The gunfire was loud and the distance short.

"We have to go now," Sawyer said as his forehead sweated. "They're close."

Monique didn't move. Her face was pale and her lips quivered as she looked toward the sound of fighting.

"We have to go," Sawyer repeated himself. "Quick. Now."

"Ils sont très près," Monique said as she shook her head, "mon fils. Pourquoi les hommes nous ont renoncés?"

Sawyer grabbed his mother by the hand and told her to move. Monique eventually heeded his pleas and the pair grabbed a few of their remaining possessions as they moved deeper into the forest, keeping far from established trails and well beneath cover of treetops. Sawyer stopped every few minutes to catch breath while his mother moved without break since she was long accustomed to climbing the mountain (though even she sometimes slowed to take her son's hand or kiss his cheeks). Despite the fact that Sawyer worked hard to push through the brush, it wasn't long before his arms ached and legs wobbled and eventually Monique herself showed strain with an occasional slip or stumble. They pressed forward an hour before they came to a shallow pool filled with water seeping from cracks through a granite outcropping. There, mother and son alike satisfied their thirst and filled their bottles. When Monique soon motioned to leave, Sawyer balked.

"I need to rest," the boy said.

"Il faut partir."

Sawyer removed his shoes and socks, then splashed his feet. "We've no place to go," he said. "One place is as bad as another."

Mother sat down. She too removed her shoes and slipped her feet into the water. "C'est bon."

"It feels good."

Sawyer leaned back until his head rested on earth even as his legs remained bent at the knee and his feet submerged. Monique sat upright as her own feet soaked. Already the sun pierced the canopy, its light shimmering over the brush and trees of the forest. As the day warmed, exhaustion soon showed and Sawyer closed his eyes until his mouth fell open and his head rolled to one side. Monique watched her son sleep half an hour before her own eyelids also grew heavy and she too slept.

IT WASN'T NOISE that woke Monique, but silence. At first, the woman cocked an ear to pick up a sound that wasn't. Then she sat up, wide-eyed and alert as she panned the forest and stood to scour the trees. When she spotted a flock of green parrots half-hidden in the branches of a great mahogany, but no longer squawking, Monique shook her son.

"Saw-yer. Saw-yer."

Sawyer opened his eyes. "Yes?" he said.

"Vas-y."

Sawyer looked around as his mother pointed to his shoes.

"Vas-y," Monique repeated.

Sawyer didn't understand. "What's wrong?" he asked.

Monique didn't reply. Her eyes showed terror as she grabbed her son's arm and dragged him toward cover, abandoning their few remaining possessions. She pulled hard and the boy staggered and lost balance before finding his stride.

"My shoes," Sawyer yelled.

Monique paid no heed. "Vite! Vite!" she shouted. "Ils sont ici."

Sawyer didn't resist his mother's pull, nor could have if he had wanted to. Monique's grip of terror was unbreakable as she dragged her son through brambles toward nearby trees. Grass grew waist high and brush was thick, so it was more a matter of threading through foliage than actual running. Even as the pair struggled through briars, thorns, and grass sharp enough to slice exposed arms and legs, the forest remained otherwise still.

Crack.

Monique never heard the shot. She never heard her death knell. She never again heard anything. Rather, it was Sawyer who heard the whine of the bullet and jumped at the thud of its impact. It was Sawyer who saw his mother knocked against a tree. It was Sawyer whose words were mere reaction.

"Are you hurt?" the boy cried out.

Sawyer's mother lay face down in grass. Blood gushed from a hole between her shoulder blades and the ground already was soiled from the flow of her life. Sawyer dropped to his knees and rolled Monique over, only to see unblinking eyes and unmoving lips. A large gaping wound, oozing with blood, punctured her chest above her left breast. She no longer breathed.

"Mother!" Sawyer cried out.

Monique neither blinked nor twitched.

"Don't leave me, Mother."

Monique stared dead-eyed toward the heavens.

Now Sawyer turned back, scouring the forest. "God help me," he whispered. "God help me."

His face red from rage and nostrils flared from fury, Sawyer jumped to his feet and sprinted for the trees, looking toward brush from which the shot sounded. Grabbing a thick limb from the ground, the boy charged forward.

"Murderers," Sawyer screamed as loud as he could. "Parricides."

Sawyer never reached his objective.

Crack.

A second shot rang out, shattering the boy's lower rib and knocking him down breathless. Sawyer landed on his back, his breathing labored and face contorted as he choked on foam-filled blood that gurgled in his throat even as his eyes rolled to the back of his head.

A moment later, a pair of camouflaged soldiers emerged from the brush, dirt covered and sporting two-day beards. Both carried long rifles with short scopes. The first was taller by a head, but they were equally thin-shouldered. The taller soldier approached Sawyer and motioned for his compatriot to come as the latter unholstered a pistol and walked toward the mortally stricken boy.

Sawyer turned his head aside, paying no attention to the soldiers as the shock of the gunshot faded and pain intensified. Now tears rolled from his eyes and blood backed up from his lungs, running through his nostrils and filling his mouth before trickling down his neck as he gasped for breath.

The second soldier gave Sawyer a long look before taking aim as the boy coughed a mouthful of blood and tried to speak, choking out only a single word.

"Mother."

The soldier squeezed the trigger.

Crack.

The pistol fired and its bullet bored a single hole the size of an old two-bit coin into the front of Sawyer's forehead just before blood, bone, and brain exploded from the back of his skull. Sawyer never moved again, not even to close his eyes. The soldier holstered the pistol and tossed a camouflaged helmet to the ground as thick blonde hair fell to the woman's neck.

"I jerked the trigger," the blonde soldier said.

"The pistol?" the taller soldier asked.

"Long gun," the blonde said. "I thought it might be the boy."

"What boy?"

"From the briefing. The Confederate," the blonde soldier said as she wiped her brow with the back of a hand.

A moment later, the taller soldier looked at Sawyer's corpse. "Are you going to tell the captain you shot a Confederate?" he said.

The blonde shrugged. "Just a déclassé," she said. "Hook

won't care about a lost boy. Just another collateral causality. Anyway, it's authorized. He has no more rights than anyone else on this island. They're as much targets as the Chinese."

"For a minute you had me worried."

"Suppose I ought to call it in?" the blonde asked.

"I wouldn't bother," the taller soldier said. "Count him with the others. From the village."

"Makes sense. Less paperwork."

The blonde marched back to the trail and her compatriot followed. "Did you hear him?" she asked after a moment.

"Couldn't make out his words. What'd he say?"

"He wanted his mother."

"They always do," the taller soldier said. "They always realize too late that they threw away a good thing."

The blonde just shrugged.

Made in the USA
Middletown, DE
14 March 2021

35290648R00170